Admiralty Orders

M.C. MUIR

Other titles by M.C. Muir

Under Admiralty Orders - The Oliver Quintrell Series
Book 1 – Floating Gold
Book 2 – The Tainted Prize
Book 4 – The Unfortunate Isles

Other titles by Margaret Muir
Sea Dust
Through Glass Eyes
The Black Thread
The Condor's Feather
Words on a Crumpled page (Poetry)
Uncanny (Short stories)
Goats (non-fiction)
King Richard and the Mountain Goat (Young adult)

Admiralty Orders

Under Admiralty Orders–The Oliver Quintrell Series
Book 3

M.C. MUIR

PROLOGUE

1804

In the palpable dankness of the graveyard, the gentleman's features were hidden beneath the broad rim of a felt hat. Only the satin ribbon on his powdered queue was visible. From his shoulders, a dark velvet cloak fell to his knees but when the moon emerged from between the clouds the white silk stockings, accentuating his shapely calves, glowed as did the silver buckles on his shoes.

Standing next to him was a much younger man – bareheaded, with an anxious expression on his face. His fingers were locked tightly together to prevent his hands from shaking. Two shabbily dressed men, armed with the tools of their trade, padded along the path ahead of them.

'Which one is it?' the taller fellow asked.

His accomplice, skinny as a barge-pole and stinking of ale and stale tobacco smoke, walked on slowly peering into the shadows before kicking the toe of his boot into a mound of newly dug earth.

'This one 'ere,' he said. Dropping to his knees, he removed the stones that decorated the dirt and placed them aside carefully replicating their positions.

'Don't dilly-dally,' the older gentleman in the cloak advised. His cultured voice was low but demanding.

There was no response, save for the crack of a twig snapped underfoot and the breeze whistling the Lord's vengeance through the treetops.

Digging with wooden spades and heaping the soil neatly into a pile, the men ignored the rustling in the bushes. Most likely a fox or badger making its nocturnal rounds. Having repeated the ritual many times, the sack-'em-up men were not distracted.

They knew exactly where to dig and how much dirt to remove before they would strike the head of the coffin.

After scraping the loose earth from it, one of the resurrectionists cracked the lid open with a single blow. Then, with an iron bar, he prized up the splintered timbers ignoring the smell of death released into the night air.

Standing with his legs apart over the hole, the taller of the pair reached under the cadaver's torso whilst his assistant took a firm grip around the head. With a single practiced movement, they slid the body upwards and out of the casket and deposited it onto the grass. Like a butterfly emerging from a chrysalis, the shroud, which had cocooned it, was stripped away. This was tossed back into the coffin and the body rolled up in a length of canvas.

During the theft, which took but a few minutes, not a word was exchanged between the two exhumators. As soon as the job was finished, the grave was quickly returned to its previous appearance. The damaged remnants of the coffin lid were replaced. The soil shovelled back. The stones, which had decorated the mound returned to their original positions. Finally, a handful of leaves, pulled from the nearest bush, were sprinkled over the gravesite leaving no obvious trace that a robbery had taken place.

With one man carrying the tools and the other with the corpse balanced over his shoulder, the pair headed for their cart hidden in the bushes beyond the cemetery wall. By the time they reached it, foul fluid was oozing from the fetid body saturating the grave robber's hands and clothes. But with no knowledge of the spectre of death carried in such matter, the man was unconcerned.

The pair might have been half-drunk, half-stupid or half-mad, but they were savvy enough to know there was a ready market for the product of their labours. Although fresh cadavers were preferred, corpses in any state of decomposition were always needed and no questions were ever asked. Payment was made on delivery and prices were guaranteed. Ten pounds for full-grown adults. A lesser amount for children. Babies and still-borns were paid by the inch with a handsome bonus for a woman carrying a dead infant inside her. All-in-all, the resurrectionists made a tidy living. Their latest stiff was the result of another successful night's work.

As for the two observers, who had a carriage waiting for them, their experiences of the event were quite different. For the well-spoken gentleman cloaked in velvet, the retrieval had been performed cleanly. The cadaver appeared fresh and he was well satisfied with the outcome. Watching a robbery take place always provided a frisson of morbid excitement, even though he had witnessed it several times before.

For the younger man, however, the desecration of the grave, the disturbance of the dead and the stripping of the body were abhorrent acts. He dared not allow himself to dwell on the dire consequences should he be discovered there. With his conscience tearing at his throat, heart and stomach, his only concern was to get out of the graveyard as quickly as possible.

CHAPTER 1

Portsmouth Harbour
4 August 1804

'Captain coming aboard. Side boys! Bosun's mates, look lively now.'

The call brought an instant flurry of activity on deck. Topmen slid down the shrouds, idlers hurried up from the waist whilst those already on deck shuffled into the semblance of lines amidships. The two dozen marines who appeared from different parts of the ship made a better presentation, though their stature was less uniform than the dress they were wearing.

'Hats off! Silence!' The voice of the youngest midshipman quivered both through lack of confidence and the fact his voice had only recently broken.

As if in response to the dull thud of the captain's boat when it bumped against the frigate's hull, a cacophony of drumming sounds commenced in the hold.

In contrast to his usual placid expression, a frown of frustration creased the face of the first lieutenant who headed the line of officers waiting to greet the ship's captain on his return.

The high-pitched shrilling of the pipes carried across the waters of Portsmouth Harbour and, when the unmelodious tune penetrated the bowels of the ship, the banging rose as if in accompaniment.

Stepping onto the deck, Oliver Quintrell stopped momentarily and raised his hat respectfully to His Majesty's frigate, *Perpetual*, the vessel he had commanded for over a year. After casting a glance forward, aft and aloft, he paused, inclined his head and listened.

'Welcome aboard, Captain,' Simon Parry said.

'Has the ship suffered a mischief during my absence? Do you have carpenters working below?'

'No, sir. I have a group of pressed men confined in the hold. I can only assume they got wind of your arrival and wanted to make their presence known.'

'I trust you will attend to it, Mr Parry.'

'Yes, sir, immediately.'

'I will speak with you in my cabin fifteen minutes from now. In the meantime, I do not wish to be disturbed.'

'Aye aye, Captain.'

With the sound of hammering reverberating through the ship's timbers, Oliver Quintrell headed below.

Mr Parry thought nothing of the brevity of the conversation. He had expected nothing more. However, the senseless banging from the hold was something he had not anticipated. He glanced at the level of sand in the half-hour glass. It had only recently been turned.

'Mr Tully, go below and put an end to that diabolical din. And tell whosoever is responsible that if the noise does not cease, every man Jack of them will be flogged.'

The second lieutenant knuckled his forehead in the style of a common sailor. Although he wore an officer's uniform, many years of service before the mast had left Ben Tully with old habits.

'Mr Gibb, deliver the captain's dunnage to his steward. Mr Nightingale, attend to the boat. I trust it will not be needed again.'

With the larboard watch on duty, the sailors of the starboard watch, along with the waisters and idlers returned below. Climbing the ratlines, the bosun and his mate returned to the blackened pots hanging in the rigging and continued working aloft. On the weather deck, after cursing the men for walking on the sail he was stitching, the sailmaker resumed his job with palm and needle, carefully inserting a patch of canvas into an already heavily patched topmast staysail.

When the noise from below suddenly stopped, the caulkers took up the beat, hammering teased oakum into the seams that had opened in the deck-beams permitting water to leak through to the wardroom.

There was no wind. Not even a breath of breeze. Wood smoke from the fire-hearth in the galley hovered above the chimney before floating slowly up to the yards and evaporating. The smell of beef, boiling in iron pots, drifted back from the forward companionway.

Satisfied his orders were being followed, the first lieutenant strode along the deck observing the scene that had met Captain Quintrell's return. Aloft, *Perpetual*'s square sails were neatly furled to the yards, the main and mizzen staysails hung like flaccid members strapped alongside the masts, and the jib sails were folded neatly in concertina fashion and lashed to the bowsprit. Only the mizzen was set, but it showed no inclination to move. With the frigate hanging off its anchor on a tide that had lost its sense of direction, the vessel was as still a ship sitting on the stocks in dry dock.

For the past few hours, the lieutenant had observed the Portsmouth pound filling with the incoming tide. He had watched the flood from the Solent slip gradually across the banks of sand engulfing Portsmouth Harbour and refloating the boats and victuallers' barges that had settled in the Gosport silt. For Simon Parry, the rising tide was as insidious here as it was off the Kent coast. Seawater slowly drowning the treacherous Goodwin Sands was a sight he, like many other men aboard, could never forget.

Higher up the harbour, towards the mouth of the Porchester River, the great hulks of war-wearied fighting ships, stripped of their pride and raiments, stood in single file, their rotting keels gripped by the mud. The number of emasculated men-of-war was growing to accommodate the French prisoners whose numbers had been increasing every week since the resumption of war. Occasionally another hull was towed in and added to the line – a damaged British second-rate that had seen one too many battles or a pulverised French prize deemed uneconomical for repair by the Navy Board and of no resale value by the prize agents.

Now some of those stinking hulks provided accommodation for a rapidly growing number of thieves and felons – convicts sentenced by the Assizes judges around the country to transportation to the colonies. Because America was no longer a viable dumping ground for Britain's criminal classes, Australia was the prisoners' likely destination. While signal flags no longer flew from their salt-hardened halyards, the ships' decks were often decorated with a mismatched assortment of bed-sheets and clothing. Apparently today was washday.

Closer at hand was the bustling wharf around the Camber – Portsmouth's inner waterway where local boats tied up – an area where taverns and alehouses, chandlers' shops and stores outnumbered the houses that were home to seamen, custom officers, fishermen and tradesmen. The Camber was always busy. It was where Jewish merchants wandered the docks, quick to tempt recently paid-off sailors with gold baubles that were not real gold or pocket-watches that stopped ticking soon after the ship left port. Other equally useless knick-knacks were sold at exorbitant prices. Harbour doxies, whose painted faces looked the same in any port, roamed the Camber hiking the price on their purses for hungry sailors home after months at sea. If they had coins rattling in their pockets, the women weren't choosy about their clients' age or appearance.

Carts rumbled back and forth on the dockside with the occasional post chaise or coach rolling to a halt, discharging a paying passenger or sea captain, or a rich merchant heading to his ship. Toothless old tars, cudding on tasteless tobacco leaves or hobbling on wooden pegs, littered the wharf side begging for the opportunity to return to sea. But even the press-gangs ignored them.

Simon Parry checked the sand in the glass. Half of it had slipped through. He headed below.

'Come.' Oliver called, in response to the knock on the door.

'Welcome aboard, Captain.' The first officer's greeting was polite but genuine.

'What was the confounded racket that greeted me when I stepped aboard?'

Mr Parry apologized for the disturbance and vowed he would make sure it did not happen again.

'Tell me about these men confined below.'

'There are twenty pressed men, all sailors. They were brought aboard in the early hours of this morning.'

Oliver leaned back in his chair. 'Please sit, Simon.'

The lieutenant sat down and continued. 'Mr Tully took the gang out last night. I had received news an Indiaman had arrived in Spithead the previous day. Having ascertained it had paid-off some of its crew, I dispatched the gang to the Northport Gate after midnight to await those heading for the London Road under the cover of darkness. I am told it was not a difficult task. The sailors were easy to identify.' He paused. 'I will have them mustered on deck for your inspection, when you see fit.'

Oliver nodded. 'Have they been fed?'

'Yes, they have.'

'And what caused the noise? I trust they are doing no damage.'

'There appears to be two or three who are not happy with the accommodation and they are stirring up the others. Mr Tully tells me they are using their shoes as hammers.'

'Then I suggest, if you haven't done so already, you collect every man's shoes and stockings and let him go barefoot. Let us see how long they persist with their merry games. Knocking on the hull with swollen toes and bleeding knuckles is unlikely to create too much of a disturbance.'

'It will be done.'

'Has the doctor examined them?'

'The doctor has not yet come aboard.'

'What? I understood he would arrive two days ago, while I was in London. Any message from him to explain this tardiness?'

'No word, sir.'

The captain shook his head. 'I presume we still have the surgeon's mate in the cockpit?'

Simon nodded. 'Abel Longbottom.'

'Abel – eh? Never was a man more inaptly named,' the captain mused cynically.

'And I'm afraid the loblolly boy is missing. He appeared to be a reliable fellow, but he never returned from his shore visit so I have entered an *R* against his name.'

Oliver sighed. 'If Longbottom is all we have in the sick berth, then pray to God we meet no serious action on this coming cruise.' He paused for a moment. 'Apart from the cockpit, is everything else in order? I trust the rest of the hands are all come aboard and the women returned to the dock.'

The lieutenant acknowledged, 'All is as it should be.'

'Thank you, Simon.'

Without knocking, the steward poked his head around the cabin door. 'Coffee now, Capt'n?'

'Thank you, Casson. That will be most welcome,' Oliver removed his coat and loosened the buttons on his waistcoat.

'How was your journey to London?' Simon asked.

'As tedious as ever,' Oliver replied. 'I dislike it more intensely every time I make it. The coach was uncomfortable and overcrowded with four passengers perched on top with the luggage. The London Road is either a muddy quagmire or the wheel ruts are baked as hard as navy tack, and it seems to make little difference what season of the year it is. The only noticeable changes are the colours of the crops in the fields that sail by. Unfortunately, they do not sail by fast enough.'

Quintrell shook his head and continued. 'As such, I was not surprised when the coach cast a wheel. Though the passengers were thrown from the roof, no one was injured, but the driver was unable to repair the damage and a replacement had to be found. Despite being less than a few miles from Guildford, the incident delayed us for over three hours and resulted in me reaching Grosvenor Square well after my sister's household had retired for the night. Apart from that, as if to break the monotony while we waited for the wheel to be replaced, the coach was set upon by an angry mob. Quite an eventful journey, to say the least.'

'Footpads? You were robbed or hurt?'

'Thankfully, no. It was a group of angry villagers seeking the Church sexton who, I learned, had been in the habit of passing word to the London resurrectionists of recent deaths in his parish.'

'Resurrectionists?'

'Grave-robbers eager to lift the corpses from newly dug graves. It seems they make a tidy living from the practice. It is a dangerous occupation. I would not envy the man his fate if the irate relatives of a recently deceased victim ever caught up with him. To be skinned alive would be the least of his worries.'

Oliver sniffed the air when the coffee arrived. 'Excellent, Casson.'

'You want something to eat, Capt'n?'

'Thank you, no. You may leave us.'

After sipping his drink, Simon put the next question tentatively. 'Might I venture to enquire if your attendance at the Admiralty was fruitful?'

Oliver had been anticipating the question and, knowing his first lieutenant was eager to receive news, he was surprised he had taken so long to ask. He, too, was eager to divulge the information he was permitted to share. 'Fruitful indeed,' he said, running his hand across the chart smoothed out on the table in front of him. 'If all is well and we have a full crew, we sail tomorrow for Gibraltar, with dispatches to deliver on the way.'

'Will we be joining Lord Nelson in the Mediterranean?'

'No. We do not sail beyond Gibraltar.'

'But Nelson and the Mediterranean Fleet are responsible for the Gibraltar station. Is that not so?'

'That is the situation at present. However, as you are aware, Lord Nelson's fleet is fully occupied in the northern Mediterranean. Every ship under his command is engaged in the blockade of Toulon ensuring the French fleet doesn't slip out. I was also reminded that war with Spain, which as we know has been looming for some time, is now considered imminent.' He was tempted to continue but hesitated to divulge anything more. 'My instructions are to proceed to Gibraltar, where I will receive further orders from the garrison commander there.'

'The Duke of York is in command of the fortress, is he not?'

'In name only. He departed the Rock about a year ago for Canada and is unlikely to return. However, he was unwilling to relinquish his title – much to the chagrin of Sir Thomas Trigge, the present Lieutenant-Governor and commander of the Gibraltar garrison. I understand His Highness's ideas were somewhat unorthodox and proved very unpopular amongst the troops.'

Simon raised his eyebrows.

'Of the ninety taverns in the town, he restricted the troops to frequenting only three of them. They were not allowed to drink gin or rum. Instead he insisted they drink Bristol Beer which was locally brewed on Windmill Hill. He had the morning gun brought forward to three-thirty and was a stickler for regular parades and uniformity. He even ordered the soldiers to shave off their beards and whiskers.'

'An unpopular move, no doubt,' Simon said.

Oliver nodded. 'The Duke of York's measures resulted in a threat to his life and a mutiny. And although he has retained the title of Governor, it is well known that he will never return to Gibraltar. Since taking up his post as Lieutenant-Governor, the new commander has repealed most of those regulations in an effort to reclaim the confidence of the troops.'

'In interesting situation,' Simon said. 'I trust we will not be remaining there long.'

'That is not for me to question,' Oliver replied. 'Gibraltar has proved itself to be a British military stronghold where the navy plays only a minor supportive role. As you will know, the garrison established its superiority during the Great Siege against French and Spanish bombardment from both land and sea.' He sipped his coffee. 'But, apart from the dockyard and stores, there is no permanent naval establishment in Gibraltar. The navy uses it as a place to refit and refurbish, and an Admiral's flag is only raised when one is in residence on the Rock, as Earl St Vincent was a few years ago.'

'Indeed.'

'My orders are to proceed to sea and deliver dispatches in person to Admiral Cornwallis off Brest before sailing south to Ferrol, where I will attend Lord Cochrane.'

Simon Parry was intrigued. 'I assume our mission entails more than delivering messages to the squadron commanders.'

Oliver grinned. 'The motives behind the Admiralty's orders are often veiled in secrecy, or contrived in such a way to hide their true intent. I am aware of some of their Lordships' concerns but, at this juncture, I am not at liberty to share that information with you.'

The lieutenant nodded. 'I understand.'

Oliver's mind was leaping ahead. 'How soon before we are ready to sail?'

'The fresh supplies have all come aboard in your absence, plus two new midshipmen.'

'Their ages?'

'Not long weaned.'

Oliver did not reply.

'We are fully watered and the additional shot you requested was brought aboard yesterday. The only matter requiring your attention is those pressed men confined in the hold. Do we ship them all or cast half of them adrift?'

'Until they have been examined, I cannot say. I will come on deck shortly. In the meantime, keep a look-out for any sign of the surgeon on the wharf.'

'Aye aye, Captain.' Simon Parry said, as he departed the cabin.

There was no doubt in Oliver's mind as to the admirable qualities of his first lieutenant, both as a naval officer and a gentleman. He was trustworthy, astute, dependable and honourable. He was also unassuming, perhaps too much so for his own advancement. Oliver also respected his first lieutenant for his personal loyalty, for his loyalty to whatever ship he was serving on, and his loyalty to King and country. That he was still without his own command was a travesty in Oliver's eyes but, that he was serving aboard *Perpetual*, with responsibility for the welfare and performance of the crew, was a definite bonus.

The captain welcomed the news the ship had been resupplied and watered and was ready for sea. After six months cruising the northern reaches of the Channel and the North Sea, as part of a squadron, he looked forward to sailing south alone.

But his recent visit to the Admiralty had raised a few questions in his mind and left him feeling somewhat deflated. Things had changed in the corridors of power since his previous visit. The government had changed. Lord Addingham had been ousted and

William Pitt the Younger was now Prime Minister. And, in an unexpected and unpopular move, the position of First Sea Lord was no longer held by Earl St Vincent. It had been given to Lord Melville, a soldier, a military man, born of a wealthy aristocratic family. A land's man. A lubber.

Oliver asked himself: *How can a man who has never served aboard a navy ship, let alone commanded one, possibly comprehend or appreciate the needs of the Navy and its sailors?*

Here was a soldier who would serve the government with visions of military supremacy, while ignoring the role of the Royal Navy in preventing the French invasion of Britain taking place.

Oliver knew he was not alone in his concerns. Many high-ranking naval officers were uncomfortable with Lord Melville's appointment, but nothing could be done to change the situation. The Lords Commissioners were a group of highly respected men and, like the officers aboard any ship, were made up of men from various backgrounds, ages and experiences – though, at least on a fighting ship, all its senior officer were seafaring men.

The previous Sea Lord, who, as the young John Jervis, had come from humble beginnings, entered the navy at twelve years of age and during his sixty years of naval service risen to the rank of Admiral, been created a Knight of the Bath in '82 and received an Earldom following his victory at Cape St Vincent. But now, like a worn-out hulk in Portsmouth Harbour, he had been cast adrift and replaced.

Earl St Vincent was a man Oliver had always held in high esteem and he felt privileged the previous First Sea Lord had rewarded him with missions he would not have offered to other captains.

Only a few years prior to his retirement, St Vincent had spent time in Gibraltar where he had raised his flag and documented numerous urgent matters that needed to be addressed such as the problems of sanitation, the need for reservoirs to collect drinking water, the need to improve the naval dockyard and the need for shipwrights in order to build gunships to serve on the bay. His vision for Gibraltar was as something more than just a place for ships of the Mediterranean Fleet to refit. He also wanted to see the power wielded by the military moderated.

As he sat in his cabin alone, Oliver wondered if it was ill-health or the vehemence of St Vincent's demands that had led to his withdrawal from the Rock, his recall to England, and his subsequent retirement from the service.

The appearance of his steward interrupted his thoughts.

'Beg pardon, Capt'n, but Mr Parry said for me to say there is a boat just pulled away from the Camber and heading this way. From the number of boxes and bags heaped on board, he thinks it's likely to be the surgeon you're expecting.'

'Thank you, Casson, that is indeed good news.' Reaching for his cup, he drained the bitter dregs and was about to rise but reconsidered his decision. 'Tell Mr Parry, if it is indeed the doctor, I would like to speak with him as soon as he is settled in his quarters.'

Although good surgeons were invaluable in the King's navy, it was common knowledge that men of repute were few and far between. Skilled physicians worked from private rooms charging exorbitant fees to operate on their patients. Some held teaching posts in the major London hospitals. Having suffered the services of some dubious characters posing as physicians, it was not hard for the captain to resist the desire to go on deck but he did not wish to inflate the surgeon's ego before he had the opportunity to learn if his services warranted such attention.

'It will be interesting to discover what manner of man the Navy Board is subjecting us to this time,' he said cynically.

CHAPTER 2

Dr Whipple

'*Perpetual*!'

The call came from a small boat that had swum from the Camber and was being rowed towards the frigate. The single word prompted the sailors on deck to shuffle to the starboard side to take a gander at the approaching wherry as it drifted up against the frigate's hull. Apart from the two men on the oars and a sailor sitting in the bow, the boat conveyed a well-dressed gentleman.

Sitting upright in the stern sheets, his left arm rested on the rail, his right hand on his walking cane. A substantial wooden chest, an assortment of boxes, several large glass jars and other baggage were stowed between the thwarts.

'Looks like the surgeon we were waiting for,' the second lieutenant commented.

'I believe you are correct, Mr Tully,' Simon Parry replied.

Although the surgeon's stick, decorated with a brass ferrule, was the first item to be handed up the ladder, the man to whom it belonged was in no way infirm or aged. He was a sprightly young man appearing little older than the average lieutenant. The cane, however, provided no indication of his professional prowess. Tarnished brass was a poor substitute for the gold-topped walking sticks carried by physicians as a mark of their status.

Mr Parry greeted him as he stepped aboard.

'My apologies, I am a little overdue. Jonathon Whipple. At your service. Ship's surgeon.'

'Welcome aboard, Mr Whipple. Mr Smith will show you to the cockpit. Then, as soon as you are familiar with your quarters, the captain wishes to speak with you.'

The doctor bowed his head politely before casting a glance over his shoulder to ensure all his luggage was being hoisted onto the deck.

'Mr Tully, kindly attend to the doctor's dunnage. Make use of Mr Gibb and Mr Hanson. The rest of you men who are not required, go below or find yourself some useful occupation.'

The second lieutenant knuckled his forehead and turned to the two new midshipmen. 'You heard the lieutenant. Make doubly sure all the baggage is out of the boat before it casts off. I've known stuff disappear before it's even stepped foot aboard. If you want me, I'll be on the orlop with Mr Parry.'

'Aye aye, sir,' Mr Hanson, the taller of the two replied.

No sooner was the lieutenant out of sight than an argument began at the entry port.

'You there. Get back in the boat,' Mr Gibb ordered. 'You're not allowed to come on deck.'

'But I'm a sailor and I want to sign.' The demand came from a youth who looked little older than the new middie. He had a bag slung over his shoulder and he was attempting to climb the ladder.

'We don't need any more hands,' Mr Hanson insisted. 'We've got more than enough already.'

'Well, I'm sure you can squeeze in one more. Go tell the captain it's me, Tommy Wainwright, and tell him that when I last spoke with him, I said I'd be back. He'll remember. Go on.'

The midshipmen exchanged glances.

'Less of your cheek. I don't care what your name is or what your cock-and-bull story is, the fact is you're not coming aboard.' With that, Mr Hanson grabbed the youth by the wrists and tried to dislodge the firm grip he had on the rail. 'If you don't let go, I'll get a pole and push you overboard.'

From the forward rail a voice boomed: 'Hey, you young scallywag! What do you think you're up to?'

Everyone stopped and turned in the direction of the voice.

'Go sling your hook on another ship! Who do you think you are, throwing your weight about like you've got a warrant? Chuck him in the harbour. Let him drown. That's what I say.'

While Gibb and Hanson were unable to see who had issued the command, some of the sailors applauded and a smile broke out across Tommy Wainwright's face.

'Bungs – you old codger!' he yelled, grabbing the opportunity to wriggle his way on to the deck. 'You ain't forgotten me then?'

The young middies exchanged puzzled looks.

'I never forget no one,' Bungs said, striding abaft like he was lord of the manor, his false scowl mellowing with every step. 'Do as I say and let the lad alone. You don't need to ask the captain, I'll vouch for the young fella. But you best let Mr Parry know.'

With sniggers and jeers from the sailors enjoying the exchange, Mr Hanson spun his head around anxiously searching the deck for an officer. 'Go get Mr Tully,' he whispered to his mate.

'Looks like you've sprouted a bit,' Bungs said, as he neared the group. 'Knee-high to a flea you was when you was last aboard. Grow another few inches and you'll be as big as the rest of the crew. That ma of yours has been feeding you too well, I reckon.'

Running the final few paces to greet him, Tommy embraced his old friend.

'Hey – get your hands off me. I ain't your father.'

'Nearest I've got to one,' Tommy said, punching his fist into the cooper's belly. 'Where's Eku? Is he aboard?'

'Aye, and Muffin and the rest of the lads. Wait until they see you. Sight for sore eyes, you are. So you've decided to come back and mess with us?'

'Watch out!' a voice warned.

Mr Parry leapt up the companionway two steps at time and headed for the group gathered near the entry port. 'What is all this about? I could hear the upheaval from below.'

'This man says he's a sailor and he's come aboard without permission. I couldn't stop him, sir,' the midshipman explained.

'You couldn't stop him? Then I hope we never come into close action with you in command, Mr Hanson.'

'We got us another volunteer, Mr Parry,' Bungs said. 'You remember young Tom. He says the captain'll speak for him like he did once before.'

'Thank you, Bungs, I will have words with you and the midshipmen later but, for the present, I think the captain has more important things to attend to.' He looked at the new arrival with a glint in his eye. 'Perhaps I should lock him in the hold with the other pressed men.'

'Not bloody likely,' Bungs argued adamantly.

'Be careful, Bungs! I was speaking in jest.'

'Sorry, sir.'

'Bide your time and your temper. The choice of hands from the pressed men has yet to be made. I need a dozen men to make up a full crew, and who stays and who goes will be for the doctor to determine. However, I see no reason this young sailor can't be included in that selection.'

Tommy liked the fact he was referred to as a sailor.

The lieutenant addressed him. 'Behave yourself and remain on deck. Mr Gibb,' he called, turning his attention to the midshipman, 'is that wherry still alongside?'

'Yes, sir.'

'Then I suggest you have it cast it off as quickly as possible. Isn't that what you were instructed to do?'

'Yes, sir. Aye aye, sir.'

'And clear this rabble. I shouldn't have to tell you twice.'

The two young middies dithered over which job to attend to first. The events of the previous few minutes had completed befuddled them. Arriving on their first ship they had been warned there was a lot to be learned, but it was quickly becoming evident that not everything was written in the handbooks.

When the wherry had pushed off and was pulling for the Camber, they breathed a little more easily but real relief didn't come until the lieutenant had returned below and all of the surgeon's dunnage had disappeared from the deck. Only then was the pair of thirteen-year-olds able to retreat to the sanctuary of the quarterdeck.

Leaning against the windlass, Bungs threw a glancing punch that skimmed across Tommy's chin. 'You look too healthy to have been working underground. Are you still breathing that coal dust? And where's that brother you said you was going to bring with you?'

Tommy shook his head. 'No way was I going down the pit again, especially with prize money rattling in me pocket. Instead, I bought meself a hand-cart and started fetching and carrying stuff.'

Bungs was surprised. 'So you're a barrow boy now, eh?'

'Yes, but I'm not working for some thieving merchant like them that hangs around the wharves. It's me own cart and me own business and I make me own wages. I ain't fussy. I'll cart anything that needs carting, furniture, sacks of oats, rhubarb, coal, coffins, even night soil – anything that folks will pay to have shifted from one place to another. I've worked hard and built up a tidy little trade.'

'I don't doubt you have, lad, but, tell me this, Mister Clever Dick, if you're such a clever little businessman, what brings you back here?'

'I promised I'd be back, didn't I? I wanted to see you and Eku and Muffin. And there's always the chance of a bit more prize money.'

'Chance of getting your head blown off too,' Bungs said.

Tommy shrugged. 'Like you said, I've grown a bit so I won't be taken for a powder monkey anymore, so I'll make more wages. And I've got this to prove I've seen action,' he said, proudly holding up his left hand minus the little finger. 'As for me brother, he wouldn't leave ma back home alone but he was happy to quit the pit and take on the carting job. And me ma was happy about that too. Real proud of me she is. She thought she'd never see me again when I took off last time, and she didn't want me to go again, but I told her I'd be back. I couldn't say when, but I promised I'd have more money in me pocket and I said I'd buy me a horse and a real cart next time.'

Bungs face took on a serious expression. 'You can forget that idea, lad. For your information, apart from our wages, we've made no money worth speaking of in the past six months. And there'll be no more prizes like the last one we got. The blockade fleets have got the Frenchies tied up so tight they can't even sneeze and, I hear, there'll be no more treasure ships. I guess we were just lucky last time.'

'Never mind,' Tommy said sagely. 'So where are we heading?'

'How should I know? The captain hasn't said. He's just back from the Admiralty but he's in a big hurry to put to sea, so we'll know soon enough.'

Tommy remembered his first encounter with Captain Quintrell in London. That seemed like a long time ago.

'What did you do with your prize money, Bungs?'

'Never you mind, that's my business. But I didn't waste it, not like some I know.'

'Do you think Mr Parry will have a place for me?' Tommy asked quietly.

'Sure he will. I'll make sure he does.'

Tommy laughed. 'You ain't changed much, Bungs, have you? Still as bold as brass.'

'And you're still as talkative as ever, young Tom.'

In his cabin, Oliver folded the sheet of writing paper neatly and slid it into the envelope he had addressed to Victoria, his wife, at their home on the Isle of Wight.

Lifting the candle from its holder, he held the stick of sealing wax over the flame and allowed it to heat, but not burn. The coil of dark smoke drifting up from it scented the air with the smell of beeswax mellowed by a hint of musk. It reminded him of the strange, but not unfamiliar, odour of ambergris.

Dripping slowly but rhythmically, like blood from a severed finger, the dark drops of red wax pooled to the size of a shilling on the back of the envelope. Blowing across it, to cool it slightly, he breathed warm air onto the metal seal before pressing it firmly into the soft wax. The imprint was excellent. His wife would recognize it instantly.

Replacing the candlestick on the top of his writing bureau, he immediately reached for another envelope. After addressing it, he placed it aside. Picking up the quill, he dipped the nib into the well but, before he had put pen to paper, the ink dripped onto the desk. Wiping it, he gazed down at the blank page.

The letter he had just written to his wife had flowed easily – a little like writing to another post captain, the content informative and courteous, worded with a degree of formality afforded by respect, but with the comfortable familiarity of years of interaction. Yet those words never conveyed his closely guarded inner feelings – his joys, his hopes, his fears. As at home, he had learned to guard those jealously. Nor had he written of his aspirations. Preserving his ship and the lives of the men under his command was the most he could wish for. He had no desire to return home – at least not until his present commission had been completed. Victoria was already aware of that.

For Oliver Quintrell, life aboard a frigate of His Majesty's Navy was well regulated and duty bound, and his correspondence, like an entry in the log, related to aspects of day-to-day life at sea. But, in letters to his wife, this information was recounted only at a superficial level. It was not that he feared offending her sensitivities, but because his wife was not interested in either the mundane or the more sordid sides of sea life or of the officers or crew aboard his ship, even men who had sailed with him for many years. It was a fact he knew their character traits and understood their moods more intimately than he knew his wife's.

He shook the excess ink from the nib.

With Susanna, however, it was different. Although he had not seen her for nigh on two years, she was always close to him, in thought if not in person. With her, even on paper, he felt free to share his inner desires, confide his doubts, express his wishes and reveal his regrets all without fear of recrimination or rebuke. Though, when committing thoughts to paper, he was careful in case his correspondence was misdirected.

Where was she now? He wondered. *Still at the house, perched on the mountainside in Madeira, overlooking Funchal and its peaceful harbour? Was she standing beneath the vine in the garden, her black hair spilling over her right shoulder? Were her bare feet bathed in a sea of spent magenta flowers? Was she alone?*

The distant, but unmistakable, sound of chimes of the ship's bell rudely reminded him of the hour. He had other more pressing matters to attend to and this was no time to allow his mind to drift. He must hurry. Dipping the pen carefully into the inkwell again, he wrote:

My dearest Susanna,

Once again, I must beg your forgiveness as I tender my apology. You cannot comprehend how much it grieves me that I cannot contact you in person, but my orders, received only two days ago from their Lordships in London, are to proceed from this harbour to Gibraltar, where I will remain for some months or until the impending war with Spain is declared.

Should that event transpire, every ship in the Royal Navy will be called into service. How long such a conflict will continue cannot be determined, and which side will emerge victorious is in the hands of God. I pray that Portugal will not be drawn into the war and Madeira will forever remain a safe haven.

If you still hold a place for me in your heart and are liberty to write, your correspondence should be directed to me care of the Commander of the Garrison at Gibraltar. It would uplift my spirits, if I were to receive some communication from you.

No words can express my feelings for you and I pray that one day we can meet and be together.

I am, as always,
            Your Obedient Servant,
                        Oliver Quintrell
Aboard His Majesty's frigate Perpetual, *Portsmouth Harbour*

The ambiguity in the last line was not only in his words, but in his mind. He was unsure of Susanna's present situation, but he trusted that her feelings, although unlikely to be as raw as his own, were still smouldering and she would interpret his words in the manner they were intended.

After quickly reading the letter for a second time, he was dissatisfied with its composition and the formal way he had signed it, but there was no time to pen it again. If his correspondence was to be dispatched before they sailed, he had no time to waste. Without the need to blot the page, he folded it and placed it in the addressed envelope, reached for the candle and allowed the vermilion drops of sealing wax to spill onto the back.

'Casson!' he called.

'Aye, Captain.'

'We will be discharging some men to The Hard shortly. Kindly pass these two letters to my coxswain and have them delivered to the Post Office in town.'

With those obligations attended to, all thoughts of his wife and Susanna were immediately put from this mind. Preparations to sail on the morrow were now his primary concern.

'Captain Quintrell?'

Oliver looked up to find a man standing in his doorway.

'Ah, Mr Whipple, I presume. Or should I call you Dr Whipple? You must have been delayed. The Navy Board advised me to expect you some days ago.'

'That is correct, Captain, and I offer my profuse apologies. I trust it has not delayed your departure.'

'Very nearly,' Oliver admitted bluntly. 'We sail tomorrow. Your papers, if you please.'

The surgeon handed over several documents, including various certificates and letters of recommendation along with a warrant from the Navy Board.

'I was detained in London. There was an accident and I was called to attend a child who had fallen beneath the wheels of a wagon. The boy's leg was crushed and required amputation.'

'I trust the operation was successful.'

'The operation was successful, but the patient died yesterday, two days following the removal of the limb. I left when my services were no longer needed.'

Oliver withheld the cynical comment he was tempted to make. 'Thank you, Doctor. These papers appear to be in order, but if you will leave them with me, I will peruse them again more thoroughly when I am less pressed for time. I trust, by now your dunnage has been taken below, and I am sure you are anxious to familiarize yourself with the sick berth. However, before you return to your quarters, I have a group of men I require you to examine for any obvious defects that might render them unable to perform their duties as seamen. You have sailed before, I notice.'

'Yes, sir. After a period of twelve months abroad, I disembarked the ship in Plymouth a little over a week ago. That was my first naval appointment.'

'And you are prepared to sail again so soon?'

'I did not wish to refuse the Navy Board's offer to serve aboard *Perpetual*.'

Oliver wondered about the man he was addressing. His clothes were of quality cloth, but appeared a little shabby and well worn. He was fresh faced and young – probably of little more than 23 years. His pale blue eyes and the unnatural pallor in his cheeks were troubling, but he had known other surgeons who, after serving many months in the tropics, had returned to England as lily-white as the day they left. Working constantly below the waterline was enough to drain the colour from any man's cheeks. He could not condemn a man for having blue eyes or a pale skin, it was his ability with the lancet and saw which was of importance on a fighting ship.

'Then, all that remains is for me to welcome you aboard. Perhaps this evening you will do me the honour of dining with me. It will provide the opportunity for you to meet my officers and to enjoy the pleasure of a meal one does not have to chase across a pitching table.'

The surgeon smiled. 'Thank you. I am pleased to accept your kind invitation.'

'Casson! Pass a message to Mr Parry. I will inspect the pressed men now. Kindly ask him to have them mustered on deck immediately. Inform him I will join him directly.'

As the doctor reached for his cane, bowed his head slightly and departed the cabin, Oliver observed him keenly. Like the silver buckles on his shoes, the brass ferrule on his cane shone. His hands were clean and appeared soft, which was appropriate for a man unaccustomed to manual work. His hair was also clean, neither greased nor powdered, and was cropped close to his head in the latest fashion of the *bon ton* of London Society. Or perhaps his head had been shaved recently to combat the infestations of nits or lice, which find the scalps of sailors appetising? As his scalp appeared quite white beneath the bristling black hair, he decided the London fashion had determined the surgeon's coiffure. Or perhaps, he was in the habit of wearing a wig.

As to Dr Whipple's facial features, they were pleasant enough, for a young man, although unremarkable. No scars or pockmarks and a straight nose. Obviously not a fighting man.

From a very brief perusal of his papers, it was evident the doctor had attended University in Edinburgh. It could be assumed, therefore, that he was a learned man. His diction was clear and his enunciation lacked any evidence of anything other than City living. His papers indicated he had qualified, first as an apothecary, and later studied to be a surgeon spending several months working at the two Borough Hospitals – St Thomas's and Guy's. His warrant from the Navy Board was dated only a few days ago.

Everything appeared satisfactory and, as he had served in the West Indies for a year, Oliver assumed he would be fully conversant with the requirements of a surgeon serving aboard one of His Majesty's vessels. Hopefully, if they saw action in the coming months, Dr Whipple would be an asset. Hopefully, too, the new arrival would offer some conversation at the dinner table to stimulate and entertain the officers who had served with him both aboard *Perpetual* and on His Majesty's frigate, *Elusive*, prior to that.

'Casson.'

'Yes, Capt'n.'

'Pass a message to the sergeant of Marines. When the pressed men are brought up, I want them guarded. We are little more than a stone's throw from the Camber and it's likely there will be at least one of them sorely tempted to chance his luck against the tide in preference to another year at sea.'

'Aye aye, Captain.'

CHAPTER 3

Pressed Men

When the grating was removed from the hold and the men released from confinement, the smell of bilge water drifted up from the darkness with them. Whether the sudden rush made by the men was to escape the stale air, to see daylight, to attempt to run, or merely to find out where they were was uncertain. Only one sailor hung back while the others shoved and pushed, cursed and tumbled over each other in the effort to be first up the ladder to the waist, then up the companionway to the weather deck.

'Line up along the rail,' Mr Parry called, as the men taken by the gang emerged, eyes scanning the ship, the harbour and the ancient fortifications.

'I've seen him before,' one whispered, nudging the man standing next to him and pointing at the doctor. 'Can't rightly remember where, but it'll come to me.'

'Why should I care?' his mate replied.

'Stand upright! No talking.'

With a knotted rope's end swinging from the bosun's fist, the noise subsided.

Striding along the motley group of men, the captain glanced briefly at each man. Most eyes refused to meet his gaze preferring to stare blankly ahead or down to their bare feet. One fellow coughed several times, releasing the gunk from his chest, washing it around in his mouth before tossing his head back and swallowing. The man, who had been last to arrive, spat on the deck.

Standing directly in front of him, Captain Quintrell addressed the sailor. 'Name?'

The reply was mumbled.

'I asked you your name. I shall not ask again.'

'Irons. Zachary Irons.'

'So, Mr Irons, you choose to spit on authority – at the very service which, so far, has protected this country from invasion. Men give their lives willingly to protect cowards like you. And I don't doubt it was you tapping on the ship's timbers attempting to imitate a woodpecker.' He turned to Mr Parry. 'This man's wings need clipping and he needs to learn that freedom is not a right, nor should it be taken for granted. Freedom must be fought for to be deserved. Let this man's name be the first to be added to the muster book.'

'Damn your eyes, all of you,' Irons yelled. 'You don't give a sod. Twelve months I sweated in the West Indies. I've got a family at home. Now you sentence me to another year of Hell. I'd have more chance of freedom if I was in Newgate Prison.'

'Silence!' the lieutenant ordered.

'I warn you, Mister,' the captain said. 'Your name may not be in the ship's book as yet, but one more outburst and you will be seized up at the grating before this inspection is complete. Impressment is not my choice but, with men of all rank and file sacrificing their lives for England, it is a necessity of the service. Marines, when he has mopped up that foul deposit, take him below and secure him.'

There was little point in struggling. Zachary Irons knew his fate was sealed.

'Dr Whipple, if you would kindly examine these men.'

The young surgeon retraced the captain's footsteps, pausing in front of each man, looking briefly at his hair, eyes and opened mouth, instructing each to cough but not physically touching a single one of them. Then he returned to join the captain on the quarterdeck.

'In your opinion, Doctor, are any of these men unfit to serve?' Oliver enquired.

'Two or three. Do you wish me to indicate which ones?'

'If you would be so kind.'

'If the surgeon points to you, step from the line and wait by the windlass.'

The men shuffled about, one coughed loudly and let his chin fall onto his chest, saliva drooling from his mouth. Either he was unhealthy, or he was trying to appear so. But the doctor had already made his selection and pointed to three others. One had eyes that were crossed. Another had a large cauliflower-like growth protruding from his bottom lip and the third appeared to be little more than a bag of bones tied up in a shirt. They didn't need asking twice to leave the line and go forward.

'From that brief inspection, I can safely say the rest appear sound, but I would prefer to conduct a more thorough medical examination later.'

'Thank you, Doctor. That will suffice for the present.' Oliver turned back to the sixteen who remained. 'Raise your hand if you have spent time in prison or suffered jail fever.'

Two hands went up. The others glanced along the line.

'Stick your hand up,' one sharp-looking lout whispered to the man standing next to him, as he raised his own. 'They don't want thieves and murderers.'

After thinking about it for a moment, his mate – a red-headed Irishman sporting a recently broken nose and bruised cheek received a sharp elbow in his ribs. Not sure what he was letting himself in for, he lifted his hand.

'Four,' Mr Parry announced.

Oliver noted the faces and addressed the dozen who remained. 'Are any of you recently returned from the Indies?'

Not knowing the reason behind the question, the men were reluctant to admit to anything.

Mr Tully marched down the line. 'Raise your hands if you've ever sailed to the Indies. East or West, it don't matter.'

Six more hands went up.'

The captain considered his selection. 'Then it appears we are left with six fit and healthy men who are either lubbers or have never sailed beyond the Lizard.'

There was no answer.

'Discharge them, Mr Tully.'

'Begging your pardon, sir, but which ones?'

'The six healthy men, along with the three deemed unfit to serve. Ready a boat. Give them their shoes and deliver them back to Portsmouth with all speed.'

'That gives us a total of eleven,' Mr Parry noted. 'Four from the jails, six from the Indies and the man down in the hold.'

'That is well. I have made my choice. Eleven will suffice. After their names have been entered in the book, I suggest Mr Gibb or Mr Hanson read them the Articles of War and then have them returned below. I do not want to see them on deck until we have The Needles in our wake.'

'Begging your pardon, Captain, there is a volunteer who came aboard at the same time as the doctor. He has asked permission to sign. He would make up the round dozen and he's served with you before.'

'Name and rate?'

'Thomas Wainwright. He was powder money when he sailed last but he's now almost seventeen years.'

With a sharp prod in the back from the cooper, Tommy stepped forward.

Oliver showed no signs of recognition, but he did glance down to the sailor's left hand. 'You may add this man's name to the muster-book, Mr Parry. I believe the surgeon is in need of a loblolly boy.'

Tommy opened his mouth. 'Thank you, Captain, I just wanted to—'

'Silence there!' Mr Parry ordered. 'Mr Tully, a boat if you please. Have the captain's crew row these men ashore. Mr Gibb and Mr Hanson lend a hand. Look lively now!'

While the men waited for the boat to be lowered, it suddenly dawned on the fellow with the red hair what his lie had sentenced him to.

'Why did you make me stick me hand up?' he yelled, swinging a punch at the man next to him. 'I ain't never been in jail in my life.'

Within seconds the pair was tearing at each other's throats but a few clouts about the head and shoulders from the bosun's starter quickly brought the fight to a stop.

'Marines, escort these two below!' Oliver ordered. 'And make sure, when the Articles of War are read to them, they take special notice of the penalty for fighting.'

Purposely detaching himself from any further commotion, the surgeon removed himself to the taffrail at the stern of the ship. He chose to cast his eyes over the silky smooth water and observe the ship's boat lolling lethargically as it waited to receive its passengers.

Like the men the press-gang had brought in, he was somewhat perplexed by the captain's method of selection. It appeared to make no sense at all. But he was in no position to argue. In times of war, many seamen served as cannon fodder and it made not the slightest difference whether they had sailed to Spithead, the Saint Lawrence or the South Seas, or if they had spent time in Newgate Prison or the Black Hole of Calcutta.

A few hours later, the captain's choice of pressed men was argued over by the foremast, but the heated discussion was short lived. It was a situation that had happened before and would happen again and no matter what was said the opinions held by the men would have no bearing on the selection.

When Bungs had had his say, which everyone was obliged to listen to, he slapped Tommy on the back. 'Don't worry about what the captain said about you being the loblolly. I'll put in a word for you.'

'But I don't mind.'

'Don't be daft,' the cooper argued. 'What do you want to be a loblolly for? Think of the constant moanin' and screamin' in your ears, and bleedin' skulls peeled back like turnip skin, and the rasp of the saw as it chews through bone. I can tell you now, there'll be times you'll be tempted to murder them that won't lie down and die quietly. I'll speak with the captain. I'll tell him I'll teach you an honest trade – coopering. Then, when the war's over—'

'And when might that be?' Smithers piped up.

'Shut your trap, you old cockfart! I ain't talking to you.' Bungs turned back to Tommy. 'Like I said, when this war's over and long forgotten, you'll always get work as a cooper. There'll always be a need for barrels, you mark my words.'

'Aye. That's if the lad survives long enough.'

Bungs swung around and lunged for Smithers leaning against the pin rail grabbing his throat with both hands. 'One of these days, I promise, I'll stick a stave up your arse and weld an iron girdle around your neck and you'll never open your mouth again!'

Smithers pulled himself free, sneered, turned his head and spat into the harbour.

'Stow it, Bungs,' Tommy said. 'We all know Smithers' advice ain't worth a spoonful of snot. And, I thank you for your offer, and me ma would probably say you're right, but since the day me little finger was blown off and I spent a spell in the cockpit watching the old surgeon busy slicing and stitching, I thought it would be good to help in there – better than snorting gunpowder and cracking fingernails scraping rusty shot. Funny how things work out,' he laughed, 'but I never thought I'd get a chance. Besides, I don't mind the sight of blood or the cries and curses – it's better than a lungful of coal dust and the silence of a grave.'

Tommy looked around, pleased as Punch. 'Imagine the likes of me, a short-arse, no-good pit urchin, working for an educated toff like the surgeon. Wait 'til I get home to tell me ma.'

'Aye, and wait till the doctor learns that you never stop yapping. He'll nail your tongue to the slab to shut your blab.'

Tommy laughed. 'I can see nothing's changed since I was here before. It's good to be back.'

CHAPTER 4

Midshipman Gibb

'Mr Hanson. Mr Gibb. Hats off! Take a seat. The captain'll not bite you. Not this evening anyway.'

With little alternative, the pair of newly appointed midshipmen did as Mr Tully instructed taking their places for dinner, one on either side of Jack Mundy, the sailing master.

Captain Quintrell was already seated at the head of the table and, although engaged in conversation with Mr Parry, his eyes appraised every man as he arrived. Most were familiar faces, seasoned officers who had served under him for the past two years. Absent was Midshipman Smith or, more correctly, the Honourable Archibald Biggleswade Smythe. Mr Smith was on harbour watch together with Mr Nightingale – the third lieutenant, and the other middies.

Once seated, there was little conversation. Everyone was waiting for the final guest to arrive. Oliver did not need to draw his pocket watch, the ship's bell having sounded only five minutes earlier. The doctor was late. This was the second time.

When he arrived, some five minutes later, Dr Whipple offered his host an apology and bade the company good evening. After a polite bow, which was little more than a nod, he took the only vacant chair alongside one of the new midshipmen. Being the only civilian at the table, and not wearing naval uniform, he looked decidedly out of place.

The captain remained seated. 'Gentlemen,' he said, directing his words to the younger members of the crew, 'before we enjoy a sumptuous feast which, I might add, cook has taken hours to prepare, and before we drink a fine wine and some of you become totally distracted from your designated duties, I take this opportunity to introduce to you, Dr Whipple, ship's surgeon. For those of you who have not yet had the opportunity to speak with him, you will be interested to learn he has recently completed a lengthy sojourn in the Caribbean during which time he, no doubt, accrued many stories. I trust he will share some anecdotes with us over the coming weeks.

'Furthermore,' the captain continued, addressing his other table guests, 'I must welcome Midshipmen Gibb and Hanson who came aboard in my absence. As yet, I have not had the opportunity to acquaint myself with either of these young gentlemen, however, that matter will be rectified in the next day or so.'

The pair, dressed in brand new, slightly oversized uniforms and aged around twelve or thirteen years, smiled self-consciously.

The arrival of the steward with another bottle of wine broke a little of the early evening's polite silence. But the captain had not yet finished with the middies.

'Mr Gibb, pray tell us, what are your ambitions in the King's Navy?'

With all eyes directed at him, the lad shrank into his coat's collar.

'Come along, man, we are waiting for your answer.'

'To have my own ship, sir,' the midshipman said tentatively, not knowing what was expected of him. 'Then, perhaps one day, to make Admiral,' he added.

'Lofty ambitions, would you not agree?'

The company around the table laughed.

'Perhaps, passing the examination for lieutenant should come first,' Oliver quipped, his face showing no change of expression.

'Yes, sir. Of course, sir,' the boy admitted, a rosy flush spreading from beneath his jaw-line to the mass of curly white-blonde hair that rolled down his forehead and over his eyes. At a glance, he had the features of a girl, and a pretty one at that.

'Might I suggest the addition of a ribbon to your hair, Mr Gibb, or you could have it cropped in the manner adopted by some of the *beaus* in London. We have more than one barber on board who will be happy to oblige you.'

The surgeon acknowledged the jibe, rubbing his hand across his short bristle-brush *coiffure*.

The laughter subsided.

'Answer me this, Gibb,' the captain continued. 'Did you never go shooting with your father?'

'Yes, sir. Often, sir.'

'Then I do not need to tell you how difficult it is to recognize a stag's antlers when gazing through a hedgerow.'

Obviously embarrassed by the laughter and lacking sufficient worldly experience to comprehend or respond to the comment, the midshipman attempted to push his unruly locks behind his ears. But the angelic mop had a will of its own, springing back, determined not to be restrained.

Captain Quintrell turned his attention back to the surgeon. 'Doctor, let me now introduce the officers of His Britannic Majesty's frigate, *Perpetual* to you.'

Going clockwise around the table, he began with Mr Parry sitting on his left. 'My first lieutenant, whom, I believe, you have met.'

Simon Parry nodded to the surgeon.

Next is Mr Benjamin Tully, who will admit to being a little rough around the edges, but is an excellent seaman and well deserving the rank of second lieutenant. Mr Nightingale, my third lieutenant, could not join us as he is providing a watchful eye over the ship. He is a young man with a fine artistic hand, an admirable skill that is both commendable and very useful. Mr Nightingale has provided me with some remarkable illustrations, for both the ship's log and my personal journal, from our previous voyages.

'Mr Mundy, our sailing master has served with me the longest of all my officers. I could not wish for a better navigator, although he can be a little feisty at times.' The captain raised his glass to the Master. 'And we do not see eye to eye on all matters. Would that be a fair assessment?'

'Well I don't know about that,' Jack Mundy replied, with a sly grin.

'Exactly,' Oliver quipped. 'Mr Smith, one of my midshipmen is also biding his time on deck, probably counting each grain of sand as it slips through the hour-glass and adds to his time in the service.'

'Finally, Casson,' he turned his head to his steward who was standing near the cabin door. 'Step forward, man, and be introduced. John Casson, my personal steward, is possibly more familiar with my habits than I am myself. Like Jack Mundy, he has sailed with me for several years. A more trusted steward, I could not wish for.'

Casson didn't wait for the patter of applause to stop. 'If you'll excuse me Captain, I fetch some of the dishes in now.'

Oliver nodded and continued addressing Dr Whipple. 'Then of course, there are the warrant officers and their mates who you will come to know over time – hopefully not as names entered on your sick list.'

'I trust that is not the case,' the surgeon replied.

With the formal introductions over and glasses refilled, the atmosphere mellowed.

Although no one put the question, Oliver was conscious the company was eagerly anticipating news of his visit to London and his subsequent sailing orders. 'Gentlemen, if we gain some wind overnight, we sail tomorrow. And, you will be pleased to learn we will not be spending this coming winter in the northern reaches of the English Channel but heading into warmer, less fractious waters.'

His announcement was met with a buzz of approval. 'So, gentlemen, I suggest you enjoy your meal. The fresh delicacies, we are about to receive, will not last long!'

Another rumble of applause greeted the arrival of the captain's steward with his assistants carrying an assortment of dishes.

A steaming suckling pig, garnished with crab-apples, was placed in the centre of the table and next to it a potato and carrot pudding seeded with raisins and topped with green olives. The *coup de grâce*, however, was a long platter of five roast pigeons perched in a row.

Casson looked pleased. 'Them birds is stuffed with plum pudding and chestnuts and baked in the oven with gravy from their own juices. Cook said I should tell you.'

'Excellent,' Oliver said, 'I am sure they will be delicious. Perhaps you would do the honours, Casson, and assist those who are ready to partake.'

The midshipmen were eager with their plates.

'Patience gentlemen, there is enough for everyone.'

After thanking the Lord for his bounties, the meal commenced. For a short while, it was interrupted only by the clatter of knives and forks, smacking of lips and the sound of wine glugging from the bottle.

Setting his cutlery aside, Dr Whipple wiped his mouth and sat for a moment. 'I hope it would not be out of turn to congratulate you on your previous cruises, Captain. I heard they were very successful.'

The forthright nature of the comment took Oliver by surprise. 'I can only presume you are referring to the taking of prizes, Doctor, and the subsequent sale of the vessels and their contents by the agents?'

'Indeed, Captain. But I did not mean to speak out of turn. However, the success of your last mission was documented publically in the Kingston Chronicle – treasure from the Spanish vice-royalty, if I am not mistaken. The article also reported this was not the first time you had been well rewarded for your efforts.'

Oliver shot the doctor a disparaging look. 'Prize money, sir, is an entitlement within the British Navy and it provides the major incentive for men to sign as volunteers. This *reward* is absent in the French Navy whose crews are little more than a mob of disorganised and dissatisfied scallywags – men who have been dragged from their villages and forced to serve on a fighting ship against their will. The majority of them have no prior knowledge of the sea and are offered no financial incentive whatsoever. The only reward they can look forward to is a quick death, if they are lucky.'

'But,' the surgeon replied, 'if I might be so bold as to point out you have eleven men in the hold who I examined only a few hours ago. I understand they were given little choice when pressed into service.'

The company around the table stopped eating.

'That measure, sir, was taken out of necessity. It requires a certain number of hands to man a frigate such as this. In times of peace, it is not hard to attract volunteers, but in times of war, sailors die and have to be replaced. When there are no volunteers, we must look elsewhere to fill their shoes. The choice of men who are pressed into service is not as indiscriminate as you might think. The navy requires experienced seamen not landlubbers and the impressment gangs can easily identify a recently disembarked sailor by his clothes, his gait and the colour of his skin.

'It is unfortunate for those, like the group held below, that they have recently returned from a long period away from home, so to be taken from the London Road and placed on a navy ship may seem unjustifiable to you. However, these men will be paid wages for their time and rewarded for their toil. They will be treated well – unless they misbehave, in which case they will be punished. They will be well fed with regular, adequate rations and if they fall sick on a voyage, or are badly injured in battle, they will receive care from a ship's surgeon such as yourself. If, as a result of a permanent injury, they are disabled and deemed unfit to serve, they will be retired from the service and granted a pension for the rest of their lives. But above all, they will play their part in defending Britain from that megalomaniac, Napoleon Bonaparte.'

The captain did not release his gaze on the ship's surgeon.

'But further to your comment about prize money, the news sheets would be better employed in concentrating on the navy's successes in battle and not on the amount of prize money awarded to its senior officers. It is the direct result of such information appearing in the Portsmouth papers that my wife has been submitted to a constant line-up of nefarious characters turning up on our doorstep at all hours that God sends. All appear to be beggars and, while a few are deserving the others are scoundrels, fraudsters and opportunists. Being in a delicate state of health, such invasions of privacy are distressing to my wife, to say the least. One should not be called upon to defend one's private abode from such intruders.'

The doctor opened his mouth to speak but the captain had not finished.

'I would remind you, sir, that according to the division of prize money received from the prize agents, all the men who served with me received their appropriate allocation. But,' he continued, raising his voice slightly and addressing, not only the surgeon but also the two new midshipmen, 'for those amongst you who have been attracted to the service expecting to reap rich rewards, let me warn you that nothing is guaranteed. The past twelve months have returned only a meagre pittance in prize money to everyone aboard this ship. Furthermore, I do not anticipate my coming cruise to be any different.'

With the company around the table shuffling uncomfortably in their seats, Mr Parry posed a question to the surgeon in an attempt to moderate the tension.

'Perhaps you would care to share a little of your last voyage with us, Doctor. The West Indies is a hornet's nest of action, is it not? What were your expectations of the Royal Navy when you first applied to join a ship and were those expectations met?'

Pushing his plate away from the edge of the table, the surgeon placed his napkin alongside it. 'That was the first time I had travelled abroad, in fact it was the first time I had been on the sea in anything larger than a rowing boat. I admit, the experience delivered something of a shocking revelation to me. The sick berth in a man-of-war, situated below the waterline, is a far cry from the light and airy wards of the London Borough Hospitals. Although we sailed in tropical waters, I saw very little of the islands we circumnavigated.

'However,' he explained. 'It was an opportunity I would not have missed for, in that time, I became more intimately familiar with the workings of the human body than during all my time spent in London. Of course, the ship was engaged against the enemy on several occasions and at times the fighting was intense, the smoke from the gunpowder blinding and the noise deafening, but nothing was as unnerving to me as the speed by which infectious diseases ran rampant on those tropical islands.'

'Which diseases in particular are you referring to?' the sailing master asked.

'You could take your pick,' Dr Whipple replied. 'Often it was impossible to know. Swamp Fever, cholera, measles, smallpox, Yellow Jack – they all have some similar features, but the Yellow Jack was by far the worst. It claimed a quarter of the ship's crew. Even I succumbed to the illness for a time but, with help, I managed to recover. After exhausting all the medicines on board, and resorting to the use of local remedies, there was little I could do for the men who were sick, beyond segregating them and maintaining cleanliness throughout the ship. That is not a situation I would wish to return to.'

'Indeed,' Oliver commented with a degree of cynicism.

The doctor went on: 'I learned, from the Navy Board, Cadiz is suffering an epidemic of a similar nature.'

Oliver assessed the frowns on the faces at the table.

'Gentlemen,' the captain announced, attracting everyone's attention. 'Here is a question for you to consider. Let us think positively and not negatively on this score. If Spain was to enter the war tomorrow, it would not require a sea battle to defeat them. If the disease is spreading unabated, as Dr Whipple suggests, then King Carlos's Navy will be hard pressed to find enough fit sailors to man its fighting ships.' He turned to the sailing master. 'I regard that topic as a worthwhile question for these young men to ponder over during the coming days. Would you not agree?'

Before the sailing master could reply, another round of dishes was delivered to the table. The well-timed arrival distracted everyone from the topic of conversation.

'What do we have here, Casson, which cook has hidden beneath the crust?'

'Sea pie, Capt'n. From fish landed on Portsmouth dock only this morning. And a serve of pickled quail eggs, and periwinkles picked fresh from the beach. Cook sent his apologies and said they should have come up first.'

'Well done, Casson. Please thank cook for the excellent fare.'

The air hung with appetising smells.

'Eat up, Gentlemen, do not let any go to waste, although I am sure my steward and his mates will be able to dispose of any left-over servings, not forgetting the officers on watch.'

'A veritable feast,' Simon Parry added, helping himself to a slice of pork.

'Excuse me, Captain,' Mr Hanson said, 'If we are heading down the Channel, will we be joining the blockade fleet?'

'Not unless the situation changes. Admiral Cornwallis is adequately supplied with ships. Currently he has fifteen off Ushant, although I am sure some of his men would appreciate being relieved. Many have been on that station for a year and a half.'

While the captain was speaking, Mr Gibb took a large mouthful of fish pie and swallowed but, within seconds, it was obvious the bolus of food had not gone down his gullet as intended.

The captain chose to ignore the boy's spluttering but, when the half-chewed contents of the midshipman's meal was projected across the tablecloth towards him, Oliver cast the boy an extremely disdainful look. Attempting to ignore the lack of table manners, he continued his conversation.

'Eighteen months is a long spell,' he said. 'That is equal to the time Napoleon has been amassing his armies in France for a proposed invasion of Britain. It is well that the Channel patrols have proved a successful deterrent to his evil plans.'

Struggling to stop himself from coughing, the midshipman clapped his hand across his mouth. But the heaving continued.

'Take a drink,' the doctor suggested, pushing his glass of wine towards the young man.

'Mr Gibb,' the captain growled. 'If you cannot control your coughing, kindly withdraw yourself.'

With all eyes on him, the colour in the midshipman's face was no longer that of embarrassment. Unable to breathe properly, his skin had taken on a strange grey pallor, he was gasping for air. His lips tinged with blue.

Oliver persisted. 'Napoleon cannot launch an attack from either Toulon or Brest. He is completely hemmed in. Bayonne is his next alternative.'

'Will Lord Nelson stay in the Mediterranean?' Mr Hanson asked. But his question remained unanswered.

'For goodness sake, Mr Gibb, kindly remove yourself from my table until you are able to behave in a more acceptable manner.'

Heaving behind his napkin, the young man attempted to offer his apology, his head moving up and down like a tethered goat.

Rising from his seat beside him, the surgeon assisted the midshipman to his feet. 'If you will excuse me, Captain Quintrell, I will accompany the young gentleman to the deck. A little fresh air might help.'

'I see no necessity for you to leave the table, Doctor. He has two good legs, has he not?'

'In this instance, I prefer to lend some assistance. Gentlemen,' he said, inclining his head to the table. 'I beg you to excuse me.'

With his hands placed under Mr Gibb's armpits, Dr Whipple supported him through the doorway towards the ship's waist. The disturbing sounds continued for a while before slowly fading, as the pair struggled up to the deck.

For the company at the captain's table, the conversation was renewed, but the disruption to the evening's meal had not only left two empty places at the table but reduced the mood to one far less convivial than unusual.

'Well, I hardly think that performance was sufficient to necessitate the services of a surgeon,' Oliver said, trying to make light of the matter. 'But the doctor's loss will be our gain. Casson!' he called. 'Kindly open a bottle of that fine French brandy that I brought aboard with me. Unless the doctor returns shortly, I'm afraid he will miss out on an excellent drop.'

Early morning brought a welcome breeze blowing up from Spithead through the entrance of Portsmouth Harbour. It also brought with it heavy drenching rain making it impossible to see more than thirty yards. The massive chain gate, which was raised across the harbour entrance every night to protect England's premier harbour from enemy vessels, had already been lowered to the seabed but, despite the entrance being clear, no ships were sailing out. A few fishing boats headed in taking advantage of the flood tide and the southerly blow, the tired skippers relying on instinct to bring their boats to the fisherman's wharf.

Having been advised of the weather conditions at first light, Captain Quintrell had come on deck briefly to check for himself. Before returning to his cabin, he had left word to be called when the tide reached its full or if the rain stopped.

An hour later, the rain eased to showers and Oliver was again on the quarterdeck relieved to see the clouds breaking up and patchy pockets of blue colouring the grey.

'Wind's dropping and shifting to the east,' Mr Mundy confirmed. 'Still half-an-hour to the full. Shall I pass the order to make ready to sail?'

'Thank you, Mr Mundy. I have spoken with Mr Parry already.'

When the rain stopped completely, hammocks were immediately piped up – a little later than usual – and by the time the larboard watch came on deck, visibility had improved with the sun attempting to break through the clouds.

Across the Solent, the rolling hills of the Isle of Wight were visible as a hazy grey outline. Although he spent little time at his house on the island, it was Oliver Quintrell's home – the place he often thought of when he was far from England's shores.

On the left bank of the harbour mouth stood the old stone fortifications which had guarded the port in a long gone era, from the time when close action was fought from the decks of fighting ships with bows and arrows. Although the latest ships were different in their contours, the enemy from across the Channel was still the same one.

Away to the right, the Haslar Hospital reminded both officers and sailors alike of the wounded who were brought there to die or to recover, depending on the skill of the surgeons, the Hand of God and the will of the individual to survive.

Directly across from the Camber was Gosport with its military battery, assorted warehouses, docks and small jetties. From there, the victuallers' barges came and went serving the naval vessels anchored in the harbour and in Spithead.

After wasting no time in discharging their night's catch, a small fleet of fishing boats, with pots or nets piled high on their decks, prepared to head out again. They could not afford to miss the tide's reflux.

'Good morning, Captain. Fresh, isn't it?' Dr Whipple commented, rubbing his hands together.

'Come now, Doctor, it is not cold. It is summer. I fear your blood has run to water after lingering too long in the Caribbean.'

The surgeon smiled politely but did not engage in further conversation. He inhaled deeply but the breeze drifting from the Camber delivered only the unfortunate smell of fish.

Aloft, the topmen on the yards were making preparations to sail. The topsails and t'gallants were already ungasketted. On deck, the lashings on the ship's boats were secured, and any loose items were hurriedly taken below.

'I have not seen Mr Gibb on deck this morning,' the captain noted. 'Are you aware of his watch?'

'He is not on watch, Captain. He is in the cockpit.'

'He should be on deck. Why was I not informed?'

'I intended to inform you. I am afraid he is still unwell. I was hoping his condition would have improved so he could return to his duties.'

'Surely, he is not still coughing.'

'No.'

'Then I suggest you bring him here, immediately.'

'I am afraid he is sleeping.'

'Sleeping. At this hour? Then wake him up this instant.'

'That might be difficult. I have administered a dose of laudanum to sedate him.'

'Mr Parry,' Oliver called. 'The deck is yours, I am going below.'

Far from pleased, the captain headed down to the orlop deck surprising the hands who were still in the mess. 'Have you men nothing to do? On deck this instant!'

When they reached the door to the cockpit, Oliver stepped back and indicated for the surgeon to go ahead of him.

'The door is locked,' Dr Whipple said. 'I did not want the young man to be disturbed.'

'I suggest you open the door immediately!' Oliver demanded. 'I wish to speak with him.'

'That is my sick berth, Captain.'

'And this, sir, is my ship!'

The surgeon retrieved the key from his pocket and turned it in the lock. Although it was a spacious area, the sick berth was lit only by a single lantern hanging from the deck beam in the centre. When at sea, it swung like a pendulum over four chests pushed hastily together to form the table on which the surgeon operated.

The captain glanced around. Of the six cots suspended from the beams only one was occupied. A mop of soft white-blond curls heaped on the pillow identified the midshipman.

'As I said, Mr Gibb is sleeping. I respectfully ask that he is not disturbed.'

Oliver rubbed the soul of his shoe on the floor. 'You have sand on the deck. Did you perform an operation on this young man?'

'No, Captain. The sand was used to absorb the vomit. It makes cleaning easier.'

'And how do you intend to treat this man?'

'Purge him, perhaps. A dose of salts will allow his system to release the blockage and flush away the poison.'

Oliver regarded him quizzically. 'But you said the bone was stuck in his throat.'

'At this stage the poisoning in his blood is spreading through his body. Therefore, I will bleed him later,' the doctor said.

'Surely such treatment will weaken the fellow more. How much have you drawn already?'

'Only ten ounces.'

'And how much yesterday?' The captain's tone was cynical.

'Captain Quintrell, I do not tell you how to sail your ship. Kindly do not advise me how to treat my patients. I adhere to the practices commonly employed by the best surgeons of the London Borough Hospitals.'

'Then tell me this, sir. You bleed a man in an effort to improve his health, yet I have seen dozens, if not hundreds of men, wallowing in enlarging pools of blood on a gundeck. These men invariably die, yet according to the mode of treatment the London surgeons practice, they should be the healthiest men on the ship.'

The doctor did not reply.

Oliver turned. 'I wish to see Mr Gibb in my cabin when his condition improves. And, as he appears to be your only patient at the present time, you will accompany him.'

'I will be only too pleased to do so,' the doctor said, his pale blue eyes flickering in the lantern light.

'Your assistant, Mr Longbottom and the loblolly – young Tommy Wainwright – where are they?'

'Mr Longbottom is at the grindstone in the carpenter's shop sharpening my knives. Mr Wainwright is in the waist cutting strips of bandage from a bolt of linen.'

'It appears you are expecting the worst.'

'I am preparing for whatever might eventuate.'

CHAPTER 5

English Channel
5 August 1804

Soon after ten o'clock, on the morning of 5 August, the British frigate, under the command of Captain Oliver Quintrell, proceeded from Portsmouth Harbour on the ebbing tide. Once clear of the heads, more sail was added and, with a freshening breeze from the south-east, *Perpetual* headed across Spithead and down the Solent to the English Channel. Apart from local fishing boats, there were only two naval ships sitting in the roadstead and a handful of merchant vessels anchored in St Helens Road and on the Motherbank.

The course, which the captain had discussed earlier with his sailing master, followed the English coast until they were south of Plymouth. From there, they would bear diagonally across the Channel towards Ushant on the north-eastern tip of France. The lookouts would need to be vigilant. The English Channel was a busy waterway, even during peacetime, frequented by ships of various European navies, Indiamen, merchants and coastal traders.

With lookouts on both the fore and main mastheads, Oliver was acutely aware of the importance of the dispatches he was carrying. The written instructions he had received from the Admiralty clearly stated:

You are to keep a weight constantly affixed to the dispatches and in case of falling in with an enemy of superior force – you are to throw them overboard and sink them.

Such a command was not unusual and, if such a situation came about, he would do as instructed. It would not be the first time.

With the squares braced to bear, the wind drummed on the canvas while the jibs and staysails crackled, as they were hauled across the deck obliterating all other sounds. But once *Perpetual*'s head turned and the courses were sheeted home, the only sounds were the gentle hum from the vibrating rigging and the regular *thrap* and gurgle of the bow plunging into the swell flowing in from the Atlantic Ocean.

Standing near the helm, the captain inclined his head to windward and listened. To the men on deck, the sounds were imperceptible, but to the captain and his first officer, the dull distant thunder carried on the wind, was the unmistakable sound of guns.

'Do you hear it, Mr Parry?

'Yes, Captain. It's coming from the French coast.'

There was no way of knowing what the action was and very soon they were out of earshot. No doubt, it would be reported in the Naval Chronicle.

By early afternoon, *Perpetual* had left The Needles in its wake and the eleven pressed men, who had been confined in the hold, were released armed with the knowledge their fate was sealed. Five were allocated to the larboard watch, the remainder to starboard. An issue of slops clothing was supplied by the purser to those who needed them and each man was issued two hammocks plus a plate, knife, spoon, wooden tankard and a cake of soap.

After being allocated a place in the mess to sling his hammock, each man's initials were marked on the beam from which he would lash it. According to the rules, only 18 inches of space was allowed per man, as determined by the Navy Board. However, with the hammock on either side designated to hands from the opposing watch, there were few occasions when the sailors were occupying them at the same time.

Finding a place to sit in the mess at mealtimes was not such an easy task. No rules applied here. Each swinging table had space to accommodate six or eight men, the sailors sitting where they chose. Most tables were occupied by mates, men who had sailed together for months or even years. As such, most groups didn't take kindly to having newcomers in their midst, eavesdropping on their private conversations, stealing their jokes, telling tales or spreading malicious rumours. With few choices, the newly signed hands wandered the length of the mess looking for a place to sit but being merchantmen and pressed men to boot meant they were doubly unpopular.

'You shift yourselves across,' the bosun's mate shouted at two of the regular crew. Brandishing his knotted starter, he swung it in front of their faces. 'If you don't, you'll feel the sting of the rope's end across your head,'

With an undercurrent of curses and grumbles, a few men reluctantly slithered along their sea chests and a made space available.

The pressed men were not happy either. Seeing the Isle of Wight disappearing from view meant they had lost their freedom – lost the chance of escape and of seeing their wives and children. Now they were stuck on a navy ship loaded with stores for a six month voyage, heading to sea. It would be a long time before they would be returning home. The only reason they controlled their fists and tempers was to avoid being locked in the hold again.

'We don't want you here,' Bungs yelled. 'Find another spot.'

Muffin shrugged. 'Give it up, Bungs. As long as I've sailed with you, you've always been the same. At least, let the man sit down and eat. You don't have to talk to him or even look at him.'

'So, what's up with you, Muffinman?' the cooper sneered. 'What's brought on this sudden burst of goodwill? He won't return you no favours, you mark my words.'

'Let him be,' Eku said, moving along the sea chest to allow room for one man to sit down. 'Plenty of space here for young Tommy and room for another.' The other messmates at the table held their tongues as usual.

'I don't mind you, young Tom,' Bungs said. 'I saved a place for you all the months you was ashore. You didn't know that, did you?'

'It's true,' said the big Negro, 'while me and Muffin had to put up with his yapping all the time.' He turned to the pressed sailor. 'What's your name, man?'

'The name's Zachary Irons, and don't you forget it.'

'Else what?' Bungs challenged.

'You'll find out soon enough.' Irons barked.

Eku looked down at the man's hands. They were calloused and brown and his nails blackened with pitch. 'Off a merchant ship, are you?' he asked, having served on several himself in the past.

'How do you know?' Irons replied, suspiciously.

'He might be black as the ace of spades,' Bungs said, 'but he ain't dumb. Eku 'ere knows a thing or two. Including a bit of Voodoo magic.'

Tommy laughed. 'Not that again. Come on Bungs, if Zac has been in the Caribbean, likely he knows as much as Eku does. Maybe more.'

'Have it your way then, I'll find another table where they'll appreciated my company.' The cooper stood up to leave.

'Don't be daft, you old fool. Sit down,' Muffin ordered. The others were surprised to hear him speak his mind. Bungs, however, threw a deaf ear to the mess table and lumbered off.

'Don't worry,' Tommy said, 'He'll be back.'

'I ain't worried,' Irons said.

'So where have you been put?' Eku asked.

'The main,' he mumbled in reply.

'Top?' Muffin asked.

Zachary Irons nodded.

Tommy was impressed. Good topmen were the elite of the working crew. On most ships, they messed together and didn't tolerate newcomers easily. More than any other group on a fighting ship, the life of every man on the yards depended on the skill and strength of the man working alongside him. Zachary Irons would have to prove his worth in the frigate's rigging, and do so quickly, if he was going to be accepted into that fraternity.

'Why were you put up top?' Eku asked.

''Cause that's where I work. I don't work anywhere else. And that's what I told the lieutenant.'

Eku winked at Tommy. 'Well that'll keep him out of Bungs' locker at least.'

The following morning, standing in the doorway to the captain's cabin, the surgeon coughed to attract attention.

Oliver glanced up. 'Come in, Dr Whipple and bring the midshipman with you. He *is* with you I trust.'

The surgeon entered. 'I'm afraid not. He took a bad turn through the night. I did all I could to help him but to no avail.'

Oliver stared straight into the pale eyes. 'Are you telling me Mr Gibb is dead?'

'Yes, Captain.'

Oliver was shocked. 'But he was a fit and lively young man only two days ago! Goddamit, he only came aboard a week ago. This cannot be!'

The doctor closed the door behind him. 'You must understand what happened,' he said softly. 'In attempting to swallow a fish bone, it became firmly lodged in his throat and, as a result of his coughing and retching, the bone pierced his gullet and became wedged. By constantly poking his finger down his throat, the young man succeeded in exacerbating the matter. It was for that reason I sedated him.'

The captain shook his head.

'I tried everything, but I could not avert the raging infection which quickly took hold, nor prevent the blood poisoning from spreading throughout his body. The administration of laudanum eased his breathing and soothed him in his final hours. I did all I could.'

Nothing could be said or done which would change the course of events surrounding the midshipman's untimely death. Sitting at his writing desk, staring down at a blank piece of paper, Oliver pondered the irony of naval service. Death in battle was an accepted part of life. Death by misadventure was occasionally inevitable and accidents happened when least expected. Yet the waste of a young life, by whatever cause, was always a tragedy. Such an event had happened on his last cruise, although the malady and circumstances had been entirely different. In future, there was nothing to guarantee something similar would not happen again.

Writing a letter to the boy's family, whom he had never met, explaining the nature of their son's death, was difficult in the extreme. Oliver pictured them, at the time when their son had prepared to leave home for the first time. He imagined the boy parading himself across the floor in his oversized uniform. A fine-looking midshipman. No longer a child. He visualized the tears and affectionate kisses bestowed on the boy by his mother and grandmother when they finally said their fond farewells. He imagined the father's grand ambitions for his son, fully expecting him to rise up through the naval ranks to make his family proud.

To be felled fighting the enemy would have provided for an acceptable and glorious epitaph, but that was not the case. Midshipman Gibb had choked on a mouthful of fish pie and Oliver was bearing the guilt of having reprimanded him for coughing at the dinner table. Had he coughed the bone out instead of trying to withhold the reflex, his death may never have resulted.

'Sir, you have no reason to feel guilty,' Casson said, as he removed the Captain's untouched cup and saucer. 'I was responsible for dishing out his portion on the plate. What if that serve had gone to you or Mr Parry? That bone could have stuck in your throat just as easy. It's fate – that's what it is. There's no accounting for why this sort of thing happens and there's no one to blame but the lad himself for eating too fast without chewing his food. My mother used to say to my brother and me, "Chew your food a hundred times then you'll think you've eaten a hundred spoonfuls instead of only one."' Casson chuckled. 'If truth be told, we'd be lucky if we got more than one spoonful some days.'

Oliver pondered on the sheer luck of birthright – of boys born into households, where substantial meals were served several times a day, while others begged on street corners for scraps, or starved. Although the food served to the crews of His Majesty's ships was considered unpalatable, monotonous and insufficient by some, to others it represented a feast.

'Thank you, Casson.' Oliver said, with a half-smile. He knew his steward's intentions were good, yet doubted any words would absolve him from guilt at this time. The boy had been placed into his care and had been his responsibility.

'Pass the word to Mr Parry to assemble the men at noon for the burial service. I shall require my dress uniform.'

'Aye aye, sir.'

'There weren't much left of the lad, were there?' Bungs said, when recounting the burial service that evening in the mess.

Abel Longbottom, the assistant surgeon, who had carried the young midshipman in his arms from the sick berth to the deck, had told Tommy Wainwright the boy weighed no more than four stone.

'There was hardly a dent in that hammock he was sewed into. The round shot took up more space.'

Next morning, with *Perpetual* south of Start Point, waiting on a wind to carry it across the Channel to Ushant, all hands were called and preparations were made to exercise the guns.

Mr Tully addressed the gun crews.

'Captain wants to see how useful the new hands are who haven't sailed with us before. They'll be divided between the crews. You all know what's expected of you. Teach them well. They are your responsibility now.'

Splitting crews that had served together for years, and substituting inexperienced sailors was even more unpopular than seating new men in the mess. Pressed men were despised on the gundeck, not because they were ignorant of working the guns but because they were often troublesome, argumentative, lazy or downright careless. Such attributes were the ingredients for serious accidents.

'We'll have the deck bouncing and you all dancing to its beat in no time,' Mr Tully shouted, his former foremast-Jack voice easily carried the length of the gun deck. 'There ain't no finer hornpipe!' he quipped.

The gun captains and regular members of the crews watched the pressed sailors as keenly as a hawk eyes a field mouse. Powder and shot were not items to be played with. One false move could be fatal for them all.

Bungs, Eku and Muffin were still with Hobbles, the near deaf-as-a-post gun-captain, who had devised a system of hand signals for the firing sequence. Much to Bungs' disgust, Lompa and Styles were allocated to Hobbles' gun crew – the pair who'd lied to avoid selection by saying they had been in jail. It was soon obvious they were lazy and not prepared to pull their weight either on a gun or any other job aboard the frigate. Zachary Irons, who now messed on Bungs' table, had been excused from gun practice, because he was a topman.

With preparations to fire underway, the powder monkeys scampered along the deck delivering cartridges to the gun captains. The gun ports were opened and secured. The guns loaded, primed and run out. Then everyone waited for the order to fire.

Having grown almost two inches during his time back at home, Tommy Wainwright was no longer seen as a boy and, having the post of surgeon's loblolly, he no longer had to act as a powder monkey. Despite it being one of the most vulnerable locations on a ship during battle, his place was now with the idlers in the waist, the area of the frigate affectionately known as the slaughterhouse.

Better than being stuck in the magazine scraping shot, Tommy thought.

When gun practice was over, Tommy returned to the cockpit. He liked his new job. He liked the surgeon too.

'Carry the bucket carefully and tip the contents into the sea,' Dr Whipple said. 'But be mindful it doesn't spill and keep the lid closed. The smell is not pleasant and I don't want to hear any complaints from the sailors on deck.'

After only two days, Tommy was used to carrying the ungainly wooden pail with its rope handle, and was becoming quite adept at preventing the fluid from spilling every time the ship pitched and rolled when climbing the ladder. But this time the bucket was heavy. It was filled near to the brim, and the wooden lid wasn't fitted tightly enough. As he made his way to the weather deck, bilious green fluid slopped out, trickled down the sides and left a trail of drops along the deck. Tommy ignored them. Such spots would scrub off far easier than bloodstains could be removed after a fight.

'Make way!' he yelled, as he headed to the frigate's lee side.

'Make way for the milk maid!' one of the sailors mocked.

'Anything tasty in there?' Smithers cried.

'Captain's tea coming up!' Brickley joked.

'Back to work you louts!' Mr Tully reminded. 'If you're so keen on having a bucket, then you can help yourself to one, and get a broom while you're at it and swab the deck again.'

The men returned to their duties.

'Only 'aving a bit of fun,' Smithers jibed, his upper lip raised to reveal his toothless gums.

Tommy ignored the banter. Usually he was quick with a smart reply but only if there was no officer in sight. This cruise was his second aboard a naval frigate and already he was learning more than the ropes. Working with Dr Whipple and Abel Longbottom, in the cockpit, made him feel special. He'd grown not only in height, but in his attitude and way of thinking. The cooper had been the first to notice the differences in him but wasn't sure he liked what he saw, and he had been quick to remind him of it.

Securing one end of a line to the caprail and the other to the pail's rope handle, Tommy waited for the right moment. When the ship heeled, he tipped the contents into the sea. After checking it was empty, he let the salt water wash over it. Having learned an early lesson, after losing his grip on one bucket, he was careful not to let the sea grab it and drag it away.

'Hey, look at that!' The voice came from the shrouds, the topman pointing to the ship's wake.

Immediately, heads spun around to see what the man was pointing at. With *Perpetual* barely making three knots, it was easy to pick the spot in the ocean that was bubbling like a pot on the galley stove.

'See the fish,' the sailor on the ratlines shouted.

There were dozens of them. Big fish leaping, diving, flipping while fighting over the generous feed tipped from the bucket.

'Ain't you never seen a fish before,' Mr Tully yelled, leaping onto the caprail to get a better view.

'Them's innards!' a voice yelled.

'Back to work!' Mr Tully ordered, 'Or you'll find your name at the top of the morning list!'

In less than a minute, the shoal of frenziedly fish were lost to the rolling swell and the sailor, who wandered casually across the deck to find out what the commotion was about, found nothing of interest to see.

'I saw it myself,' Mr Tully admitted to the captain. 'I'd have thought little of it, but some of the topmen also seen it and recognised the coils.'

'Coils?' Oliver queried.

'Aye, coils of innards, like the sort you see hanging out of a man's belly after he's been sliced open with a cutlass.'

'I appreciate your description, Mr Tully. Your observation will be noted.'

'But that's not all,' the second lieutenant added rather apologetically, 'I've overheard murmurs. The men say the doctor is butchering his patients. Them rumours have got some of the hands too scared to answer the sick call.'

'Thank you, Mr Tully. I will speak with the surgeon. In the meantime, I trust you will assure the men that we have adequate provisions on board and there is no necessity for Dr Whipple to cannibalise the crew.'

The lieutenant knuckled his forehead and closed the cabin door as he left.

Oliver thumped his fist onto the deck. 'Damn, damn and damnation. What is it about this ship's surgeon that aggravates me so?'

Casson poked his head around the door. 'Did you call, Captain?'

'No, I was merely clearing my throat. Coffee however, would be most acceptable.'

'Coming up in two ticks.'

'Dr Whipple,' the captain said objectively. 'I have been informed by Mr Tully that earlier today the men on the deck witnessed the contents of a pail from the cockpit being emptied over the ship's side by your young assistant, Tommy Wainwright. I am also advised that what the men saw appeared to be human intestines floating on the surface of the sea and being gorged on by hungry fish. What is your response to that claim?'

'What they saw was correct, Captain. In hindsight, I should have told the lad to empty it after dark. But, I can assure you the intestines were not human. They were from a pig butchered the day before we left Portsmouth. I begged the cook to save the intestines for me and he kindly obliged.'

'Isn't it customary for the galley to use that commodity to make sausages?'

'Cook said he was too busy to do so, because of the preparations for your excellent meal. He also said they were beginning to smell, and he intended to toss them out.'

'Indeed,' the captain said, with a sigh. 'I will speak with the cook regarding such wastage, but for the present, what is your interest in the contents of a pig's belly?'

'Pig, goat, sheep or man – apart from the number of stomachs, we are all very much the same inside. Anatomising this type of specimen is an interesting challenge.'

Oliver frowned. 'Might I remind you, Doctor, you have a duty on this ship to serve your King and His Majesty's Navy. When a man enters this disciplined way of life, he must say farewell to his favourite haunts, habits, hobbies and, indeed, even those who are dear to him. Perhaps you have failed to realize this.'

'Captain, I respect the Royal Navy and am trying to improve my knowledge in order to advance myself in the service. My tutor, the very well respected surgeon, Mr Astley Cooper – a highly regarded London surgeon, anatomised a whale, a kangaroo and even an elephant at his home in central London.'

Oliver was not impressed. 'It may surprise you, sir, but I do not care for the dissection habits of such men or where they choose to conduct their outrageous experiments.'

He continued. 'I would remind you, this is my ship and the welfare of every man aboard is my concern. Anything which unsettles, or troubles them, likewise unsettles and troubles me. In future, I will be grateful if you will restrict your so-called *interesting challenges* to bed bugs, rats and 'roaches. Good day to you, sir.'

'Come on, Tommy,' Muffin begged. 'You call tell me what was in the bucket. I shan't say a word.'

'I don't know,' Tommy answered in all innocence. 'Whatever it was it was already in there when I went down to the cockpit. I just did what I was told and got rid of it. I never looked inside.'

'Huh! I thought you were a mate of mine,' Bungs said. 'But since you were made loblolly, I think you fancy yourself as being a step above your old mess mates.'

'That's not true,' the lad argued. 'I was just doing my job. All this talk about what the doctor is supposed to be up to ain't fair. He's a good man and he does all he can for them he attends to. But, he said to me that if some are too far gone, no amount of medicine will cure them.'

'Bollocks!'

Eku nudged Tommy in the ribs. 'Ignore Bungs, he'll come around.'

Unfortunately, by being one of the last to hear about the pig's intestines tossed to the sea, it was obvious Bungs' nose had been put out of joint.

'Next time you throw an arm or a leg overboard, tell me first. I want to be on deck to see it swim.'

Eku nudged again and Tommy couldn't stop a smile from curling on the corners of his lips. Sitting opposite the cooper, the pair watched Bungs scratch the outline of a fish on the mess table with the point of his knife. He appeared to be ignoring them. Then he lifted his head and pointed his knife at Tommy.

'Tread careful, lad,' Bungs threatened. 'I warn you. Keep your hands out of the bodies of the dead. There's no telling what evil will jump out and grab you.' Then turning the blade towards Ekundayo, he hissed. 'I shouldn't need to remind *you*. Leave the dead to the dead. That way they aren't doing anyone any harm.'

CHAPTER 6

The Blockade Fleet

'Deck there! Sail ho!'

The officer of the watch waited for more information.

'British. Tops'l schooner. Come away from Plymouth. Heading south.'

The midshipman hurried to the bow but without a glass he was unable to read the schooner's name.

The midshipman noted the time of the sighting on the board but, because of the size of the vessel and the direction it was sailing, he was not unduly concerned.

Since leaving Spithead, they had noted fifteen ships. The English Channel was a busy thoroughfare, not only for British naval vessels, but for ships from many European countries including France. Barques, sloops, brigs and Indiamen serving the East and West Indies were regular sailers, as were local coastal traders, coal carriers and fishing boats. Three-masted merchant ships, loaded with cargoes from the Baltic, regularly headed out across the Atlantic, while dilapidated slave ships returned home from the New World their holds loaded with sugar, coffee or rum, their masters' pockets stuffed with the tainted profits from their inhuman trade.

With *Perpetual* having veered to southward, following in the wake of the schooner, the gap between the two ships narrowed sufficiently for the captain to read the name.

'HMS *Pickle*,' Oliver noted.

Simon Parry took the glass. 'Six guns. Appears to be heading for Brest, as we are.'

Oliver agreed and recounted the gossip he had overheard in the Admiralty's reception room. 'A week ago one of its seamen was flogged around the fleet in the Hamoaze. Another had been accused of mutiny, but the court had dismissed the charge, however he also received a severe punishment for insolence, disobedience and desertion.' The captain paused. 'Perhaps that message can be conveyed to the newly signed hands.'

'Breakers a mile off the port bow!' the lookout shouted.

The north-western tip of the French coast was naturally protected by hidden reefs and rugged rocks which rose from the boiling sea like giant claws ready to rip apart the hulls of unwary ships. Of the scattered islands broken from mainland France to resemble the ragged tail of the Andes at Cape Horn, Ushant was the largest.

Over the centuries, the treacherous reefs that surrounded it had claimed numerous ships and many lives, a concern which Oliver had discussed with Mr Mundy when they had plotted their course. The quickest passage and the one taken by the schooner, *Pickle*, ran between Ushant and the mainland. It was a broad stretch of water but the winds and currents funnelling through it were unpredictable and frequently fickle.

In taking into account the fact the ships of the Channel Fleet would be scattered over many miles of ocean, Oliver opted to take a broad reach. Mr Mundy argued such a course would add considerable time and unnecessary sea miles to the voyage. Although usually confident of his sailing master's navigational skills, and being aware Mr Mundy had served with a previous blockade of Brest in the '90s, on this occasion, he decided to steer well clear and head west.

Two hours later, after rounding the coast, the call, which everyone had been waiting for, came down from the foremasthead lookout. 'Two sail of ships on the port bow!'

It was met with a cheer from the men on deck.

Soon after, another ship was sighted, *Neptune* 98 guns. Carrying 28 thirty-two pounders on her main gun deck, 60 eighteen pounders on her other two gun decks, and twelve pounders on her fore and quarterdecks. She was a formidable fighting ship.

Fifteen minutes later, four more ships were sighted – two men-of-war and two frigates. It was indeed the British blockade fleet under the command of Rear Admiral of the United Kingdom, Sir William Cornwallis, the sixty year old affectionately known to his men as, *Billy Blue*.

As anticipated, although *Perpetual* was twenty miles from the French estuary, the ships of the fleet were scattered over many miles. Some were patrolling far out in the Atlantic, others in the Bay of Biscay, while several were hove to almost within gunshot of the Brest batteries.

Reducing sail, *Perpetual* swam between them, everyone eager to be first to spot the Commodore's broad swallow-tailed pendant. But before it could be found, the frigate was hailed by *Indefatigable*. Using the trumpet, Mr Tully spoke the ship advising that Captain Quintrell was carrying urgent dispatches to be delivered to Lord Cornwallis and requesting his location within the fleet.

The answer was not what Oliver had expected. His Lordship had been taken ill and had returned to Torbay to recover. Although it was likely he would be returning to duty in a matter of days, in the interim, command had been passed to Vice-Admiral, Sir Charles Cotton. Such situations were not unusual. Commands changed frequently in times of war.

The message was promptly acknowledged, the location of Captain Cotton's ship provided, and the two frigates parted company. Armed with a bearing and approximate distance, *Perpetual* adjusted sail and headed away to locate the acting fleet commander.

From the deck, the captain watched as a stream of coloured flags travelled up *Indefatigable*'s signal halyard. His frigate's arrival within the fleet was being broadcast to the ships of the fleet and his attendance with Captain Cotton would not come as a surprise.

Oliver turned to Jack Mundy standing beside the binnacle. 'I trust this mission is not to be dogged by ill-health.'

His comment did not receive a response.

Despite being deprived of the opportunity to attend Lord Cornwallis in person, the meeting with Vice Admiral Sir Charles Cotton proved informative. After handing over the dispatches from the Admiralty, Oliver could not refuse the offer to dine with Sir Charles and his senior officers aboard the flagship. It appeared to Captain Quintrell, that the officers of the Channel Fleet were as pleased to receive his company as he was to join them. It made for an enjoyable and entertaining evening which Mr Parry, Mr Tully and Mr Nightingale attended with him.

'Did you meet with any action in the Channel?' Sir Charles asked.

'No, sir, we steered clear of the French coast purposely,' Oliver replied. 'However, there has been considerable activity on the French coast recently. Le Havre was under attack for the second time on the day we departed Portsmouth. Only a week before, a convoy of bomb vessels delivered a tremendous bombardment of shells to Le Havre pier. I heard the action lasted for one and a half hours. Although the enemy's batteries had been increased recently, the town was razed. The guns were manned by the officers and men of the Royal Artillery and I understand their conduct was exemplary.'

Oliver cast his mind to the group of young marines he had on board. *How adept are they on the guns?* he wondered.

'And where are you heading now, Captain?'

'From here, I sail for Ferrol with dispatches for Lord Cochrane. The Admiralty is aware that troops are mounting at Bayonne.'

'Indeed they are,' Captain Cotton replied. 'Hundreds of French troops are arriving in small detachments and amassing there. Four French ships of the line have been observed sailing in that region. But, I fear, this part of the coast is receiving less attention than it deserves. Rochefort is a busy port and we have seen some action on the coast south of here. Lord Cornwallis sends regular patrols to keep an eye on activities, while Lord Cochrane does what he can from Ferrol to monitor the north coast of Spain.

'Two weeks ago, *Aigle* fell in with a large brig and two French Corvettes of 20 guns each, heading south. Captain Wolfe succeeded in driving them ashore a few miles from Bordeaux. But a great gale of wind off Biscay forced them high on the beach. Despite Wolfe's efforts to refloat them, with a view of returning them to England as prizes, he did not succeed and had no alternative but to set fire to them both. From the prisoners he took, he learned the ships were from Rochefort and were heading for Bayonne. I beg you to pass this information to Lord Cochrane when you meet him.'

After sampling the congenial hospitality of Sir Charles and his crew, Oliver did not wish to delay any longer. Early on the morning of August 9, *Perpetual* headed across the Bay of Biscay, the strong westerly wind living up to its reputation, stirring up a huge swell and threatening to push the frigate east across the bay to the coast of France.

With *Perpetual* burrowing its beak into the huge swell and waves crashing across the deck like a winter sea over a breakwater, Oliver was anxious to test the ability of the marines on board. Although trained to fire heavy guns on a parade ground, a firing platform, or a defensive wall, he doubted they would be capable of either handling or firing a cannon on the pitching, heeling gundeck of a fighting ship at sea. But he must wait until the sea calmed and it was safe to proceed with the gun ports open. He knew, it would not be a popular exercise with either his own gun crews or the marines, but from what he had heard of the action off Le Havre, the Royal Artillery had done a splendid job. The marines he had aboard were neither soldiers nor sailors but, in his estimation, they must prove to him that they could live up to the standards of both.

On the evening before they sailed into the broad bay on which Ferrol was situated, Captain Quintrell gathered his officers in his cabin.

'Gentlemen, I am now at liberty to divulge a little more of my meeting with the First Sea Lord – Lord Melville who replaced Earl St Vincent. However, I remind you, Lord Melville is a military man who has never served on a navy ship.

'What I learned in London, is that almost two months ago, the Admiralty received information that a fleet of Spanish ships was preparing to depart from Monte Video on the Rio de la Plata – carrying treasure.'

Grins broke out on the faces around the table.

'That convoy was due to depart from South America on 7 August – two days ago – heading across the Atlantic bound for Cadiz. According to the Admiralty's estimations, the ships will be off the coast of Spain early in October. Because of the number of days the voyage will take, there is no immediate urgency.'

'Are we going to attack them?' young Mr Hanson asked eagerly.

'No, decidedly not. When the time is right, ships from the blockade fleet off Brest will be dispatched to intercept the treasure before it can be landed.'

'But to attack Spanish ships in time of peace would be an act of piracy,' the sailing master commented boldly.

Oliver nodded. 'I said, *intercept* and not *capture*. But you are correct, Mr Mundy, Lord Melville was specific in his instructions – "the ships are not to be taken by force but intercepted and detained, then accompanied into a British port". According to the information the government received, the wealth contained in these ships is destined for Bonaparte's dwindling coffers, to enable him to escalate the war against Britain. It is the Admiralty's intention to deprive the Spanish Crown and Napoleon of those finances.

'The rumblings, which are currently being heard from both France and Spain, indicate we are drawing closer to the brink of war with Spain. War may even be declared before the treasure ships arrive. Only if that occurs will Britain be at liberty to attack and plunder the Spanish ships.'

'Will *Perpetual* be included in the fleet sailing to detain the treasure ships?' Simon Parry asked.

'I asked the same question of the First Lord. His answer was *no*. The Channel Fleet presently comprises fifteen ships and can afford to release three or four to provide a reception party.'

'But what of *Perpetual*, Captain?'

'My orders are to proceed to Gibraltar to support the colony's defences. When we arrive there, I will take further orders from the military commander on the Rock.'

The captain's words were met with some questioning looks and frowns of disappointment.

'Let me remind you,' the captain said. 'Gibraltar is a veritable fortress. First and foremost it is a military stronghold attended by navy ships. Twenty years ago, the garrison withheld the onslaught of a combined French and Spanish attack. That action was the Great Siege and it was fought over three years. It was a remarkable military, not naval victory, which confirmed Britain's sovereignty over the Rock.

'Before his retirement, Earl St Vincent spent a year residing there and during that time made many recommendations for the enhancement of the facilities, not least improving the naval dockyard and building a fleet of gunboats. It was his fervent desire to elevate the navy's position on the Rock and establish Gibraltar's name as a naval stronghold, not just a military one. During his time there, St Vincent uncovered many deficiencies, not least the absence of fresh water, the inadequate victualling yards and the lack of shipwrights. Without food, water and wrights, how can ships be refitted and resupplied?'

'Have any water storage tanks been constructed?'

'Work has begun but is not yet complete. Which reminds me, Mr Parry, we must replenish our water barrels when we leave Ferrol.'

Oliver continued. 'St Vincent was not alone in his concerns. As you all know, the Mediterranean Fleet is dependent on Gibraltar for refitting his ships, and when Lord Nelson last visited, he also made recommendations for improvements. His major concern was the inadequate conditions of the shipyards and lack of skilled shipwrights, plus the need for new victualling yards.

'Without adequate yards, the fleet cannot be properly fed, and without decent shipyards, battle-weary ships of the Mediterranean Fleet must sail to Falmouth or Plymouth for repair.'

'What will we be doing when are there?' the midshipman asked.

'What our duties will be while under the command of the Lieutenant-Governor remains to be seen.'

The next day, on the morning tide, *Perpetual* sailed into the mouth of a broad bay on the north-western coast of Spain and dropped anchor. Overlooked by castles and fortifications and surrounded by docks and shipyards, Ferrol was the centre for the Spanish Navy. Unlike Brest, Ferrol Harbour was an impregnable inlet, impossible to blockade due to the prevailing westerly gales that forced patrolling ships dangerously close to the rugged coast. For the Spanish fleet, however, it was a safe haven for an impressive fleet.

Three first-rates, a second-rate, ten third-rates and six fourth- and fifth-rates wallowed on the placid waters in company with 16 gunboats each armed with a long 21 pound gun. Apart from *La Conception*, 130-guns, which was without her masts, the other ships' yards were crossed with all sails bent. All were in good repair with guns on board. Should Spain declare war on Britain and join forces with Napoleon's navy, the fleet was ready to sail at any time. If so, they would present as a formidable fleet.

Taking his boat, Oliver attended Captain Lord Cochrane and delivered the Admiralty's dispatches. The meeting was brief and, in comparison with the reception Captain Cotton had extended to him and his officers, was less than cordial. On the surface, Lord Cochrane seemed interested in the news of recent activity off Rochefort and the build-up of French troops near Bayonne. But, beneath the surface, he seethed. He was not happy with his commission and was convinced he had been treated shoddily and made no bones about it.

'This penal hulk, the Admiralty had the audacity to grant me, is an insult. It cannot sail to windward and is likely to end up dashed to matchwood on a French beach taking me and my men with it.'

Oliver did not respond. Lord Cochrane's commission, *Arab*, was a refitted French prize. Its history was well-known having been well documented in the *Gazette*. As such, he had no desire to enter into an argument about it.

'The Spanish fleet is remarkable,' Oliver commented, in an attempt to distract his host and change the tone of the conversation.

Cochrane glared. He was not about to be sidelined. 'I have written repeatedly to Cornwallis and the Admiralty but I get no response. I have warned them about the French build up and the fact the Spanish have been baking ships' biscuits in Ferrol for months now. I smell them every day. All the ships have been watered and are in a state for immediate service. England cannot continue to be indifferent to the amassing of men and ships in this area. Why do my warnings go unheeded?'

The tirade was endless and when the opportunity to excuse himself arose, Oliver was not sorry to part company. His mission was to proceed to Gibraltar.

Although, *Perpetual* was not short of drinking water, Oliver was aware of the absence of fresh water on the Rock and anxious to refill his empty barrels. The rugged Portuguese coast was an opportunity too good to miss. With plenty of secluded bays on the northern coast, the water spilling from the mountains was crystal clear and easy to collect.

But the hours spent filling and ferrying dozens of small barrels cost them dearly. After passing Lisbon and raising Cape Saint Vincent, they headed east towards Cape Saint Mary then bore across the Gulf of Cadiz. When they were within sight of the Spanish port, the wind died completely. Without a following wind they could not make it through the Gibraltar strait.

Next morning, the conditions had not changed. The sky was perfectly clear with not a wisp of cloud or breath of wind in it. The thermometer registered a pleasant 74 degrees. Outside the Spanish seaport, the usually busy roads were empty. For two days, nothing entered or left the harbour.

Standing on deck, Oliver reminisced on the first time he had visited Cadiz. He remembered how impressed he had been with the number of ships crowded into a relatively small harbour. Not only ships of the Spanish Navy but large West Indiamen moored adjacent to the magazines and arsenals. He remembered striding the ropewalk that stretched for 600 yards and marvelling at the port's well-equipped dockyards.

The other naval facilities were no less impressive – the School of Navigation, the Naval Academy and the Observatory. Not surprisingly, Cadiz was envied as one of the best naval establishments in Europe. Had Earl St Vincent and Lord Nelson been similarly impressed when they had visited the port? Were the facilities at Cadiz the basis for their vision of a strong naval establishment in Gibraltar? He wondered.

But apart from its naval prowess, Cadiz was primarily a commercial port with over a thousand merchant ships entering its roads every year from Europe, America and the Baltic. However, its richest imports came from the Spanish islands of the Caribbean, Monte Video, Honduras and Cartagena – the sources of its consignments of gold and silver bullion and minted specie.

Because of its mercantile reputation, the city boasted many foreign business houses, the greatest number being Irish, followed by Flemish, Genoese and German. English and French houses were fewer by far.

In both its buildings and its inhabitants, Cadiz epitomised a city built on the fortunes of both the old and new worlds. It exuded elegance, wealth and good taste and was one of the most opulent cities in Spain. It had everything in abundance to meet the needs of its 75,000 residents – except one thing, like Gibraltar, it lacked fresh water.

Overnight, *Perpetual* drifted south and east carried on the long slow Atlantic swell. By morning, the frigate lay off Cape Trafalgar. At midday, a fresh breeze blew up but it was blowing from the east and in danger of driving the frigate back into the Atlantic. *Perpetual* needed a westerly to carry it safely through the Strait of Gibraltar.

The easterly, however, was favourable for a small squadron desiring to leave the Mediterranean and head west. Soon after six bells, a call came from the foremast lookout. The three ships had been sighted.

'British man-o'-war. Third-rate.'

Oliver reached for his glass.

'And two frigates.'

'*Triumph*, Captain Barlow, 74-guns,' Oliver observed to Mr Mundy who was standing beside him. He was unaware of the identification of the frigates.

The three vessels, part of the Mediterranean Fleet, were designated to patrol the Strait as far as Cadiz and along the North African coasts of Tangier and Morocco, taking care not to sail too close to the coast of Algiers where the Dey's reception was not always friendly.

With their canvas filled and heading north-easterly, the three British ships had no reason to heave to. Brief signals, exchanged with the third-rate, revealed the squadron was heading to Ferrol. As the two frigates passed, the names *Amphion* and *Medusa* were noted, and recorded in the log.

Later that afternoon, the wind changed and before the sun dipped into the Atlantic, *Perpetual* was carried through the Strait. It dropped anchor off Ceuta, the sheltered port on the Moroccan coast that supplied much of the garrison's daily needs.

Although the Rock of Gibraltar presented an aura of permanence and stability, Oliver was aware of the strong currents of water running around it, evidenced by the sea thundering into the natural hewn caves around its base. He was aware, too, of the easterly winds capable of forcing unwary ships onto the rocks of the Spanish coast and dashing them to pieces. Morning was the best time to enter the Gut. Oliver knew it and was prepared to wait.

It was almost dark when Tommy tipped the last bucket of dirty water over the ship's side. After refilling it, he hauled it up to the deck and scrubbed the inside. When satisfied, he sloshed the seawater to the scuppers and watched it run away. After returning the rope to its rightful place, he wiped his hands down his trousers and wandered to the scuttlebutt for a drink of water not realizing someone was watching him.

'Hey, you!' Bungs shouted. 'I want a word in your ear.'

'I've got to get back to the cockpit or the surgeon will wonder what I'm up to,' Tommy said, dipping the scoop into the water butt. Just as he did, Bungs thumped the lid down with his fist, knocking the scoop out of his hand.

'What did you do that for?'

'There's a murmur going about the ship saying it was the surgeon what finished off that young middie, not the bone that was stuck in his throat.'

'Don't be daft,' Tommy said, not wanting to get into an argument.

Bungs grabbed him. 'Don't you walk away from me, lad.'

'Let go! You're hurting.'

Bungs' grip tightened on Tommy's arm. 'Rumour says the floor was awash with blood and the lad's face was the colour of his curly white locks. It's said he was a ghost hours before he snuffed it.'

'Who said that?' Tommy demanded. 'It's not true. I should know, 'cause I was there.'

'So these tales didn't come from you?' Bungs demanded.

'Of course they didn't. I might have been away for a while, but I haven't changed.' He wrenched his arm out of the cooper's grip. 'I thought you knew me better than that. I don't tell lies and I ain't one for spreading gossip. Anyway, I ain't got time for your silly tittle-tattle. Save it for the mess. I've got a job to do.'

Brushing past his old friend, Tommy shook his head and headed to the companionway without looking back.

'You think you're everybody now, don't you.' Bungs yelled. 'Well, we'll see.' With that, he grabbed the scoop and thrust it back into the water butt, splashing himself in the process.

'What's going on here?' Mr Nightingale asked, striding forward from the quarterdeck.

Pretending he had not heard him, the cooper wiped his forearm across his face and walked away.

'Time will tell,' Bungs whispered under his breath.

CHAPTER 7

Bay of Gibraltar
20 August 1804

Hanging, like a grey pendant from the precipitous promontory, the tear-dropped shaped cloud was a product of the easterly wind. Blowing off the Mediterranean, it had rolled up the eastern face of the Rock, slid over the ridge but got caught by its tail on the summit. It was a wind that carried with it a disturbing feeling of foreboding.

'The Levanter,' Simon Parry commented, standing beside the captain on the quarterdeck.

Familiar with the formation, Oliver turned away and looked across to the coast of North Africa, burnished in gold by the rising sun. Directly across the Strait, eleven miles apart, stood the opposing Pillar of Hercules – Jebel Musa, a sentinel in the Atlas Mountains of Morocco. From the ports along the North African coast, traders sailed daily to the British colony to barter their wares.

The distant boom of a cannon distracted him.

'A little premature for a salute, is it not?' Oliver said.

'The morning gun,' the lieutenant advised. 'Fired every morning to announce the opening of the Land Port Gate.'

'Your knowledge of the territory will prove invaluable during our stay. Let us see what the Lieutenant-Governor has in store for us. Make sail, Mr Parry, if you please.'

Flying topsails and staysails only, *Perpetual* crossed the Strait and entered the broad Bay of Gibraltar, or Algeciras Bay, as it was known to the Spaniards who lived on the western shores.

The prevailing wind in summer invariably blew from the east and in winter from the west with the absence of north or south air currents at any time. But this being late August, and with autumn approaching, the winds were becoming unpredictable, often contrary and confused, just like the swirling currents turning beneath the frigate's hull. As *Perpetual* sailed through the Gut and into the long morning shadow cast by the Rock, the easterly wind died but the tide was sufficient to carry the frigate in.

As they neared Rosia Bay, Oliver gazed across the water to the town of Algeciras only six miles away on the opposite shore. The old Spanish town, with its colourful history, dated back to the time of the early Greek and Phoenicians voyagers. Today, its harbour was packed with a tangle of masts making it impossible to count how many ships were moored there. The tall masts of two Spanish men-of-war towered clearly above the rest. On the open waters of the bay, but closer to the British side, three hulks swung on their anchor cables – a retired second-rate, an aged sixty-four, and a brig. While the masts were stepped, they lacked spars and sails. They also lacked guns pointing from the open ports.

Mr Parry scanned the surrounds.

'Has anything changed, Simon?' Oliver asked.

'The number of dhows and feluccas in the bay is far fewer than before. The harbour is usually awash with them at this time of the morning.'

As preparations were made to drop anchor, Oliver sniffed the air. 'I notice the smell of this place has not improved. If anything, I think it is worse.'

'Human effluvia, I fear.' Simon Parry sighed. 'This is the time of day the scavengers collect the night soil from the streets. They transport it in barrels to the neutral ground beyond the North Mole. That is where it is emptied to await the arrival of the locals who dig through it, collect what they want for their farms and gardens, and carry it away. They seem oblivious to the stench.'

'Disgusting,' Oliver said, but his attention was distracted by a group of soldiers climbing into a boat at the short South Mole. Dipping their oars and pulling away from the defensive wall, the boat's bow was turned towards the frigate.

'A welcome from the garrison commander, perhaps,' Oliver said.

'And not the only one,' Simon added, indicating another boat being rowed from the North Mole, plus five Spanish gunboats which appeared from behind the small island sheltering the port. They were heading across the Bay of Algeciras towards Gibraltar.

'Have the lookout keep a watch on those gunboats. Muster the men and have the sergeant present his marines on deck. As he was speaking, the cable rumbled through the hawse hole. *Perpetual* was sitting in six fathoms of water, a cable's length from the small beach at Rosia Bay.

Being the only natural harbour on the coast, it was protected by the guns of the Parson's Lodge Battery on the southern end. Beside the fortification was the huge vaulted roof covering the new victualling yard and water tanks that had only recently been completed in response to the demands of Earl St Vincent.

In response to the whistles and calls, over a hundred pairs of feet thumped up the companionways. Once the shuffling was stilled and the whispering hushed, there was silence. Within minutes, the boat carrying members of the Queen's Regiment was swimming twenty yards from the frigate.

The corporal, standing in the bow, hailed the frigate. '*Perpetual*. Be advised, no one is permitted to leave the ship until it has been inspected. Is that understood?'

Oliver turned to his lieutenant. 'Tell the officer to come aboard and deliver his message in person.'

Simon Parry relayed the captain's words however the boat made no attempt to come up alongside.

'You cannot disembark,' the corporal reiterated. 'All ships are subject to inspection. Until then, you must stay aboard. By order of the garrison commander.'

Oliver moved closer to the rail. 'What is the name of your commanding officer?'

'Major General Sir Thomas Trigge, Lieutenant-Governor of Gibraltar.'

'Then kindly inform Sir Thomas that my orders, from London, are to meet with him as soon as possible. I suggest you convey that message. Advise him Captain Quintrell is arrived from England aboard His Majesty's frigate *Perpetual*. Inform him that I sailed directly here and made no landfall on any foreign shore. Furthermore, tell him that my surgeon will confirm we are carrying no infectious diseases. Relay the message directly and advise the general that I seek an urgent audience with him in accordance with my orders from the Lords Commissioners of the Admiralty.'

'I understand, Captain, but I still can't let you to go ashore. I have my orders too. I'll convey your message personally to General Trigge and return with a reply.'

There was nothing more Oliver could say or do. Frustrated, he turned to his first lieutenant. 'We did not encounter this situation last year. What do you make of it?'

'It's unusual,' Simon Parry said. 'Gibraltar has long been a free port which has no customs restrictions and levies no import or export duties.' He turned to the captain. 'Shall I dismiss the men?'

'Not for the present.'

The progress of the boat from the North Mole was slow. The men were rowing against the current of the incoming tide and, while the water of the bay was deceptively flat, a line of white foam curled along the tiny beach at Rosia Bay.

'If I am not mistaken, this may be the port's medical guard,' Oliver said. 'Mr Smith, kindly ask Dr Whipple to join me on the quarterdeck.'

The Mediterranean air was hot, far warmer than any August day in England and already the officers were sweating under the heavy weave of their woollen uniforms. With the last breath of breeze gone, it was going to be an uncomfortable day even on the water.

Oliver removed his hat and poked the one remaining digit on his right hand, through his hair. Thinking of the three ships they had encountered in the Atlantic, he added: 'A visit from Captain Barlow, while we are in port, would be most welcome. He served at the Nile amongst other victories.'

'Perhaps the frigate captains will be able to join us also,' Simon added.

'I fervently hope so. It is reassuring to know we are not alone in this region and if the Straits' squadron is in the vicinity, I feel certain they will make contact with us. Good conversation over dinner is always welcome.'

The quarterdeck offered a good view of Rosia Bay. Oliver studied it carefully. He was impressed with the navy's huge victualling store and the recently completed water. Dug into the ground out of solid rock, the tanks, when filled, promised to collect rainwater from the mountain and provide ships the opportunity to refill their empty barrels. But apart from the nearby gun battery and fortifications, there were few houses.

The road passing the bay wound up to Windmill Hill, a flat plateau on which the main barracks building was situated. Europa Point was skirted by precipitous cliffs which dropped 60-feet to the sea below. It was the southern tip of the peninsula.

Heading north, from Rosia Bay, was the main road, which lead directly to the colony's town. Behind the road, the Rock rose steeply, its bare face scarred only by an old defensive wall and a track which slowly zigzagged to the ridge on the very top. At the summit, poking up like a scrawny finger, was a 200-feet high lookout tower. A short distance from that was the signal station. Unlike the animated semaphore towers criss-crossing France, this device, elevated on a platform, consisted of an arrangement of large black drums along the yards of a mast. For the present, the position of the drums remained static.

Leaning on the caprail, the *Perpetuals* were more interested in the town to the north and what it might have to offer them. Their only question was when they would be allowed to go ashore.

After watching one boat leave, the officers on deck awaited the arrival of the second boat.

Oliver was becoming impatient. 'As soon as this matter has been completed, have my boat ready. I intend to pay the garrison a visit.'

His assumption the boat carried the health guard was soon confirmed and within two minutes of coming aboard, the inspector was taken below. Dr Whipple escorted him to the sick berth where he presented to him the only patient under his care.

Standing alongside the only occupied cot, the surgeon was anxious to share his diagnosis and discuss his patient's condition – an old rupture in the groin, which had recently been aggravated resulting in lumps the size of a man's fist protruding from the sailor's belly. The guard, however, was not interested in the man's anatomy or malady but, once satisfied no contagion was being harboured in the sick berth, he thanked the doctor and returned to the deck.

Following a cursory examination of the mustered crew, and receiving a signed declaration from the captain stating he would abide by the quarantine regulations of the Gibraltar Port Authority, Captain Quintrell was handed a note attesting to the good health of the frigate.

With the inspection completed, the health guard returned to his boat and with the Spanish gunboats keeping their distance in the bay, it was time for Oliver to step ashore.

Compared with the midday heat and the dusty condition of the garrison's parade ground, the air inside the stone barracks' building was cool and clear.

'Welcome, Captain Quintrell.'

Oliver bowed politely to General Sir Thomas Trigge, the ruddy faced, rotund Lieutenant-Governor of the Rock – a man who had seen many years of successful military service.

'I must apologise for the inconvenience you suffered on your arrival. After a long and tedious voyage, I am sure such delays are frustrating. However, you will come to appreciate why such measures have been deemed necessary.'

Oliver acknowledged 'It was no inconvenience whatsoever, sir.'

'As you are probably aware, I was advised in advance that you had been ordered to Gibraltar, so your arrival today was not entirely unexpected. You have sailed directly from England, I understand.'

'Yes, sir.'

'Then you will not be aware of the situation on the Rock at the present moment.'

'Although I have sailed into the bay previously, I admit to being unfamiliar with the colony and its people. According to my orders, His Majesty's frigate *Perpetual* is at your disposal and I trust that while in port, I will be able to provide whatever assistance is required.'

The general scratched his temple beneath his powdered wig.

Oliver continued. 'A few days ago, I encountered three naval vessels south of Cadiz, but we only came to within hailing distance. My only other encounter was with the gunboats in the bay. They appeared interested in my arrival, but we have sighted no French ships since leaving the Channel.'

'The Spanish gunboats are an aggravation,' the general replied, 'but nothing more. There are dozens of them and they are prone to firing warning shots if you sail close to Algeciras. But, they are fairly harmless – merely another minor annoyance we have to contend with – like scorpions, venomous reptiles and mosquitoes.'

'And the French, are they a problem around the peninsula?'

'Recently, a pair of privateers has been aggravating the fishermen on the Mediterranean coast off Catalan Bay. I have received reports of stolen fish and nets and even a couple of small boats being sunk. A few months ago, His Majesty's Armed Cutter, *Swift*, was approached by a lateen-rigged vessel posing as a Spanish coastal vessel. Until she touched against the cutter's side, it had appeared there was only a handful of men aboard. But 50 men were hiding below and took the cutter. She was carrying dispatches to Lord

Nelson. Her captain, Lieutenant Leake was cut down while trying to protect them.

'For the most part, however, the French stay in the Mediterranean and do not round Europa Point or attempt to enter the Gut of Gibraltar. No doubt, they are aware that the lookouts at O'Hara's Folly monitor their every move. They are also familiar with the positions of our gun batteries, including those within the Rock itself. Those embrasures, high up in the face, are invisible from the water and totally invulnerable to attack from either sea or land. They have saved this territory from previous attacks.'

The general smiled. 'As you may know, I commanded the 12th Regiment of Foot against the Franco Spanish forces during the Great Siege. A combined fleet of 49 sail of the line, plus fireships and other boats threw everything they had at the Rock but they could not topple the garrison.'

'A great victory indeed, Sir Thomas. I trust both France and Spain learned a lesson from it.'

The general nodded.

'And what of Admiral Lord Nelson? Is the Mediterranean Fleet still blockading Toulon?' Oliver enquired.

'To the best of my knowledge, although none of his ships have been here for some weeks. Had they suffered any damage in action, they would have come here to refit.'

The expression on the Lieutenant-Governor's face clouded over. 'There is one other matter,' he said, after ordering the guard to leave the room.

Oliver was unsure of what to expect.

'You may have heard the garrison now boasts a magnificent new library. It is stocked with a vast selection of books and housed in a new building.'

'Indeed,' Oliver responded politely, surprised at the general's clandestine tone. 'I would welcome the opportunity to visit and browse the bookcases, if I am permitted.'

'Of course, and I would invite you to donate a book if you are so inclined. A request I put to all visiting officers.' He paused. 'The matter which I must speak with you about concerns the body of a beggar that was buried in the library garden last week.'

Oliver was intrigued.

'A few years ago the southern coast of Spain was ravaged by an epidemic – a fever which could not be controlled. Thousands died, including many residents here is Gibraltar.'

'I remember reading of it.'

'Presently Gibraltar is under threat of the same thing happening again. Residents in Cadiz and Malaga are reportedly dying of fever at a rate of 100 a day, and the infection is spreading across Andalusia. Fortunately, in August there have only been three deaths in the garrison so far. But should word of a possible epidemic take hold, fear will spread like wildfire and prompt an exodus from the territory. Hence the reason the body was buried in the library garden and not removed by the undertaker and taken to the cemetery in the usual manner. The beggar had arrived from Malaga and Dr Pym, the colony's medical officer, was certain he was carrying the contagion.'

'What is the population here?' Oliver enquired.

'Almost 5000 troops in the garrison and 10,000 residents in the town.'

'Have any precautions been put in place?'

'For the moment, I have ordered all ships to be inspected but, if the number of deaths increases, it may be necessity to quarantine all vessels when they arrive. As a last resort, ships will be stopped from entering Gibraltar Bay. I cannot allow the contagion to take hold. Unfortunately, this will have a dire effect on the colony as most of our local trade comes by sea from the north coast of Africa, Cadiz and Malaga.'

He continued. 'Gibraltar consists almost entirely of a rocky promontory joined to Spain by a narrow sandy isthmus which becomes a swamp in winter. Because of these physical features, the peninsula is not self-sufficient and, apart from fish in the bay, we rely on our foreign neighbours to supply us with all the necessities of life.'

'But if the worst should eventuate and the contagion is introduced here—?' Oliver enquired.

'I hope this will not be the case but, if it happens, the land-gate to Spain will be closed to prevent people crossing the border and stop residents from leaving.'

'Turning Gibraltar into a virtual island.'

'Indeed. Isolation will be our only defence. But I beg you to keep this information to yourself. I trust and pray we will escape another epidemic, but I will advise if the situation changes.'

'Thank you, Sir Thomas. I appreciate your candour.'

Over the next four days, with no additional restrictions introduced, members of *Perpetual*'s crew were allowed to go ashore throughout the day. Numbers were limited to three divisions at a time, and a midshipman or warrant officer accompanied the men. Most sailors were eager to step ashore, armed with the money sewn into the lining of their coats or hidden amongst the possessions in their sea chests. It was an opportunity to taste flavours other than salt beef or pork. A chance to get drunk. And a chance to throw their legs over something other than a stuffed oakum pillow stinking of sweat.

The frigate's boats delivered the *Perpetuals* to the old commercial mole where numerous small craft were moored. From there, it was only a short stroll under the grand arches to Casemates Square – once the old Pickett Yard had been a place of public executions. It was dominated on one side by the 30 foot Line Wall and, on the other, by the new bombproof barracks building which gave it its name.

However, like any English square on market day, it was throbbing with crowds milling around a shambles of market stalls. But the mode of dress, the languages spoken and the behaviour of the residents was far different from any square in Britain. Gibraltar was saturated with the exotic and vibrant influences of many distant lands.

Grand Casemates resonated with a cacophony of sounds. North African merchants, their skin reflecting the colour of the dates they were selling, bartered with sandy-haired Irish artillerymen. Women argued in Spanish or Turkish at the top of their voices. Chickens squawked from behind the bars of cane baskets awaiting a buyer to ring their necks and carry them home. A sheep with three legs bound lay exhausted on the hot pavement after turning in never ending circles. A female goat screamed as it struggled to loosen the tether tying its horns to a cart's wheel. The multi-coloured kid running around its feet cried like an infant to get on the udder but the nanny would not allow it.

It was hard for the sailors to walk without stepping on something. Raffia baskets, set out on exotic rugs, overflowed with figs, dates and nuts. Freshly caught turbot and John Dory, tunny and sardines attracted flies, as did the meat, delivered by the dhows from North Africa, where it had been butchered.

In one quarter, Jews huddled together conducting their nefarious business in a secretive fashion, always remaining separate and seemingly aloof from the other foreigners especially the Moors. In Gibraltar they were despised for being the dirtiest of the colony's citizens. Yet they were also the richest.

The vibrant colours were remarkable. Cloth woven from brightly dyed yarns. Tanned goatskins in shades of yellow, brown, white and black. Felted hats and soft yellow Moroccan slippers reflected the hue of a Saharan sunset.

The aromas were amazing too. Smells rising from bubbling pots generously flavoured with exotic spices attracted customers. The sweet sickly smell of human sweat and the earthy odour of mules and Andalusian horses were less than appealing. The smoke from fires burning wood and camel dung disguised the smell of opium.

With an oversupply of tobacco always available, hardly a mouth in the square was without a cigar hanging from it, including the women's. Few smiles revealed teeth not stained the colour of sailors' hands. The faces reflected the mixed backgrounds.

The colonial town of Gibraltar was a far cry from Portsmouth, Plymouth or Falmouth.

Clambering back on board after spending four hours ashore, the sailors boasting a bellyful of ale were loud and boisterous. Those less inebriated behaved cautiously aware they were under scrutiny. Most of the banter, boasts, complaints, and details of sexual activities were saved for the mess where their exploits were regurgitated, repeated, reviewed and exaggerated.

'Foreigners,' Bungs said. 'They're all alike. Noses stuck up in the air. Won't even talk to a common sailor until they hear the clink of a coin in your pocket. Then the cockfarts swarm round you like flies round a corpse.'

'They ain't foreigners – most of them,' Muffin said. 'They might look it, but they live here.'

'If they don't speak English, they're foreigners in my book,' Bungs said.

'Well, you can't blame them for disliking the English. This place ain't a colony. It's a fortress ruled by the military. You must have seen the soldiers parading about the place and lining up along the walls. Big guns they've got, too, that's for certain.'

'Sure I saw them, but I saw lots of others too. I've never been in a port with so many Jews.'

'Well, at least they speak English and live in the town.'

'But they aren't English are they. Aye, and they're canny. And that goes for the Arabs too prancing around in nightshirts and lazing about on mats puffing on opium pipes. It's like something you read about in them *Arabian Nights*.'

'Didn't know you could read,' Smithers smirked.

'He can't read,' Muffin said. 'He just looks at the pictures.'

'Hey! You want to keep your teeth? Then shut your yap!'

Muffin had a glint in his eye. 'But I liked the look of them Spanish senoritas with nit combs stuck in their hair.'

'Aye, and skirts all a-crackly,' Smithers added.

'I wouldn't say no to crackling a few of them,' Muffin said. 'It don't matter what language they speak, they all got the same between their legs.'

'Aye, and they'll smile sweetly when your back's turned and give you a dose of the Spanish pox for free.'

Smithers shrugged his shoulders. 'I'm not afraid of the pox. A dose of mercury will cure it. You ask the Doctor.'

'Don't be too sure,' Bungs said, sniffing the air. 'This is as unhealthy place as I ever set foot in.'

'And what makes you an expert? There ain't naught wrong with my nose,' Muffin said. 'If you ask me, it don't smell no different to any other port.'

'You mean you can't smell evil when it's served up on a plate.'

Smithers sneered. 'Rubbish!'

'It's everywhere, not just on the dock. It's in the streets. In the square. You can fairly smell it oozing out of the houses. I know it when I smell it. There's an unholy stench of evil hanging in them streets.'

'Is Bungs right?' Tommy asked quietly.

'Don't take no notice, lad,' Muffin said. 'He just likes to hear his own voice. It's the smell of night soil. And they only clear their courtyards once a year when the pile is too big to climb over.'

Smithers cackled.

Bungs inclined his head. 'I'm telling you. No good will come from us being here. I worked in Gibraltar once before, and I've heard stories of what happened in the past.'

'Tell us then,' Smithers taunted. 'Is the Rock about to explode and blow us all to Kingdom come? Or are the apes going to attack the garrison and drive the troops out?'

'As far as I can see,' Eku added, 'there's only one worry and that's if Spain decides it wants to take the Rock back.'

'Why would they want to?' Muffin asked. 'It's just a lump of rock sticking up from the sea.'

Smithers laughed. 'You talk a load of rubbish, Bungs.'

'You can laugh, but I'm warning you, something's going to happen. I can feel it in my bones and, unless we sail from here soon, we'll find ourselves floating like a turd in a bucket with nowhere to go.'

As usual, Bungs had gathered an audience who scoffed at his predictions. Because he always worked alone and kept to himself, he was not the most popular man on board and, apart from the group at his mess table, he had few mates he could count as friends. But he was one of the oldest seamen aboard. He knew the coopering trade inside out, and he'd lost count of how many ships he'd served on or ports he'd visited.

But it wasn't the sight of his bunched fists that made his messmates take notice of him. There was just something about him. He had a nose for danger and was hardly ever wrong. When he made a statement about anything, few argued, and although they wouldn't admit it, most of them took heed of what he said.

'Sorry to disturb you, Capt'n, but Mr Parry thinks there is something you should see.'

Oliver put down his pen, and took his hat from his steward. 'Thank you, Casson.' He trusted his first lieutenant's judgement well enough to know he would not demand his attention unnecessarily.

On deck, the men who had swung the last of the boats aboard were gathered around a package lying on the deck. Mr Hanson appeared to be guarding it.

'What's all this about?' the captain asked.

Mr Tully answered on behalf of the midshipman. 'Seems this package was tossed into the boat when it pulled away from the jetty. Mr Hanson said the man who threw it just pointed to *Perpetual*. He also said he didn't touch it, or open it, he just left it in the bottom. The men fished it out a moment ago when the boat came aboard.'

Oliver turned to the midshipman. 'Tell me about the man who delivered this. Was he a soldier? A naval officer? Did he wear a uniform?'

The midshipman returned a blank expression.

'Think man.'

'No, sir. He looked like a fishermen off the dhows. He was dressed in a long white shirt and had a curved dagger hanging from a cord around his waist.'

'Hmm,' Oliver said, glancing down at the parcel. 'And you didn't remove any of the wrappings?'

'No, Captain, I just left it in the bottom and told Mr Tully about it when he asked me.'

'Is appears to be wet.'

The midshipman looked sheepish. 'I think it might have taken in a bit of sea water from the oars.'

Oliver studied the package that was sitting in a small puddle of brown water. Wrapped in a square of salt-hardened canvas, it was bound with strips of linen resembling bandages.

'A pair of fat cigars?' the sailing master quipped flippantly.

No one laughed.

'A dead fish perhaps?' Mr Tully suggested.

'What do you think it is, Mr Hanson?'

'I couldn't say, Captain.'

'Then, perhaps, you should have asked the man who threw into your boat. However, you may have the dubious honour of unwrapping it.'

The sailors gathered around and watched as the midshipman squatted on the deck and unravelled the lengths of binding. When the final corner was peeled back the middie jerked backwards, lost his balance and rolled onto his back with his feet in the air, much to the amusement of the boat's crew.

'Get up, Mr Hanson,' the captain ordered. 'I can assure you that hand is quite dead. It is not going to jump up and grab you by the throat so there is no reason to be afraid of it.'

'But sir?'

'Back to work,' Mr Tully ordered. 'You've all seen this sort of thing before.'

It was true, seeing arms and legs that had been blown off in battle was an accepted part of the naval mural. Heads separated from torsos. Bodies with innards more out than in. Fingers, lodged between deck beams, dripping blood. All familiar sights during close action. But this neatly packaged hand showed no evidence of injury, save for a fine brown line around the wrist where it had been sliced from the wrist and forearm. The cut was as smooth as when a wire was sliced through a large cheese. This was not the ragged remnant of a hand blown off with a four-pound shot, a picture that resonated in Captain Quintrell's memory, although he did not dwell on it.

'What do you make of it Dr Whipple?' Oliver enquired, inviting the surgeon to take a look.

Without a second thought, the doctor picked it up by the wrist and rested the dead fingers on his left hand. After briefly examining it, he turned it over so it was laying palm upwards.

'A seafaring man, no doubt,' the surgeon said. 'There are tar stains engrained around the nail beds. The palm is heavily callused and the distinct yellow colouration of the skin is from contact with pitch, which I attribute to contact with ships' rigging. There is no doubt in my mind this hand belonged to a sailor.'

'Could it be one of ours, Mr Parry?'

'I entered R against the names of Lompa and Styles – two of the pressed men. They have been absent for two days.'

'Do you have anything more to add, Doctor?'

The surgeon examined the wrist more closely. 'This is not a surgeon's work but the cut was fast and skilfully administered.'

'What leads you to that conclusion?'

'The bone has not been sawn through. I would suggest it has been severed by a single swift blow, the sort you would expect from a sharp axe or a meat clever.'

'Why would anyone do such a thing and then send it to the ship?' the sailing master asked.

Oliver cast his eyes to the town. 'The population of Gibraltar is mixed. On the surface it is a British colony but not all its residents are God-fearing Christians. You need look no further than across the Strait to the coast of Barbary to find customs and habits very different to those we know and expect. In parts of Africa, if a man is caught stealing, his hand, and sometimes his foot are chopped off to advertise to the world that he is a thief.'

He turned to the sailors who were gathered on deck. 'I think this hand is delivering a message from the residents of the Rock. It is a warning and I trust every man aboard will take heed of it.'

CHAPTER 8

The Hulks
24 August 1804

'A depressing sight,' Oliver commented, gazing from the deck to the three hulks anchored almost a mile from the King's Bastion on the British waters of the bay. With only the twinkle of a few glims flickering from their stern windows, the aged hulls were barely visible in the moonlight.

'They were once fine ships, with proud histories,' Simon said, directing his gaze to the nearest and largest of the three.

'French, I would say, by her lines,' Oliver observed.

'*Peuple Souverain* – French third-rate convincingly beaten at the Battle of the Nile.'

'Ah,' Oliver mused. 'Nelson's greatest victory. I have studies the formations many times. She lost her fore and main and was severely damaged, if I am not mistaken.'

'And was considered not worthy of repair,' said Simon. 'Hence, she was towed here from Aboukir Bay to serve as a prison ship. When she arrived at Gibraltar, she was recommissioned, H.M.S. *Guerrier*.'

Oliver was puzzled. '*Guerrier* – surely that was the name of the French ship that stood first in line. Burnt and sunk with a great loss of life.'

'Three hundred men,' Simon added, shaking his head.

'But from all appearance, her namesake is no longer a prison ship.'

'During my time spent here last year, I learned she served as a prison ship until the Peace of Amiens. Then, when the prisoners were released, she was used as a supply ship and later a guard ship. Earl St Vincent raised his flag on her, when he was stationed in Gibraltar. But now, she serves as a repository for the main commercial commodity of Gibraltar – tobacco. I believe the other two hulks are also tobacco stores. It is the mainstay of the local smugglers.'

'Smugglers!'

'Smuggling is an accepted trade here in Gibraltar. It has gone on for decades right under the nose of the garrison yet no one seems willing, or able, to do anything about it.

'An ignominious end to the career of a fine ship. The only consolation is the crew will be content if there is plenty of tobacco to be had at a cheap price.'

When eight bells sounded the end of the second dog watch, it didn't bring the familiar thunder of feet along the decks as it would at sea. Instead, the lookouts from two mastheads climbed casually down the rigging, jumped down to the deck and stopped to talk with the sailors from the starboard watch who had come to replace them. Beneath the foremast, a group of sailors perched on the windlass and lit their pipes, the distinctive smell drifting across the deck. From the frigate's waist, the murmur of voices, occasional burst of raucous laughter and the melodious notes of a fiddle were reassuring to the captain. The crew of *Perpetual* was relatively content. At least for the present.

With no desire or necessity to go below, Oliver and his first officer stood at the taffrail in silence.

The evening air was warm, with barely a waft of movement in it, yet on the distant slopes of the mountains of Andalusia bursts of lightning flashed on a backcloth of indigo but the sound of its thunder failed to reach them.

Directly across the bay, dancing pinpricks of light, from the houses of Algeciras reflected on the water giving the impression the town was afloat. On the Gibraltar peninsula, the glow of lanterns and flicker of yellow candles from the nearby town's windows provided a welcome sight.

'Humph!' Oliver exclaimed involuntarily.

Simon Parry raised one eyebrow and looked directly at the captain. 'Am I right in thinking you are considering the integrity of the ship's surgeon?' It was not a difficult assumption to make after the conversation they had shared during dinner.

'You have sailed with me for too long, Simon. You read my thoughts too well.'

The lieutenant did not answer.

'What is it about Dr Whipple that puzzles me?' Oliver said. 'He is a gentleman of good breeding with credentials that testify to all he has told me. He displays the accomplishments and attributes of a naval surgeon. He has studied with learned men and, from what I have heard, is adept in the performance of his duties. Yet, there are certain expressions and turns of phrase he uses that lead me to sense there is something questionable in his history, something he prefers not to reveal.'

'We all sail with a crew of private ghosts,' Simon added.

'Forgive me,' Oliver said,' I do not wish to stir memories you may not wish to be reminded of.'

Simon Parry acknowledged the apology with a slight nod. 'Do you wish for me to speak with the doctor? And, if so, is there something in particular that concerns you?'

'Thank you, no. If there are any questions to be put to him, then it is I who must do it. As to specific concerns, I cannot point to a single one. In the meantime, I shall oblige him with the benefit of the doubt. Were it not for him joining the ship, we would only have the services of that fellow, Abel Longbottom, who, I understand, is incapable of pulling a loose tooth without causing dire consequences.'

Oliver frowned. 'You must forgive me, Simon, I cannot write about such matters to my wife nor record such thoughts in the log, so you are the only outlet for my frustrations. I remind myself that our fortunes could be far worse than they are. Sitting here on this bay reminds me of the frozen inland sea we visited in the Southern Ocean. There is something reassuring about a flat sea at night when there is no threat against us and no enemy ships within many miles.'

Glancing back to the Rock and the black silhouette of the tower on its highest point reaching up to the dark sky, he laughed. 'When you consider the great distance the soldiers on the ridge can see, our masthead lookouts are rather superfluous.'

The lieutenant smiled. 'I heard it was built with the intention of seeing Spanish ships sailing from Cadiz.'

'That is almost sixty miles away!'

'An error of judgement. It appears General O'Hara had failed to notice the range of mountains standing between here and Cadiz. Hence, his men gave it the affectionate title: *O'Hara's Folly.*'

'Well, I for one am grateful to General O'Hara's resourcefulness, even though his geography and geometry did not prove to be totally sound. However, while the arms of the signal tower are sleeping, I will take my leave, and bid you good evening, and pray the night remains without incident.'

During the night, however, the barometer fell and strong winds drove into the bay from the Strait, whipping the water and sending waves breaking against the artificial moles.

'I trust we did not drag or sustain any damage,' Oliver asked his first officer, when he came on deck.

'No, sir. Considering the strength of the gusts, *Perpetual* fared well.'

'And the men. How are they?'

'A few sore heads,' Simon said. 'Not unexpected after several hours in the local taverns yesterday afternoon.'

'Do you intend to allow another two divisions to go ashore today?
,

'If that meets with you approval.'

'Indeed. It does the men good, although I doubt they can justify their excesses in the clear light of dawn.'

'Will you be going ashore today, Captain?'

'I am undecided,' he said, focussing his attention on Rosia Bay, the barracks and victualling yard.

'You ran some of the boats up on the beach opposite, did you not?'

'Yes, sir. From there it's only a short walk into town.'

'Did the men report any unusual activity?'

'No. There was the usual chatter and complaints about the prices the traders were charging. But tobacco was readily available so most were happy. What activity you were referring to?'

'Take a look,' Oliver said, passing the glass to his lieutenant and pointing to the road leading from the town. 'It winds south up to the barracks at Windmill Hill.'

Simon Parry placed the glass to his eye and scanned the shoreline. 'A convoy of carts under military guard.'

'Well-laden carts at that. I am wondering what it signifies. As we are the only naval ship in the bay, it's unlikely they are moving supplies.'

'Perhaps those dhows by the North Mole delivered meat early this morning. They would need to transport it to the garrison before the sun was too high.'

Oliver paced the deck. He was puzzled.

'Are they moving guns?' the lieutenant asked.

'I have not seen any,' Oliver replied. Taking the glass he scanned the length of the coast from the nearby South Mole along the defensive Line Wall with its fortified bastions, to the newer North Mole and the town. Beyond that, the square tower of the ancient Moorish castle clinging to the slope and beyond that to the neutral zone – the narrow isthmus, not more than a mile wide, separating the British colony from the Spanish mainland.

Between the North Mole and the distant beach, Oliver was surprised by the presence of a dozen dhows, their lateen sails furled to their masts. While a few were wallowing on the ruffled waters, most had been dragged up onto the beach. He thought it unlikely they had arrived from North Africa that morning.

Simon Parry had earlier described to him the exotic appearance of Gibraltar, not only relating to its people, but also it buildings. He had spoken of the shambles of wooden houses built close together in the older part of town and the streets which he described as narrower than those in the poorer districts of London. Being two or three storeys high, they completely blocked out the sun but withheld the heat. The newer more elegant stone buildings had balconies with wrought iron railings and carved wooden shutters reflecting the Venetian and Genoese influence, while the Moorish and Spanish heritage was ever present.

'The character of the town is as diverse as the exotic spices sold on the streets,' the lieutenant commented, 'and just as unpalatable to our conservative English tastes.'

Oliver agreed then returned his attention to the line of carts still moving south towards Windmill Hill.

'Ship entering the Gut!' The call from the masthead attracted everyone's attention.

'Spanish man-of-war,' the lookout shouted.

Its arrival accounted for the signal tower's strange gesticulations which had begun at first light.

The 74-gun ship had waited until dawn before attempting to enter Gibraltar Bay. Sailing under minimal canvas, the Spanish ship of the line was greeted by six gunboats from Algeciras. They escorted it across the bay.

While everyone's attention was on the big three-masted ship, a pair of much smaller masts, which had been hidden behind it, came into view. A tiny brig was sailing in the 74's wake.

'Portuguese trader,' Oliver declared. 'And by the condition of her canvas, I would suggest she made heavy weather of the blow last night.'

'Is she making for Algeciras or Gibraltar?' Simon asked.

'Impossible to say but she would do well to reduce sail and heave to.'

The pair followed the progress of the two very different sized vessels. The sailors perched in *Perpetual*'s rigging also stopped what they were doing and watched.

'Let us hope she is carrying a cargo of wine and spirits for the colony. My personal stores are in need of replenishing. I must speak with Casson about it.'

As the captain spoke, the 74 bore away towards the Spanish port, while the much smaller brig, *Conception*, slipped under her stern and steered for Gibraltar's North Mole. Once behind the man-made jetty, only the tops of her twin masts were visible making it impossible to see what cargo she was carrying.

For a fleeting moment, Oliver's thoughts drifted to the island of Madeira, to its sweet red wine and to Susanna at her home in Funchal. He was hungry for her and hungry for breakfast. It was time to go below.

With ribbons of ripped canvas hanging from her foremast topsail yard, the brig dropped anchor in the sheltered water on the north side of the North Mole. After being subjected to the compulsory inspection by the health guard, *Conception*'s handful of passengers was disembarked before any cargo was unloaded. The goods, stored in the hold, comprised of bolts of linen cloth, bleaching wax and salt, all items produced in Cadiz. There was no wine.

Returning home from a brief and unsuccessful business trip to Cadiz, Señor Santo, a grocer by trade, was disgruntled and extremely weary. The passage, although short, had been particularly rough and he had suffered from sea sickness throughout the voyage. This morning, he had woken with a raging thirst and throbbing head. Perhaps he had consumed too much wine during the voyage. Now his only thought was to return to his house on Gunners Parade as quickly as possible, and take to his bed.

After lining up to be examine by the health guard and waiting impatiently for his boxes and baggage to be retrieved, the shopkeeper was not inclined to talk. However, when asked about his apparent pallor, he was obliged to answer and blamed it on the rough sea stating it had robbed him of both sleep and the contents of his stomach. He exchanged a few words with the ship's master and the handful of other passengers who had travelled with him but nothing more.

There was no shortage of porters waiting with hand-carts, eager to attract paying customers and deliver their baggage to their homes or places of lodging. Within fifteen minutes of the brig arriving at the North Mole, the small stream of wearied travellers had passed through the North Port Gate and entered the town.

Santo's house was quite some distance away and up the hill. Although he had nothing to carry, he did not relish the walk.

Little did he know that within two weeks of his return he and his family and most of his neighbours would be dead.

CHAPTER 9

Quarantine
25 August 1804

Early the same afternoon, a boat bumped against *Perpetual*'s hull and a letter addressed to Captain Quintrell was handed up. It bore the official seal of the colony and required the captain to attend the Lieutenant-Governor at the Windmill Hill Barracks immediately.

Oliver had his suspicions as to what the meeting might be regarding, but nothing could be presumed in Gibraltar especially at this time.

After a polite but brief greeting, thanking the naval officer for his prompt attendance, Major General Sir Thomas Trigge invited Oliver to sit down. Although the room was elegantly furnished with several cushioned sofas, the captain choice an upright chair to sit on.

'Captain Quintrell, there are several matters I must speak with you about. First and foremost, to advise you the situation on the Rock is deteriorating rapidly. As a result, from dawn tomorrow, the Sea Port Gate will be closed and full quarantine conditions will apply from that time.'

Oliver was not unduly surprised. 'To what degree is the port closed – to local boats, coastal traders, naval vessels?'

'My order applies to all ships, including ships of Nelson's Mediterranean Fleet. Any ship that attempts to enter the harbour will be stopped and turned back to the Strait. And no persons from any vessel, apart from those already serving on ships in the bay, will be allowed to step ashore.'

'But what of Spanish ships sailing for Algeciras.'

'I have no jurisdiction over them. This order applies only to the waters on the eastern side of Gibraltar Bay and more particularly to landings on the North and South Moles.

'And what of those citizens who cross the neutral ground daily from Spain by carriage or on foot?'

'The Land Port Gate will also be closed. Those who entered this morning will be allowed to leave this evening but, after that, no one enters or leaves the territory. That means there will be no communication with the world beyond the Rock. This morning, I dispatched a messenger overland carrying word to Lord Nelson. But, as the message must await arrival of one of his ships in Barcelona, it will take several weeks before he receives the news.'

'I presume this measure is to stop the fever from being introduced.'

The general's brow furrowed. 'I fear it is already too late. The contagion is here. Only a handful of troops have died in the last few days, but dozens have been recorded in the town and the number of civilian deaths is growing daily.'

'Can the garrison's doctor do nothing to halt the spread?'

'He would be better placed if he knew what he was dealing with.'

'What can I do to assist?' Oliver asked.

'I shall not order you to stay aboard your ship,' Sir Thomas replied, 'but I suggest that the safest place for you and your men is on the water. The less contact made with the residents of the colony the better.'

'Of course.'

'Secondly, Dr Pym is working under extreme pressure, as is the garrison's surgeon, Mr Burt. His dispenser has died and currently the apothecary is serving as his assistant. Furthermore, the French doctor in town, Monsieur Jay, has disappeared. It is not known if he escaped Gibraltar in the last few days, or if he is lying in a hovel somewhere, dying. What we do know is the victims of this pestilence die within a matter of days, and very few of those affected survive.'

Oliver waited before putting his question. 'What of the threat from the French? Is the Gut of Gibraltar safe from attack?'

'While we have Captain Barlow and his ships patrolling the Strait, your frigate anchored in the harbour, and sufficient fit men to man the guns on the Line Wall, I do not fear attack from the enemy. However, when we last spoke, I mentioned the problem of French privateers in the Mediterranean, off Catalan Bay. They are becoming increasingly troublesome.'

'I can sail around Europa Point and patrol that roadstead, if you wish.'

'Thank you, Captain, but no. I prefer you remain in the bay, especially now the port is closed. Captain Barlow in *Triumph* is vigilant. Unfortunately, however, he is designated to patrol both the Strait and the southern coast of Spain from Tarifa to Cape Saint Mary. Therefore, he cannot be in attendance at Gibraltar all the time. Hence the importance of your presence.'

Oliver was obliged to agree and nodded, then took the opportunity to enquire about the movement of carts he had seen heading south along the road.

'I am relocating my men to Windmill Hill. I have ordered all the barracks in town and at Rosia Bay to be evacuated. The troops and their families will be accommodated in tents here on the plateau. As that location faces south and receives the fresh breezes from the sea, the air is far healthier here than in the shadow of the Rock. If, as Dr Pym tells me, this contagion is carried in the miasmic mist that envelopes the town, then it is essential my men are removed from it as quickly as possible.'

'That entails a lot of tents.'

'Hundreds of tents, Captain. Enough to accommodate most of the men and their families. And because the garrison hospital is too small to accommodate the men who are sick, the Windmill Hill barracks is being used to house them. As for the townspeople, the colony's hospital is already full and even the lazaretto on the boundary of the neutral zone is overflowing. A new one is urgently under construction.'

Oliver ventured the question, 'Is that the extent of the problems?'

The Lieutenant-Governor sighed. 'Far from it. The town is suffering through a lack of street cleaners to take away the dead. Because of that, night soil and bodies are piling up in the streets. Furthermore, there are no undertakers, no spare land in the graveyards, and no coffins to bury the victims in. And, I was told, most of the priests have escaped back to Spain. In September, there will be no publication of the Gibraltar Chronicle as all the newspaper's staff is already dead or dying. That means there will be no way of circulating information, either good or bad, to the residents.'

'I do not envy you your situation, Sir Thomas. But what of yourself and your family?'

The sixty-year old general shrugged, 'I am due to be recalled in December. I survived the Great Siege here, over twenty years ago, but I wonder if I will survive this.'

Oliver tried to sound positive. 'Let me assure you, sir, that my ship is at your disposal should you require to take passage. I await your pleasure.'

'Hardly a pleasure, Captain Quintrell, but seeing a British frigate in Gibraltar Bay offers some comfort. But, you must excuse me, there are many pressing matters that require my attention. In the meantime, you have a visitor awaiting you in my private chamber. I took the opportunity of offering your guest some hospitality as it was necessary for me to speak with you first.'

Oliver was puzzled. Who would be calling on him in Gibraltar? An Admiralty representative with fresh orders, perhaps? That was unlikely as no naval ships had entered the bay. A messenger arrived overland from Barcelona or Cadiz? A naval officer who had served with him on a previous mission seeking a berth on Perpetual? Or a rich merchant willing to pay any amount of money to escape the peninsula?

From the doorway, the commander of the garrison called to the guard posted on the corridor. 'Kindly escort Captain Quintrell to my quarters. And, when his audience is over, organise transport to return him to the beach.'

'Yes, sir,' the guard snapped.

'I will take my leave,' General Trigge said. 'But I am sure we will speak again very shortly.'

Oliver responded with a customary bow but by the time he had lifted his head, the general had left leaving no opportunity to ask any further questions.

'This way, Captain,' the corporal instructed.

Oliver followed, his hat held under his arm.

On reaching the general's private quarters, the soldier tapped on the door, stood back and allowed the captain to enter.

The view from the doorway was refreshing. A large French window looked out across the plateau which stepped down to Europa Point, the southernmost tip of the peninsula where sheer cliffs dropped vertically to the sea. Across the rippling waves, white sails of feluccas glided bird-like over the cobalt water of the Strait and in the distance, the irregular outline of the mountains of North Africa rose into the cerulean sky.

When the door closed behind him, a breeze teased the lace curtains.

'Oliver,' a voice whispered.

The captain quickly turned his head. 'In the name of Heaven, Susanna! What are you doing here?'

She smiled impishly. 'That is hardly the greeting I had expected.'

'But you shouldn't be here,' he cried, shaking his head in disbelief.

The smile disappeared from her face. 'I had hoped my being here would have pleased you.'

'This place is not safe.'

Her laugh was forced. 'Are you afraid of rumours being spread about us? I feared I might be an embarrassment, which is why I came here to the garrison and did not wander along the seafront searching for you.'

'You do not understand,' Oliver said. 'Gibraltar is falling into the grip of an epidemic. For your own safely, you must get away from this place, as soon as possible, and return to Madeira.'

'But, Oliver, I have just arrived.' Reaching for him, she gently took his hands in hers. 'Tell me you are pleased to see me.'

A pained expression crossed his face. 'More than anything in the world.' He drew her closer to him, 'but not here and not now.'

Closing his eyes, he held her in his arms and for a moment neither of them moved save for the rise and fall of their chests heaving together.

Oliver's mind was milling. 'How did you arrive here?'

'When I received your letter, I took passage on the first ship sailing from Funchal to Lisbon. There, I was fortunate to find a brig bound for Gibraltar.'

'*Conception*?'

She nodded.

'I saw it arrive this morning. When is it due to sail?'

'This evening, when the tide is full, but only across the bay to Algeciras. It will return to Lisbon, when it has delivered cargo there and its torn sails have been replaced.'

She squeezed his hand. 'I understand your concern and I am sorry. I only learned of the sickness, when I arrived.' She looked at him questioningly. 'But what of you and your men? Can you leave this port or must you stay?'

Oliver lifted a curl from her shoulder. 'It doesn't matter about me. I have my orders, and until I receive word to the contrary, this is where I must remain.'

From the window, the waters of the Strait appeared smooth and inviting, yet Oliver knew that the currents lurking beneath the surface could be unpredictable and destructive.

'What shall I do?' she whispered.

'How long does *Conception*'s master intend to remain in Algeciras?'

'Perhaps a week.'

'And where is your baggage?'

'On the ship. I did not know for sure if I would find you here.'

'Then promise me this,' he said, gripping her hands tightly, 'You will return to the North Mole directly and sail to Algeciras. Do you know of anyone who lives in the town?'

'Yes, I have friends who have invited me to stay with them for as long as I wish.'

'Then, so be it. Return to *Conception* immediately. Take the brig across the bay and, after one week in the town, return to Lisbon where hopefully you will be able to secure a passage to Madeira.'

'But Oliver,' she pleaded.

'Listen,' he insisted. 'Do as I say. Do not linger in Gibraltar.'

Susanna was confused.

'Do you have money?' he asked.

'Yes, I have adequate funds for myself and my maid, who is travelling with me.'

'How did you arrive here at the barracks?'

'I walked.'

'Alone?'

'Isabella accompanied me. She is waiting for me on the parade ground.'

'Then go now.'

'But when will I see you?'

Without answering, he slid his arms around her waist and kissed her. 'Promise me one thing; you will not come back here.'

Her eyes welled with tears. 'I promise,' she whispered, her forehead resting on his shoulder. 'I will not see you again.'

He touched her fingers to his lips, but again did not answer. Opening the door and stepping out to the corridor, he called for the guard. 'Kindly escort the lady to the parade ground.'

'Take this,' she said, pushing a slip of paper into his hand. 'It is the address where I will stay. If you cannot spare the time to visit me, perhaps you will write.'

'I can promise nothing,' he said.

'Then *au revoir*,' she whispered. 'Until we meet again.'

He squeezed her hand, turned and headed along the corridor without looking back.

Staring from his cabin window, Oliver's mind was churning, as he watched the brig, *Conception*, drift out from behind the North Mole and head across the bay to the old Spanish port only five miles away. Being a regular visitor to both ports, the Portuguese coastal trader failed to attract attention from either the gunboats or the fighting ships in the Algeciras roadstead.

'Captain, may I speak with you?' Simon Parry's voice came like a knife slicing through his train of thought.

'Yes. Come in,' he answered impatiently.

Casson followed the first lieutenant into the Captain's cabin with a tray in his hands.

'Put the damned stuff on the table and leave us!' the captain ordered. 'And bring a cup for Mr Parry.'

Glancing at the lieutenant, the steward's eyebrows raised slightly. 'Aye aye, Capt'n.'

'And watch your tone, Casson,' the Captain warned.

His steward shuffled out leaving the door ajar.

'I can come back later, if the time—'

'No, Simon. Sit down. But I advise you not to ask me if everything is all right.'

'Of course.' The lieutenant seated himself at the table and waited.

'What of the pressed men who ran?' Oliver asked.

'Lompa and Styles. Nothing more heard of them.'

'Then let them rot in this Hell we are presently stuck in.'

The lieutenant paused for a moment. 'Should I send a party ashore to search for them when the quarantine is lifted?

'Certainly not. That is an order. Not now and not when the ship is cleared. And if by chance they should attempt to come back to the ship with stories that they fell overboard, I do not want them within a cable's length of the hull.

'In the meantime, I will dispatch a message to General Trigge advising him that if they are found in Gibraltar they are to be taken to the garrison lock-up where they can be held awaiting a court martial. If it were not for the epidemic, I would bring them back here and keelhaul the pair of them then hang their bodies from the topgallant yard until the gulls have pecked every morsel of meat from their bones.'

Casson interrupted, placed an additional cup and saucer on the table and left closing the door behind him.

Oliver sighed long and hard. 'It's this place. This fortified colony. It's an open cesspool, smouldering with infection that is spreading like the plague.' He laughed was affected. 'Perhaps it is the plague.'

'Did the Admiralty prepare you for this?' Simon asked quietly.

The captain could not commit himself. 'I was told there had been a few cases of fever in the past. But there are many ailments which manifest themselves with fever, so a few deaths amongst a garrison of five thousand men are to be accepted.'

He continued. 'When we sailed from Portsmouth in early August, there had been no word of an increase in the number of deaths in Gibraltar. I have since learned that no official record of civilian deaths was ever kept. However, when I attended their Lordships in Whitehall, I was asked if I had ever suffered from the fever during my previous visits to the West Indies.'

Simon interrupted. 'Yellow Fever? Is that what the contagion is?'

'I did not say that, did I?'

'No, sir, I presumed.'

'Presume nothing, Simon. For the present, the nature of the infection is not known.' Oliver stood up again and walked back to the window. 'What aggravates me is that we have been sent here to face an invisible enemy potentially more lethal than a dozen ships standing in line. Furthermore, we are not at liberty to retaliate, or even withdraw but must remain here, like a straw target waiting for the marksman to pull his trigger.'

'Dare I ask if your meeting with the governor achieved anything positive?'

Oliver returned to the table and poured the coffee. After untying his neckerchief, he dragged it from his neck and threw it onto the table.

'I'm sorry, Simon,' he said. 'It appears, I always vent my frustrations on you. It is not often such matters get under my skin but I fear while we are here, we are in danger of losing some good men and to no fault of their own. Besides which, their deaths will achieve nothing in the service of their country.'

'But what of the quarantine?'

'Quarantine, indeed,' he mocked. 'Who can say I am not already carrying this infection and have brought it back onto the ship with me.'

'I think that is unlikely. You are a healthy man.'

Looking down to the remnants of his right hand, he scratched at a stain on the tablecloth with his index finger. He had no answer.

Simon continued. 'Where does the garrison's commander stand in this situation?'

'As you know, Gibraltar is regarded as a fortress, not as a colony. The town and port are merely appendages to the garrison. Despite General Trigge having less than 5000 soldiers housed at the garrison, there are around 10,000 residents in the colony, and his jurisdiction as Lieutenant-Governor extends over all the inhabitants of the peninsula.'

'Is he sympathetic to the situation?'

'As sympathetic as is appropriate for a military commander to be. Sir Thomas is an astute man who is doing all that is possible with very little outside help or support. He is also ensuring his troops are well fed and housed and has introduced strict adherence to hygiene for his men, and cleanliness in the barracks. But water is in short supply. There is no natural source of water on the promontory. This was a problem both St Vincent and Nelson insisted on rectifying when they were here.'

'Is there anything I can do to help?'

'Yes,' Oliver said. 'I want the ship fumigated from top to bottom – every deck, every beam, every grommet, gun and gunnel. Better to be choked with the fumes of brimstone and vinegar than the putrid stench of corpses and human waste.

'Also,' he continued, 'I want the men stripped naked and disinfected. The doctor can supervise that. From today, pass the message, if any man falls ill and fails to report to the sick berth, he will be flogged. I insist that the cockpit remains out of bounds for everyone apart from those admitted as patients, or those in attendance. An armed marine shall be posted outside. Should any deaths occur, the bodies will be disposed of quickly, and the burials will be conducted with little sentimentality. Am I making myself clear?'

Simon Parry acknowledged.

'Ironic, isn't it?' Oliver sighed, 'I dearly wished for a commission such as this, to be ordered to Gibraltar as part of the Mediterranean Fleet's advance guard under Lord Nelson's command. Now I curse my orders.'

Simon was sympathetic. 'Hopefully that feeling will soon pass.'

'I trust so,' the captain said, draining his cup. 'Did you have anything to report in my absence? Has the seepage in the hold been attended to?'

'It has. In the carpenter's words, "it's the product of *Perpetual*'s age soon fixed by a parcel of oakum, a dose of hot pitch and a plaster".'

Oliver smirked, 'It will take more than dab of tar and strip of timber to resolve the situation here.'

'Will there be anything else, Captain?'

Oliver shook his head. 'If only there were more officers like you, Simon. I do declare, I have never once seen you lose your temper.'

'Perhaps I have learned to hide my feelings although, at times, I think it is better to express them the way you feel.'

Oliver considered his lieutenant's words.

'I am afraid you will bear the brunt of the men's complaints. It is best to keep them fully occupied. On this occasion, an extra ration of rum occasionally might help them swallow the bitter taste of resentment. Kindly have all hands on deck in one hour. It is only fair I advise them of our situation.

'Thank you, Simon. That will be all.'

CHAPTER 10

A Warning

Jumping up and down against the rail, and pointing to the water, the youngest midshipman was attracting the attention of everyone on deck. 'See that! Over there in the water! Mr Parry, come quick!' he yelled.

'Mr Tully, Kindly advise Mr Hanson to refrain from yelling in the manner of a fishmonger's wife.'

The second lieutenant walked across to the frigate's youngest midshipman. 'With that voice, you have now managed to alert all the guards on the defences at Algeciras. I suggest you control your lip in future and try to behave like a young gentleman is supposed to behave.'

The midshipman's elation was snuffed out as quickly as a candle's flame and with all eyes on him, and the captain approaching from the quarterdeck, the colour drained from his cheeks.

From the gangway, several seamen were pointing at the water and whispering.

'You have my full attention, Mr Hanson,' Oliver said. 'What is it you want to show me?'

'There's a sailor in the water, Captain, and I think he's swimming for the ship?'

Oliver had already glanced over the side and drawn his own conclusion. 'Is that so? Perhaps your powers of observation can provide me with a little more detail.'

The middie turned from the rail, his jaw open, lost for words.

'Look again, Mr Hanson, and tell me what you see.'

The young gentleman did as he was bid, but still had no reply.

'When you sit down this evening to write this incident in your journal, I suggest you note that the man is not swimming for the ship, but that the tidal swell is lifting him and heading him this way. You should also note his face is down and his chin does not appear to be lifting from the water, therefore, it is unlikely he is breathing.'

Mr Hanson returned a blank expression.

'What you will be reporting is observing nothing more than a piece of inanimate flotsam.'

'But he's wearing common sailors' slops, not the sort of dress the folk in Gibraltar wear. That made me think he must belong to us.'

'A reasonable assumption, Mr Hanson. But there is more. I suggest you look a little harder.'

The boys screwed his eyes and rubbed them.

Oliver examined him quizzically. 'Do you have trouble reading a book?'

'No, sir, not if I hold the print up close.'

'Hum. Perhaps you should speak with the doctor about your eyesight.'

'There's blood on his sleeve,' one of the hands announced.

'Thank you, Smithers. That was the answer I was hoping I would hear from Mr Hanson.' He turned back to the midshipman. 'If you look a little closer, you will note there is no hand protruding from the end of his sleeve.'

The midshipman had no further comment to make.

'Do you want me to get some men to haul him aboard, Captain?' Mr Tully asked.

'No,' Oliver replied, turning to the bosun's mate who was standing behind him. 'You there, get a pole. When he's close enough, fend him off and turn him over. I would like to see the man's face.'

It took several minutes for the corpse to float close enough to be manipulated by the man leaning over the rail but, when the corpse was turned over, despite being swollen due to being immersed in seawater for some time, everyone recognised the face. It was Lompa, one of the two pressed sailors who had disappeared from the ship soon after it dropped anchor in the bay. A few pokes and prods at the sleeve, confirmed the man's hand had been cut off. It was a clean amputation, not the torn and ragged stump that resulted from a shark bite or powder blast.

'What shall we do with him, Captain,' Mr Tully asked quietly.

'Leave him. Let the sea finish him off.'

There was an undercurrent of whispers from the deck.

The captain turned and faced the men. 'By running from the ship, this man broke one of the cardinal Articles of War. Desertion. If he had been found alive, he would have been returned to the ship and made to suffer the fate as determined by those Articles. Death! So, what are we to achieve if we bring him aboard now? Commend his body to the waves? Toss him back where he came from? I think not.

'Furthermore, according to the strict Quarantine Regulations that exist in Gibraltar at the present, it is my duty to refuse entry to this vessel to any person, living or dead, without the written permission of Gibraltar's health inspector. How do I know this man has not been in contact with the fever during his absence? If I were to permit his body to come aboard, I would be contravening those regulations and possible infecting every man aboard.'

There was no response.

'Cast the body off!' the captain called to the man with the pole. 'Mr Tully, clear these men away. This is not a sideshow.'

For men, suffering boredom after having been confined to the ship, the arrival of the corpse delivered only a short distraction. It lasted little more than five minutes. However, the incident would provide something for the *Perpetuals* to mull over for several days to come.

'What would you think happened to him, Capt'n?' Mr Tully asked, once most of the hands had dispersed.

Oliver looked across the bay to the corrugations of swell indicating the incoming tide. Directly in line were the three hulks including *Guerrier*.

'One, if not all of those hulks are floating repositories for tobacco, although I doubt Mr Lompa knew that when he jumped overboard and headed for them. It was an unfortunate choice of destination. And if his red-headed mate, Styles, was with him, it is likely he would have met a similar fate, if not worse.'

Oliver turned to the officers and men who were within hearing distance. 'I am sure you noticed when you wandered through this town that the traders here come from many parts, Spaniards, Jews, Italians, Turks and Arabs. They have two things in common – a greed for money, and a jealous desire to hold on to it.

'If this man was caught dipping his hand into a barrel of tobacco leaves, no questions would have been asked as to who he was or where he came from. He would merely have been treated as any common thief is treated in many foreign lands. The loss of a hand is the mark of a thief.'

Only a few faces registered surprise.

'Do not forget, gentlemen, we have our own ideas of appropriate punishments which, to others, may appear equally brutal. In the

Royal Navy we haul a man up to the yardarm and hang him by the neck until he is dead – a process that can take half an hour for his lungs to run out of air or until the neck muscles can hold out no longer and the gullet is crushed.

'Or we flog a man around the fleet, merely for being insolent, until his ribs and lungs are no better than a piece of wet meat on a butcher's slab. It happened in Plymouth only a few days before we left England. That man died slowly in excruciating pain, unable to move, breathe or even cry out. What you witnessed here was not a pleasant sight, but it will serve as a lesson to any man should he consider misbehaving in this town.'

Leaning against the rail in the bow, Muffin laughed. 'What did you think about the middie's sighting? He was that excited, I thought he'd wet himself.'

'I thought he must have spotted a mermaid,' Brickley added.

Most of his mates, sitting on the deck, shared the joke.

'It's all rubbish,' Bungs said.

'What is?' Muffin asked.

'All this talk about quarantine.'

'Careful, bosun's mate might be listening.'

'What do I care? It's a fact, we're stuck here on this ship and no one is allowed to go ashore. But there ain't no quarantine from what I can see. This morning I saw a Spanish man-o'-war and half a dozen feluccas sail in from the Strait and head across the bay to Algeciras. And did you see all the gunboats? There must have been two dozen of them sniffing around like paid-off sailors after a woman's purse? And what about them three hulks in the bay. Boats coming and going to them from morning till night. Seems like the quarantine is to keep us aboard while everyone else does exactly what he pleases.'

'Well, I'd rather stay here than get a dose of the fever,' Muffin said.

'I'd rather take me chance and go ashore. I ain't going to get no fever.'

'How can you be so sure?'

'Because I've had it before, just like most sailors who've been to the Indies. In fact, I reckon the Calcutta station is the worst. Bodies float down the rivers there every day – bobbing about like fat sea lions – but it don't bother the folk who live there, they still wash in it and drink it. I tell you, that river water's worse than a twelve-month barrel of ship's water that's got so many wrigglies moving about in it, it's a wonder it don't walk out of the hold by itself.'

'I heard the lieutenant talking,' Eku said. 'Those aren't prison hulks.'

'What are they then?' Bungs asked. 'They don't look like hospital ships.'

'They're smugglers stores.'

'Don't talk out of the back of your head.'

'He's right. I heard that too,' Muffin said. 'Baccy stores they are. I'm surprised you can't smell it from here.'

Bungs screwed his brow.

'That's a change,' Muffin scoffed. 'Fancy us knowing something you don't know. Wasn't you working on the Rock a year ago?'

'Sure I was,' the cooper said. 'But I kept my mind on the job, didn't I.'

Muffin didn't say anything more.

'So, Mr Know-It-All, tell us about these so-called smugglers,' Bungs demanded. 'Where's the baccy come from? Where's it going to?'

'It comes in from the West Indies.'

'Pinched?'

'No, it's British. Grown on the plantations by the slaves. Only problem is Britain won't allow it to go to Spain, so the folk in Gibraltar make a fortune out of it. It's shipped here, loaded into them hulks, then smuggled into Spain.'

'How? When?'

'Every day. When the Spaniards come through the Land Port Gate in the morning to sell their bits and pieces, they arrive with near empty carts and pockets. But when they go out at night, the poor mules can hardly drag the carts across the border and the Spaniards' pockets are so full of tobacco leaves they can't button their coats.'

'What about the guards on the gate? They're not stupid.'

'No, they're clever. They make their own profit. They know the smugglers. They're all regulars, and they have an arrangement with them. For the price of a bribe, they let the tobacco pass through without seeing it. It happens under everyone's noses, bold as brass, and because everyone's happy, it's been going on for years. Even the garrison closes its eyes to it.'

'So if I want some baccy,' Bungs said. 'I should take a boat over to one of those hulks and get me a sack of leaves.'

'I don't think the captain would take too kindly to that.'

'Even better, we could borrow the captain's boat, fill it to the gunnels and row it over to Algeciras. I wouldn't mind selling it and getting paid in silver dollars.'

'And what about the Spanish sailors on them gunboats?' Muffin asked. 'They'd cut your throat for a pipe, and we'd never see hide nor hair of you again, along with the money, the boat and the baccy.'

'Huzza! Couldn't wish for a better outcome.'

'You shut your gob, Smithers. Just wait until I get my share, I won't sell you a mouthful not even for a bucket full of silver.'

'Bide your time, Bungs. When we go ashore you can buy yourself a ration for a few pence.'

A movement on the Rock caught Muffin's eye.

'Hey, Mr Tully,' he shouted. 'See, the signal tower. It's dancing a jig.'

The lieutenant stopped and watched.

'What's it saying?' Muffin asked.

'How am I to know?' the lieutenant replied. 'Probably telling the garrison there's a ship on the Strait.'

The sailors all turned and looked in the direction of the Gut, but nothing could be seen from *Perpetual*'s deck.

'You there,' the lieutenant said to Smithers. 'Do something useful. Get up the mast and keep a look out. If you see a sail on the Strait, I want to know what rate it is, how many guns are mounted, what flag it's sailing under, and the direction it's coming from. Right Now, Smithers, not tomorrow! Get a glass and get up there!'

'Aye aye, sir,' Smithers drawled.

Having visited the garrison with the doctor and wandered through the growing tent city on Windmill Hill, the captain and ship's surgeon returned to the awaiting boat.

'This is a diabolical disease?' Oliver observed, as the boat pulled from the beach, not expecting an answer.

'My colleagues at St Thomas's would welcome some fresh specimens,' Dr Whipple replied enthusiastically.

The captain flashed him an icy look.

The surgeon's explanation was somewhat apologetic. 'It is possible by anatomising the corpses that an answer to the nature of the disease, its indiscriminate choice of victims and what is causing it, could be found.'

'And probably kill the good doctors who are trying to treat the sick,' Oliver replied cynically.

Dr Whipple did not argue. The captain was correct. It was common knowledge in the hospital dissection rooms that if the flesh of a cadaver entered the skin of a surgeon, that surgeon would die. It had happened to several students he had known.

He continued. 'When I spoke with Dr Pym, he said he was of the firm opinion the contagion was caused by overcrowding and lack of hygiene which is seen in the poorer parts of town.'

'But the soldiers of the garrison do not live in the poor quarters, yet they are dying also,' Oliver argued.

'But they stand on the Line Wall,' the doctor replied. 'And they are posted to every gate and street corner in the town. They patrol the streets and even escort the death carts on their daily rounds.'

'And what of the argument the contagion is carried by the Levanter—' Oliver asked. '—the ill wind that carries the infection and circulates bad air to every house and hovel on the peninsula?'

'I cannot agree,' the doctor said. 'Although I have no proof to justify my assumption. Everyone on the peninsula breathes the same air yet not everyone is affected. What I can state, however, is that like Dr Pym, I have little in my apothecary's chest to treat these victims with. And, like him, I am at a loss to know what the nature of the fever is and therefore what medicine to administer. It appears, for the present, everything we are doing is proving ineffective.'

'But is there any basis for the argument that this contagion is Yellow Fever?'

'There are some similarities to the disease I saw in the West Indies. The Spanish called it the *Vómito negro*.'

'Should I be afraid for my men, my ship?'

'I cannot say. Dr Pym informed me that Cadiz has lost tens of thousands of its residents, and Malaga is suffering in a similar manner.'

'It would appear that this pestilence is creeping towards Gibraltar. A depressing situation, would you not agree?' Oliver waited for an answer, but the one he received was not what he expected.

'For myself,' the doctor replied, 'I look at the positive aspects of the epidemic. It offers a splendid opportunity to investigate the contagion and its possible causes, follow its course and assess its outcome. It is a subject I would love to study – to record every detail in my journal and deliver my findings to one of the Royal Societies in London or to the surgeons of St Thomas Hospital in London.'

'You have a strong allegiance both to the hospital and your profession, sir.'

'I was privileged to be apprenticed to one of its most respected surgeons. Although great, such highly respected men are aware of their ignorance and limitations and are always desirous of knowledge.'

'But from your papers,' Oliver noted, 'it appears you did not stay at the hospital to follow that path.'

'Unfortunately, following one's ambitions cannot be funded from fresh air, and to attend lectures cost a considerable amount of money. But that is another story.'

When Oliver saw the Portuguese brig heading south down the bay from the harbour at Algeciras, any concerns he had about Dr Whipple's opinions were immediately forgotten.

With mixed emotions, he breathed a sigh of relief. *Conception* was sailing for Lisbon, carrying Susanna away from Gibraltar and from the pestilence that was spreading like a cancer. All being well, within a week she would be safe home in Madeira.

What a cruel hand the epidemic had dealt. At any other time, the British territory was a vibrant, colourful place where the military officers and wealthy residents held regular balls and pageants, where horseracing, polo and cricket matches were played on the neutral ground. Where exotic goods from faraway places could be purchased for a pittance. Where there were no taxes or customs duties. A place where privateers and smugglers found a haven for their booty – with no questions asked. It was a hub of honest trading too and a busy commercial port attracting ships from many countries that vied for moorings along the North and South Moles or anchorages in Gibraltar Bay.

As the wind filled *Conception*'s sails, Oliver followed its progress. Although relieved to farewell Susanna, he was plagued with guilt. He alone was the reason she had made the long journey from Madeira in the first place. And although she had been residing in Algeciras for more than a week, while the brig was undergoing repairs to its sails, he had not visited her once.

In his desk drawer, he had an addressed envelope and a partly written letter, which he had looked at several times with the intention of finishing and forwarding to her. But he had never completed it.

Now it was too late.

How long would it be before he would see her again?

He did not know the answer to that question.

CHAPTER 11

Captain Gore
2 October 1804

The arrival of a British frigate at the Gut of Gibraltar led to a flurry of activity on the bay, which began half an hour before the ship came into view.

On the ridge atop the Rock, over 1300 feet above the sea, the bulbous arms of the signal tower transmitted news of the arrival, but the coded message it delivered was more foreign to observers than the languages spoken in the town.

Despite that, a fleet of Spanish gunboats made sail from Algeciras heading along the imaginary line which divided the Bay of Algeciras from the Bay of Gibraltar. With guns primed and ready, their mission was to investigate the new arrival.

At the same time, the government cutter rounded the North Mole. It was also heading to meet the frigate. On board, Gibraltar's Health Guard was carrying unwelcome news.

Having the benefit of the morning's breeze, *Medusa*, entered the bay and sailed to within a few cables' lengths of *Perpetual*. As the frigate hove to, calls were heard from the deck, followed by a flash of powder, a burst of noise and a cloud of smoke. Captain Gore had delivered a decisive warning shot across the bow of the nearest gunboat.

The small craft did not retaliate but wasted no time in veering from the fighting ship and heading back to the Spanish side of the bay. With the anchor cable hissing through the hawse-hole, the health inspector's voice resounded through a brass speaking trumpet. He delivered his instructions regarding the port's closure and quarantine regulations loud and clear.

The British frigate's unexpected arrival was welcomed as a much-needed distraction. An hour later, when Captain John Gore, *Medusa*, stepped on board *Perpetual*, Captain Quintrell extended a warm welcome to him

'You will not be going ashore, I presume.'

'Have no fear,' Gore said, 'I have no intention of contravening the orders of the Lieutenant-Governor. However, I was granted permission by the health guard to visit with you on the condition I came alone and my frigate remained a good distance from the shore. I trust all is well with you here.'

'As well as can be expected, I suppose,' Oliver said. 'With the men confined to the ship, patience is wearing a little thin and the men are becoming bored. To combat the situation, one of my midshipmen is providing lessons in reading and writing, while my sailing master is delivering lectures in geography and exploration to any man interested. I must say, he delivers his lectures with great enthusiasm and has amassed quite an audience.'

Captain Gore grinned. 'A veritable floating Chapter of Royal Society.'

'Hardly,' Oliver smiled. 'In contrast, the bosun devised a distraction which offers relief from the heat. By lowering a sail overboard every afternoon, the men are able to sink in the water to bathe themselves or wash their clothes without fear of drowning. Despite the salt, I contend I have the cleanest sailors in the whole of the British fleet, not to mention the ship.'

He continued. 'Every square inch of *Perpetual* has been scrubbed and scrubbed again. The brasses gleam, the glasses shine and, I profess there is not a mouse or louse anywhere aboard the frigate. Besides that, there is not an inch of old rope to be found in the bosun's locker. In fact he tells me we now have enough teased oakum to caulk a first-rate. But,' he said, replacing his smile with a serious expression. 'Enough of this trivia. What of *Triumph*, Captain Barlow and *Amphion*?'

'All is well. Next week, Captain Sutton and I head out to the Atlantic to join Captain Moore in *Indefatigable* and *Lively*, Captain Hammond, who will be arriving from the Channel Fleet, but I think you may be aware of those arrangements.'

'I was not aware of the precise details, but I presume this is connected with the dispatches I delivered to Sir Charles Cotton a few weeks ago.'

'Indeed.'

'The Spanish convoy from South America is expected to arrive off Cadiz within a week.'

Oliver was eager for more news. 'And you will intercept and detain them?'

'Those are my instructions.'

'Oh, to be sailing with you,' Oliver said wistfully. 'However, that is not to be. For the present, might I invite you to join me and my officers for dinner? We would all relish some new company.'

'It would be my pleasure.'

After almost two months at sea and because of the port's closure, the paucity of fresh produce available in the town meant the ingredients cook had available to prepare the meal with, provided for a far less sumptuous table than the one Oliver had shared with his officers in Portsmouth Harbour. Despite that, the assembled company quickly relaxed, each man willing to share an anecdote from his life, although not necessarily from his service. The more unusual or unfortunate the situation, the more laughter echoed around the cabin's bulwarks.

'Captain Gore,' Oliver said, turning to his guest. 'Would you permit me to share something of your naval career with my young officers? They could not find a more admirable career captain to model their actions on than you.'

'Rather gushing words.' The lilt of Captain Gore's Kilkenny accent was becoming more pronounced with every mouthful of wine.

'I confess those words are not mine,' Oliver admitted. 'That most flattering approbation was written by Admiral Lord Nelson himself, in a letter published in the Naval Chronicle.'

The visitor laughed from behind his glass before draining it. 'Then, who am I to dispute his Lordship's observations?'

Oliver thanked him and continued. 'Gentlemen, while Captain Gore is of a similar age to myself, he entered the service as a boy at the age of seven and was a midshipman from the age of nine. By seventeen he had been promoted to the rank of lieutenant, and was stepped up to commander at the age of twenty-two years, taking command of a French caravel.'

'A privateer – 16-guns,' Gore added.

Oliver acknowledged and continued. 'And being promoted to post captain six months later that prize ship was commissioned to him under British colours as HMS *Fleche*. Does my memory serve me correctly?'

'Indeed, indeed,' the Captain replied, his Irish brogue unmistakable.

'Having taken several valuable prizes during that command, Captain Gore was transferred to the Channel Fleet and served aboard *Triton* – 32-guns, and while in that ship captured not one or two prizes but thirteen privateers and man-of-war brigs.'

Captain Quintrell had the wide-eyed attention of his younger officers. 'Then the war was interrupted by the Peace of Amiens.'

'Most inconvenient, to be sure,' Gore quipped with a wink.

'And when the war resumed you were commissioned to your current vessel, *Medusa*.'

The captain nodded.

Oliver continued. 'A 32-gun frigate, which, I believe, Nelson hoisted his flag on in the Channel for a time. Then after being transferred to the Mediterranean, Captain Gore took command of the squadron off Toulon until the arrival of Admiral Lord Nelson. From there he was ordered to proceed with three other ships to act as advance guard off the Strait of Gibraltar.

'Which bring us up to date.' Oliver looked to his guest. 'Would that be a fair summary, Captain?'

'Indeed, it is.'

'Then let us raise a glass to Captain Gore.'

The toast was echoed with great enthusiasm and a clatter of feet under the table.

'Gentleman.' Gore raised his hand to silence the applause. 'If the deck beams allowed it, I would prefer to stand, not to address you but to relieve my aching back.'

The company was eager to hear what *Medusa*'s captain had to say.

'Captain Quintrell, your welcome is most congenial. Being reminded of the part one has played in securing Britain position of supremacy on the seas, is reassuring, although somewhat embarrassing.'

He looked at the faces around the table. 'What I choose to share with you here is for the benefit of the young officers who have yet to prove themselves in the King's Navy. Allow me to be serious for a moment, when I say that life in the service is not always a successful or rewarding one. Many who serve never reach the post rank that Captain Quintrell and I have achieved, and there are many who die in the trying.

'Yet, while I have benefitted through promotion and financial rewards, I should note that having Lord Cochrane for a godfather probably helped me along the way in the early days.' His smile was genuine, when he directed his next comment to the younger members of the ship's company. 'But, I can assure you, Lord Cochrane was certainly not aboard my ship dandling me on his knee throughout the last ten years.'

The sailing master spluttered into his glass of port.

'Captain Quintrell had been very generous is citing my successes, however, he has failed to mention the dismal results I achieved in the Channel while under Lord Nelson's command. Added to that was the grounding of several of his Majesty's ships, one which I placed on a rock, and another I lodged on a sand bank on the Strait.' He smiled and shook his head. 'But more recently, I almost managed to start a war with Spain single-handed.'

The captain had the attention of everyone at the table.

'Pray tell,' Oliver begged.

'It happened when I was chasing a French privateer. She was sailing very close to the Cadiz lighthouse and one of *Medusa*'s shots went high and landed in the town. It was fortunate the Spanish authorities accepted my explanation that it was an accident. As a result my men and I were graciously invited to attend a banquet and a bullfight in that fine city.'

The junior officers chuckled.

'As a result of that incident, I have a very good relationship with the Dons at Cadiz. A fortunate outcome from an unfortunate incident that could easily have been misconstrued with catastrophic consequences.'

The Irishman obviously enjoyed talking and the officers were enthralled with his exploits.

'But three years ago, aboard *Triton*, the eleventh gun abaft the mainmast deck burst. I was dining, as we are now, when I received word the gun was ready. Lieutenant Alford, who was with me, opened the cabin door and his head was blown straight from his body. Although the gunner was virtually unscathed, his mate was killed, another man was blown into the quarter-gallery and 18 seamen and marines were badly injured, including myself.

'So, gentlemen, if you notice me shuffling in my seat, I can assure you I am not infected with the French Pox, but I suffer severe discomfort in my spine.

'Life in the service is not all prize money and glory but, in order to acquire one or both, you must be prepared to pay a hefty price for your achievements. Continue to strive and learn, and you will succeed, I guarantee you.'

His address was met with a hearty round of approval.

The evening was a great success and everyone was buoyed by the visit from the naval captain whom several of the younger officers had never heard of prior to his arrival.

Oliver and Simon Parry had also savoured the visit. The light-hearted banter over dinner had broken some of the tensions simmering in *Perpetual*.

Much to everyone's disappointment, Captain Gore had excused him relatively early to return to his ship and, with his departure, the meal came to a close.

'Pray stay a moment, Mr Parry,' Oliver begged, when the other officers had taken their leave.

Once alone, the captain lowered his voice and continued. 'I learned a little more from the conversation I had with Captain Gore before dinner but I thought it politic not to share it. Word passes all too quickly and, like plied rope, it can be twisted many times before it reaches the end of the ropewalk.

'It appears Captain Barlow was planning to take *Triumph* to Cadiz, however word is out, yet again, that we are on the brink of war. I am aware the suggestion that Spain will enter the war in support of Napoleon has been made many times and until a declaration is made, it is only hearsay and speculation. But Captain Gore, who I hold in high regard, believes conflict is imminent – in a matter of weeks. As such, he felt it would be foolhardy for a 74 to be placed in a position of vulnerability. He therefore convinced Captain Barlow to remain on his current position – as advance guard for the Mediterranean Fleet.'

'While he will sail for the Atlantic to detain any Spanish treasure ships returning to port. Would that be the outcome?' Simon Parry said.

Oliver raised one eyebrow. '*Detain but not attack*,' he repeated. 'I ask you, Simon, do you really believe a Spanish captain will relinquish his treasure without a fight?'

It was a rhetorical question.

Brickley's announcement to the group of sailors gathered around the foremast had everyone's attention.

'Now I remember who he is. He's a bleedin' jailbird!'

'Who is?' Bungs asked.

'I swore I'd seen him before,' the sailor continued. 'But I couldn't for the life of me remember where. Now I know!'

'Who? Where?' Muffin asked.

'Damn your eyes! Spit it out!' Bungs yelled.

'Newgate Prison! Our hoity-toity surgeon, who feeds his patient's innards to the fish, is nothing more than a common jailbird.'

Eyebrows raised.

'Are you sure?'

'Sure, I'm sure. I remember seeing him the day he was dragged in. Blabbering that he'd done nothing wrong. Arguing that he didn't belong there. Asking to see the Governor. Demanding that a message be sent to this person or that.'

'What was he thrown into Newgate for?' Irons enquired.

'How should I know? I'm just telling you what I saw. He was brought in early one morning along with two other cons. They didn't look bothered and from the cut of their clothes, it was obvious they were regulars. But the doctor was beside himself.'

'So, what is the man? Is he a doctor or an impersonator?'

'What was his crime?'

'Maybe he's done a murder,' Smithers smirked.

'Not dressed the way he was dressed.' Brickley said. 'He looked more like a forger, a fraudster or even a crooked lawyer.'

'What happened to him?' Eku enquired.

'Another toff arrived in the afternoon and the doctor was taken out.'

'And?'

'How should I know,' Brickley said. 'Never saw him again until that day the captain had us lined up on deck and the doctor examined us. I knew I'd seen him before and it's been nagging at me ever since.'

'What of the other two men thrown in with him?'

'They were nothing to do with him. They just happened to be locked up at the same time. They were a pair of exhumators,'

'Exhumators?' Eku asked.

'Sack-'em-up men, lifters and grabs, grave robbers, whatever you want to call them. Them types are not popular even in jail and it weren't long before they got their comeuppance.'

115

'So what made you remember the doctor just now?' Muffin asked.

The sailor shrugged his shoulders. 'It was a whiff from the heads that wafted up my nose and reminded me of the smell of prison. You don't forget that sort of thing easy, but it's taken me a while to remember the face.'

'What will you do about it? Eku asked.

'What do you mean?'

'Are you going to tell the captain?'

'Don't talk daft,' Brickley replied. 'The captain ain't going to believe me. I'd probably get a flogging for telling tales. He'd say I was trying to drag the surgeon's name in the gutter.' He smirked. 'Insolence – that's what they call it in them Articles of his.'

'Well, don't be surprised if word gets about,' Bungs warned. 'These walls have got ears and someone will tell. You mark my words.'

Brickley shrugged it off. 'Capt'n ain't interested in foremast tittle-tattle. He should know by now, a bit of juicy gossip always goes down well with a double ration of grog.'

CHAPTER 12

The Cockpit

Standing by the taffrail away from flapping ears, Oliver spoke plainly with his first lieutenant.

'Our ship's surgeon is a nemesis to me.' Oliver admitted. 'Since he came aboard, I have lost a young midshipman.'

'The unfortunate accident with the fishbone.'

Oliver peered at him with a frown.

'Old Prendergast died from blood poisoning after the assistant surgeon pulled a rotten tooth from his jaw.' Oliver shook his head. 'How many men have teeth pulled at sea and suffer no more than an aching gum?'

'Hundreds,' Mr Parry replied.

'Indeed. And I learned there was an argument over what to do with the cook's mate who was unable to pass water. It seems the surgeon was eager to cut him for a stone, which he insisted was in the man's bladder. However, the seaman baulked at the sight of the lancet and said he preferred to put up with the pain. A couple of days later, I was told, the stone passed naturally and the excruciating pain the man had been suffering disappeared. I ask you to consider this, what would have been the fate of the man if the doctor had operated on him?'

'I cannot say,' the lieutenant replied.

'Perhaps the men are also becoming a little wary. I noted this morning that apart from a few festering sores and a boil or two, there was little response to the sick bell.'

'I suppose we should be thankful that the opposite does not apply,' Simon Parry said.

Oliver knew his first lieutenant's comment was valid. 'But from what I have been told, the surgeon has some strange habits. Unlike most officers who spend their private moments writing letters or reading, Dr Whipple never leaves the cockpit and dedicates his spare time to cutting up specimens – rats, mice even the fat blood-filled leeches he brought with him. I am tempted to believe the rumours that he is some sort of vivisectionist.'

Mr Parry did not commit to an opinion on that subject. 'Yet I must argue in his defence with regard to Hobbles, the gun captain. As he is stone-deaf, he never heard the chit-chat in the mess and presented himself to the surgeon, because of a pain in the side of his head. After examining him, Dr Whipple bathed his ear in a warm solution and managed to pull out enough wax to burn a candle for two hours. Hobbles, didn't say much, but he appeared to be concentrating hard to hear sounds and voices he had not heard for a long time.'

'Wait until the next time we have gun practice,' Oliver replied cynically. 'Then he will know if he is still completely deaf of not.'

Mr Parry continued. 'One of the carpenter's mates had an enormous boil on his back. He wouldn't let anyone touch it, but eventually he let the doctor lance it. Longbottom said the yellow matter shot up to the overhead beams and when the doctor squeezed it, the boil frothed over with pus and blood. He said it resembled lava running down the sides of a volcano.'

'A very vivid description,' the captain scoffed.

'The man is now back in the carpenter's shop and is as good as new,' Simon added. 'And yesterday there was the topman who fell out of the rigging? The doctor did nothing for him – absolutely nothing, even although his mates pleaded with the surgeon to treat him. Bleed him. Purge him. Do anything. But Dr Whipple refused. He said that because the man was bleeding from his ears, his skull was broken and his brain drowning in blood. He said whatever he did would not help. He argued that if he put the man through more pain and he died, he would be accused of administering the wrong treatment. "Yet, if I don't treat him and he dies, I will be accused on neglect." Those were his very words.'

'"But if you treat him and he lives?" one of the midshipmen asked.'

'"If he lives," he surgeon answered, "it will be a miracle, and miracles are out of my hands. I will make this man comfortable as possible, but he will die before morning, I can assure you." Sure enough, at eight bells of the morning watch, the topman passed from this earthly life.'

'Enough! I am fully aware of these incidences,' Oliver replied bluntly. 'You do not need to remind me.'

An hour later, Oliver ducked his head and entered the cockpit unannounced.

Seated at his tiny desk against the bulkhead, Dr Whipple was making an entry in one of his leather-bound journals. At the far side of the sick berth, the loblolly was leaning over a bucket scrubbing the doctor's surgical instruments. Abel Longbottom was nowhere to be seen. On the table, in the centre of the cabin, a stained cotton sheet was draped over a corpse. The sweet and sickly odour of death mixed with the smell of preservative fluid hung in the air.

'Leave us,' the captain ordered, glancing at the boy.

Tommy dropped the brush into the water, rubbed his hands down his apron then hurried away.

'I wish to see the body,' Oliver said.

Striding to the operating table, the captain stood alongside it and waited for a few moments.

'I do not have all day to waste, sir. I wish to see the deceased.'

Putting down his pen, Dr Whipple joined the captain and folded back the sheet to reveal the head and shoulders of one of *Perpetual*'s foremast Jacks.

The two men exchanged glances but not a word was spoken. The man's identity did not come as a surprise to Oliver. He had been informed of the death and needed to arrange a time for the burial service. As far as he was concerned, the sooner such matters were attended to the better.

'Why has this man not been sewn into his hammock?' he demanded.

'I was waiting for my assistant to return,' the doctor replied.

Oliver was unconvinced and reached for the corner of the cloth. Pulling it back in a single sweep, he slid it from the corpse. Taking one step back, he inhaled deeply.

Not only was the man stark naked, but his chest had been cut open from neck to belly then sewn back together loosely with twine. From his profile, it appeared some of the organs had been removed from the body cavities. It also appeared that the empty space has been filled with wood shavings, as fine feathers of curled wood were protruding through the line of stitches. Sawdust was also littering the deck beneath his feet.

'You have stuffed this man's body with waste from the carpenter's shop!'

'I drained off the excess body fluid. I used the sawdust to absorb the natural seepage which accumulates *post mortem*. By that means, the corpse is less likely to stain the deck when it is taken up for the burial service.'

'You say you merely drained the fluid yet, it appears to my unskilled eye, you have almost sliced the man into two parts and removed his insides.'

The doctor did not deny it. 'I did what any other London surgeon would do in an attempt to discern what caused the man's death.'

'But the man fell from the yardarm! You already have your answer.'

'I can assure you, Captain, this surgery was performed after death.'

'I am not interested in the habits of London surgeons. I want this man sewn into a hammock immediately. Do you have his clothing?'

Dr Whipple nodded.

'Then I suggest he is fully dressed before he is stitched into a hammock in order to hide this desecration.'

'Of course,' the doctor said obligingly.

Oliver withheld his temper. 'I will speak with you later.'

Frustrated and angry, Oliver returned to his cabin and pondered over what he had just witnessed and the doctor's explanation for what he had done. He pondered, too, over the rumours circulating the ship – unhealthy rumours which centred on the actions of the ship's surgeon.

Dr Whipple was an enigma to him. Was the young doctor a product of the modern Age of Enlightenment which was sweeping Europe but, so far, managing to avoid the decks of fighting ships? Was his wooden world so detached from life that existed in the towns and cities of Britain? How could he judge?

The riddle vexed him and he determined to resolve the matter immediately, however, not wishing to confront the doctor again in the sick berth and be distracted by a corpse being sewn into a hammock for burial, he requested the doctor attend him in his cabin.

'Please sit,' Oliver said when the doctor arrived ten minutes later with a seemingly lame apology for his delay.

'I examined your papers when you came aboard,' the captain said. 'From them, I learned you sailed to Port Royal as ship's surgeon aboard a 74 with Captain Appleby.'

'I was rated assistant surgeon initially.'

Oliver waited for more information.

'The appointed ship's surgeon contracted a dose of malignant fever only three days after we arrived in Kingston Harbour. He died three days later.'

'And you examined his body, I presume,' Oliver said cynically.

The doctor paused. 'I did what was necessary.'

'As a direct result of his death, I presume you were stepped up.'

'That is correct. I had no choice in the matter.'

'What illness did the surgeon succumb to?' Oliver asked.

'I wasn't sure. I had my books with me for reference, and had read of the infectious diseases that are prevalent in the West Indies but, having only worked on the wards of the London Borough Hospitals, I was not familiar with the rapid course those tropical diseases took.'

He continued. 'I cannot speak highly enough of Dr Appleby. Although he was on his deathbed, slipping in and out of delirium, he tutored me, advised me of which medicines to make up and administer to him. But even with his own help, I could not save him.'

'And the rest of the crew, did any of them contract the same disease.'

'Many of them became ill. Seventeen seamen died in the first two weeks. The others recovered with little or no help from me.'

'Humph.'

'I can imagine what you are thinking, Captain, but our ship was not alone. Three frigates in the harbour also suffered many deaths. One lost its surgeon to the illness, while another lost its captain. He had to be relieved of his duty and transferred to the hospital in Kingston. It was many months before he was fit to return to duty.'

'No doubt you were relieved when the ship eventually weighed.'

'I cannot remember,' the doctor said. 'I was ill and delirious for several days myself, but was fortunate to be nursed back to health by my assistant.'

Oliver pondered over his next statement. 'Would I be correct in saying that your limited experience in the Royal Navy has not been entirely successful from a medical perspective?'

'I shall not comment on my failure to protect the men from an epidemic that was ravaging the Caribbean at the time. That is for my superiors at the Navy Board to assess. However, I conveyed my disappointment to the Admiralty at not being allowed to remain on the island to assist the victims of the contagion. Had I been permitted to do so, my term in the tropics would have been for more instructive.'

'Instructive?'

'Working in Kingston hospital would have provided me with new skills and perhaps I would have learned how best to treat the deadly disease.'

Oliver did not reply.

'Now if you will excuse me, Captain, there are some matters I need to complete.'

An hour later, the men mustered on deck swayed uncomfortably from one foot to the other, even though the deck had no movement in it.

Despite the burial service being brief with few unnecessary words spoken, this was the second burial for the week. With hats in their hands, the men stood in attendance only because they were obliged to. Few lifted their gaze from the deck and fewer still joined in the Lord's Prayer, although every man could repeat the words by rote equally as well as they could recite every paragraph of the Articles of War. How could they forget them? They were reminded of them twice a month.

'Who died this time?' someone whispered.

'Silence there!' the midshipman ordered.

'And who'll be next?' the voice was even lower.

'Who said that?' Mr Smith demanded, but no one answered.

Captain Quintrell replaced his hat.

'On hats,' was the order. But the captain had not finished.

'We are not stationed in this bay to satisfy any whim of mine,' he said. 'Given choice, I would put to sea in an instant and be well clear of this place. But let me remind you we have only been here for a few weeks. If we were with Admirals Nelson or Cornwallis, in the Mediterranean or at Ushant, it is possible we would have been stuck in the same location for a year or more.'

'But they don't have a plague on their back doorstep.'

Oliver's ears were keen. 'Your observation is correct, Smithers, and that is something else I have no control over. My movements are restricted by a small matter called Admiralty Orders. And while you all listen to the Articles of War, you should realize anything which is contained therein is equally applicable to the most senior officers on this ship as it is to the cook's servant in the galley.

'We all serve King and country and my wishes and desires are no different from yours. I would dearly love to see the chalk cliffs of England again and thrill to the sound of the gun on the saluting platform at Portsmouth welcoming me home. Instead, I must be content with my present situation.

'We must learn to accept the mists rising up from the bay and the clouds that descend from the mountain. I have no control over the weather. But there are other things that concern me which are not always apparent to you. The cooper tells me that most of our water is gone, and the carpenter informs me this morning that the ship's hull, below the waterline, is dressed in cloak of green weed. Added to that, you men are becoming unsettled and indolent. This concerns me. Idleness leads directly to insubordination and mischief.

'Most of you men have sailed with me before. You know me and know I am concerned for your welfare. I hope and pray our stay here is drawing to a close. As such, I have spoken with the garrison commander regarding our return to England.'

The captain's words met with murmurs of approval.

'But I can guarantee you nothing. Nor can the Lieutenant-Governor. And, I assure you, his worries and responsibilities are far greater than mine. The epidemic is claiming more lives every day, both in the town and the garrison and for that reason, I suggest any man who is toying with the idea of running should consider what he would be running to.

His words were interrupted by a call from the masthead.

'Deck below! Sail entering the bay.'

Immediately everyone's attention was to the foremast lookout.

'What colours?' Oliver called.

'British. It's the same frigate what was here last week.

'*Medusa*, Captain Gore,' Oliver murmured. 'Dismiss the men, Mr Tully.' Reaching for the glass from the binnacle, he put it to his eye.

'Take a look at her canvas, Simon.'

But the lieutenant didn't need the glass. 'I think Captain Gore might be requiring our assistance. '

CHAPTER 13

Medusa
7 October 1804

When John Gore entered Oliver's cabin on *Perpetual,* it was obvious his back was troubling him.

'Welcome aboard, sir.'

The visitor nodded, but his expression was not that of the man who had joked about his exploits with the young officers only a few days earlier.

'Fighting battles is one thing,' he sighed. 'Fighting one's conscience is another.'

'Come, sit and relax for a while.'

The Irish-born captain raised his eyes and looked directly at his fellow officer. 'It was not a satisfactory outcome for either side. Certainly, we followed orders, but all in all it was a catastrophe.'

'Casson, some wine,' Oliver called. 'The least I can offer you. And, if you should need any assistance—'

'There are several matters I must speak with you about but, for the moment, if you will excuse me,' Gore said, at the same time removing his sword, stretching his back and seating himself in the wing-backed chair beside the empty fire hearth. Then he continued. 'I presume you heard what happened two days ago.'

Oliver nodded. 'The garrison received word yesterday afternoon. The news travelled overland via Algeciras.'

'What did you hear?'

'That a convoy had been attacked off Cape Saint Mary and a Spanish ship had been sunk. There was no mention of casualties or the cargo. Having come from Cadiz, the message was brief and failed to convey precise details.'

Oliver paused. 'I presume this is the mission you were engaged in.'

Captain Gore nodded. 'Unfortunately, from all points of view, the result was far from what was intended. The only positive outcome is that it has deprived King Carlos of a considerable consignment of treasure from his colonies that was destined to end up in the hands of Napoleon.'

The conversation halted when Casson entered with a tray of refreshments.

'Are you able to share the facts of the encounter?' Oliver asked.

The captain paused before answering. 'My written report is already on its way to England. Captain Moore is heading for Plymouth in convoy with *Lively*, Captain Hammond, and Sutton in *Amphion.* They are escorting three Spanish ships.

'And, might I ask, why you didn't sail with them?'

'You will have noticed, *Medusa* suffered considerable damage during the action and is on the verge of being declared unseaworthy. Because of its condition, I was not prepared to subject either my ship or my men to the Bay of Biscay. Hence, I have come here to seek your help. My stay will be brief for obvious reasons.'

'I understand your concerns.'

Gore shook his head once again. 'No, I think not. My main concern is not the damage to my ship. What I fear is the action off Cadiz will render consequences which will reverberate across Europe. I wager, the action off Cape Saint Mary will precipitate a declaration of war from Spain within the next few weeks.'

Oliver begged the captain to tell him how the events unfolded.

'When I left here, a little over a week ago, I joined company with *Amphion*, Captain Sutton, and we headed to the Atlantic beyond Tarifa and Cape Trafalgar to patrol the waters off the Spanish and Portuguese coasts.

'There, I met with Captain Moore, *Indefatigable* and *Lively*, Captain Hammond who had been sent from the Channel Fleet.

'As was prearranged.'

'Correct. We remained in that vicinity, south west of Cape Saint Vincent until 5 October. That morning, at 7 o'clock, around nine leagues south west of Cape Saint Mary, *Medusa* was the first to see the Spanish fleet – four frigates, under a press of sail, steering for Cadiz. An impressive sight indeed. The leading frigate, *La Fama*, was flying a commodore's broad pennant. Behind that was *Médéa*, flying the flag of the Rear Admiral. She was a grand ship, armed with 42 eighteen pounders. She was followed by two others, *Nuestra Señora de las Mercedes* and *Santa Clara*.

'I signalled Captain Moore, who immediately ordered us to form a line, hoping the formation we presented would induce the Spanish ships to shorten sail and heave to. I was on the weather beam of the leading ship. Captain Moore was immediately behind me in *Indefatigable*, with *Amphion* and *Lively* followed behind.

Once in position, we waited for the fleet to reduce sail but the Spaniards showed no intention of doing so.

'With orders to detain the ships and not attack them, Captain Moore ordered a shot from *Indefatigable* to be put across the flagship's bow. That was ignored, so he sent a lieutenant across by boat stating his intention of detaining the fleet and returning them to England.'

'And the response?' Oliver asked.

'As you can well imagine, the commodore was not prepared to hand over his treasure ships and immediately moved into a position of close engagement.'

Oliver waited.

'When the boat returned, a second warning shot was fired from the *Indie*, but *Las Mercedes* replied with a ball across *Amphion*'s deck wounding five of its crew. It could have been far worse. The Spanish ships were well armed and had far more guns than we did.

'At 10 o'clock, *Médéa* turned its guns on *Indefatigable*. Fortunately for Captain Moore, the aim was poor and the *Indie* suffered neither damage nor casualties but that action prompted retaliation from the other vessels and, within minutes, both sides were engaged in heavy fire.

'Ten minutes later there was the most horrendous ear-splitting explosion. *Nuestra Señora de las Mercedes* was blown to matchwood with flames leaping sky-high.'

'A direct hit on the magazine?'

'No, I learned later, it was due to careless handling of powder below deck.' Gore shifted in his seat. 'The explosion was so powerful part of one of *Mercedes*' guns was found lodged high in *Amphion*'s rigging. I am surprised the sound did not carry to Gibraltar.'

'And what of the crew of the stricken ship? Were there any survivors?'

'*Amphion* was quick to put boats in the water but to little avail. *Mercedes* had on board 240 souls including many women and children returning home to Spain. Only 40 survivors were plucked from the water. The remaining 200, including her captain, went down with the ship.'

'A tragedy,' Oliver muttered. 'But what of the other three ships?'

'In the confusion of noise, smoke, flame and debris, they attempted to escape. I gave chase to *La Fama* and quickly caught up with her. She was not prepared to fight and hauled her colours, as did the *Santa Clara*.

'And the third?'

'*Médéa,* with the Spanish Admiral aboard, made all sail and managed to escape the action.'

'Did he get away?'

Gore shook his head. 'Captain Hammond gave chase and captured the frigate before sunset. The following morning, the prisoners and wounded were taken aboard the British ships and some of the treasure was also transferred for fear the damaged Spanish ships might sink.' He leaned back in his chair. 'There was an immense amount of treasure. Gold, silver, specie and merchandise.'

'But what of *Mercedes*, the ship that blew up? Was she an escort or was she also carrying treasure?

'According to the commander's inventory, she was carrying a fortune in gold and silver coins. She went down in deep water and would have scattered her contents on the sea floor. A disaster.'

'And the commander?'

'Rear Admiral Jose de Bustamente y Guerra. One of the most experienced officers in the Spanish Navy. He had served as Governor of Monte Video and was returning to Spain with his family. I met with the Admiral the following day when Captain Moore and I went aboard his vessel. A true gentleman, if ever there was one. He expressed no malice towards us despite his losses. He introduced me to his close friend, a Major who had stood beside him during the action and watched helplessly as his wife, five daughters and three sons perished in the massive explosion. The Major's only remaining son was on *Médéa* with him. A tragedy.'

'How can I be of assistance to you?' Oliver asked.

After stretching his back, Captain Gore sat forward in the armchair.' There are three things I will beg assistance with. Firstly, the loan of your carpenter and his mates.' He explained. 'While my frigate suffered some damage, it was not nearly as much as that suffered by the treasure ships. For Captain Moore to escort them to England, he first had to make them seaworthy. I therefore gave him my team of carpenters to attend to those repairs.'

'I understand.'

'It is important I follow Captain Moore to England, as soon as possible, otherwise he will fear I have lost my ship and the treasure that was transferred to *Medusa*. That is why I need to borrow some men to repair my damage. Two or three days should be sufficient. Major repairs will have to wait until I reach Plymouth.'

Oliver was pleased. 'Take them with my blessing. I presently have carpenters aboard who are idling their time, complaining they have nothing to do. You will be doing me a favour by gainfully employing them for a few days.

'I appreciate your help. If your men could be made ready, I will return them to *Medusa* with my boat. I just pray the weather gods will look kindly on us while we are in Gibraltar Bay.'

Oliver excused himself for a moment, while he spoke with his steward requesting the carpenter and his mates be mustered on deck with their tools ready to transfer to *Medusa*.

'Is there anything else you require – spare spars, rigging or sails?'

'Thank you, no. The ship is well supplied.'

'And the second matter?' Oliver asked.

'Do you have a surgeon on board?'

'Indeed, I do.'

'After the battle, most of the Spanish wounded were taken aboard *Lively* and *Amphion* and because there were so many, Captain Moore requested I send my surgeon to help treat them.

'In all there were seven British casualties as against seventy Spanish wounded, not counting the men rescued from the sea who suffered severe burns. Many of those injured had limbs torn off or bones crushed – some terrible cases – I fear many of those men will require amputations, and many will die because the wounds have been left too long unattended. Although badly damaged, *Medusa* suffered no loss of life or injury to her crew. I therefore agreed to transfer my surgeon to help treat the wounded as best he could. However, in doing so, I have left my ship with no one to serve in the cockpit.'

Captain Gore added. 'I would not ask the garrison commander for the loan of his physician as, with this contagion, I imagine he has more than enough to deal with.'

'If you currently have no injured men on *Medusa*, might I enquire why you need the services of a doctor?'

'I need a second opinion. My assistant surgeon tells me that a number of men, who are bleeding from the mouth, are suffering from scurvy. Yet because we have been patrolling the coasts of Spain and North Africa for some time, the ship has never been short of limes or lemons. Therefore, I question his diagnosis and I need a physician to give an educated opinion as to the cause of the malaise, and to recommend what treatment is required. I have already forfeited some of my crew to sail *Santa Clara*, so I cannot afford to lose any more men to sickness.'

A tired smile softened Gore's expression. '*Medusa* will be welcome in England with its hull filled with Spanish silver, but she will not be welcome if she returns with a cockpit full by dying men.'

'It is my pleasure to offer the services of my surgeon, Dr Jonathon Whipple. I am sure he will oblige you. I will have him rowed over to you as soon as he has prepared his chest.' Oliver paused. 'And the third request?'

Captain Gore lowered his voice and spoke in a hushed tone.

'There is one other reason I came into Gibraltar Bay. When I received my orders, I was instructed should *Medusa* detain any Spanish treasure but then be in danger of sinking, the cargo should be transferred to another Royal Navy vessel bound for England.'

'Do either of those situations apply?'

Gore considered the question carefully. 'Even with the help of your carpenters and superficial repairs made to the vessel, I cannot guarantee my safe return to Plymouth. Amongst the treasure transferred to *Medusa* from *Santa Clara* are several chests containing specie – doubloons, silver dollars and Spanish reales. With your permission, I beg to transfer four chests to *Perpetual*. You will be provided with a detailed inventory of the contents, along with a copy of my original orders. When the chests are delivered, you will sign a receipt which I will deliver to the Admiralty. Are you in a position to oblige me in this matter?'

'A little unusual is it not?'

The back pain Captain Gore was suffering showed in the creases on his brow. 'This whole affair is a little unusual,' he said.

'But of course, I will oblige,' Oliver said. 'How and when would you like the transfer to take place?'

'At dawn tomorrow. Kindly be ready to receive it. The less delay the better. That will provide me with some peace of mind should *Medusa* go down on the Bay of Biscay, or be taken by the French or Spanish privateers on our return passage. At least a portion of the treasure will have been saved.'

'One question,' Oliver said. 'This treasure is not actually a prize of war, is it?'

'That is a moot point, Oliver, and something which will no doubt be argued over for some time to come.'

On the following morning, visibility was poor and although daybreak had arrived, any evidence of the sun was swallowed by the mist. The conditions were ideal for the transfer of the treasure to take place.

Four sets of oars sliced the water, making barely a ripple, each boat accommodating a wooden chest lashed to a thwart amidships. Each timber box was criss-crossed with metal straps and had a large lock hanging from the lid. Each boat also carried a pair of marine guards seated in the bow, their muskets upright between their legs. Two more marines sat in the sternsheets, much to the annoyance of the boats' coxswains. Captain Gore was passenger in one of the boats, the doctor, with his apothecary's chest, was returning in another.

Perpetual's main yard was already rigged and ready to lift the unusual delivery. Apart from water dripping from the oars, there was no sound from the approaching boats, no shouts announcing their arrival and no acknowledgement returned from the frigate.

On deck, the officers were anticipating the delivery with subdued excitement. There were few sailors about except those required to haul the cargo plus a dozen armed marines and a gun crew. The arrival of the Spanish treasure had been timed to coincide with the crew's breakfast.

Captain Gore climbed aboard without the necessary pipes and was greeted by Captain Quintrell. Dr Whipple followed him and immediately retired to the cockpit. From the quarterdeck, the two captains watched as the transfer of the four chests proceeded.

'Steady, now!' Mr Parry instructed when the first chest was hoisted, swung across the gangway and lowered into the waist. There was no indication of its contents aside from the fact it was of considerable weight.

From the waist, it took four men to carry the first chest into the Captain's cabin where it was placed into a large fixed locker. When the last box had been delivered, a lock was placed on the door and an additional marine guard was stationed outside the cabin, much to the chagrin of Casson who was halted every time he wanted to pass.

'The cases I have delivered contain only specie,' Captain Gore explained. 'Coins of various values – doubloons, reales, and silver dollars, some cut into pieces of eight. There is no gold. I have here a receipt for these goods for the benefit of their Lordships.'

Captain Quintrell accepted the receipt and read through it carefully. Turning to his desk, he flipped the lid on the inkwell, dipped the sharpened quill, shook off the excess ink and signed his name on the paper.

'And this is a copy of the itinerary,' Captain Gore said. 'It was signed by Captain Moore when the chests were taken from *Santa Clara* and transferred to *Medusa*.'

Oliver paused. 'I must admit to finding this transfer a little unorthodox.'

'No more unorthodox than me removing the treasure from *Santa Clara*'s hold. Similarly, Captains Moore, Hammond and Sutton are all carrying some of the treasure from *Santa Clara* and *La Fama*. All the treasure is being returned to England to be detained according to Admiralty orders.'

'It leaves a nasty taste, though. Would you not agree?'

'Like you, Captain. I follow orders and it is not for me to question them.'

Oliver was still slightly puzzled. 'But *Perpetual* played no part in the battle off Cadiz. Did you speak with Captain Moore about transferring the specie to me?'

'It was at Captain Moore's suggestion, when I made him aware that I intended to return to Gibraltar Bay.'

Oliver was satisfied. 'Then you have my word, as soon as I receive orders to sail, this consignment will be conveyed to Plymouth.'

'Excellent. Captain Moore should arrive in the Hamoaze within a week and, if *Medusa* remains afloat, I will follow a week later, if all goes well.'

'I pray for the safe arrival of all ships,' Oliver said.

'Amen to that.'

'In the meantime, I intend to speak with General Trigge and request permission to leave this port. I shall also write to the Admiralty and request they reconsider my orders. But, I fear, while the epidemic continues to spread, I will not be at liberty to leave Gibraltar Bay. With the current quarantine situation the colony is totally isolated.'

Captain Gore agreed. 'It is not a good state of affairs and it brings me to a less pleasant matter. This morning, I was told there are a dozen men in *Medusa*'s sick berth. After examining them, Dr Whipple advised me they are suffering from the malignant fever. It is what I had feared. In the last week three men have died and your surgeon tells me that will not be the end of the death toll. The sooner I can reach England and depart from this region, the better.'

'But how did your men contract the contagion? You did not touch land off Cadiz, I think.'

'That is correct. Before the action we spoke only with your ship but never once stepped ashore. We took no victuals or water on board from either Gibraltar or the Spanish mainland. And when we left the Strait's patrol, I had a fit crew. The sailors of the Spanish treasure fleet were fitter than mine before the battle.'

'That would confirm Dr Pym's argument that the plague is carried in the air.'

'It can only be,' Captain Gore said. 'Unfortunately your carpenter has succumbed to the illness. He is not dead but I would not return him to you in his present condition. I suggest his mates also remain on board my ship, as they have been working together.'

Oliver frowned. 'I do not like to return to England without a carpenter.'

'I am sure you will find a replacement at the dockyard here on the peninsula. In response to the request from Admiral Nelson, the Navy Board has recently allocated a dozen shipwrights to Gibraltar and, because the port is closed, they have little work to do. They are naval wrights and not attached to the garrison and I am sure there will be a few eager to grab the opportunity to sail home from this disease-ridden place.'

'Thank you,' Oliver said. 'I will make enquiries.'

As the sea mist rose and evaporated with the miasmic cloud drifting down from the top of the Rock, Oliver and his men watched the four boats return to *Medusa*. From the caprail, little was said, but there was a feeling of envy amongst the men. *Medusa* would be sailing for England later in the day. When *Perpetual* would sail was anyone's guess.

Oliver had other concerns. Although the chests of specie had been transferred to his care, Captain Gore was still carrying a considerable amount of valuable cargo in his hold. It would make a valuable prize for a privateer. In the meantime, if word of the treasure reached Algeciras, it was unlikely the gunboats would allow him to make it further than the Strait.

Despite Captain Quintrell's unanswered questions regarding Dr Whipple's background, he was pleased to have his surgeon returned to the frigate and invited him to share breakfast with him.

'The task was not too strenuous, I trust.'

'No,' Dr Whipple replied tentatively, a troubled expression on his face. 'Not physically, at least.'

'What then?'

'I examined Captain Gore's men and found they were not suffering from the mariners' disease. They were vomiting old blood – *Vómito negro* as the Spanish call it.'

Oliver was already aware of the situation. 'But you have returned after having close contact with them. Is it possible you are carrying the malignant fever and might infect my crew?'

The surgeon was forthright in his reply. 'I can assure you, Captain, that will not happen. I have seen this type of sickness before. I suffered it myself in Jamaica. Because I recovered from it, I will not contract it again. That is the case.'

Oliver inhaled deeply. 'I hope you are right. So, for the present, we must remain anchored on a pond surrounded by infectious disease. And I am now minus my carpenter and several of his mates.'

He continued. 'I would give me right teeth to see real action rather than being stuck here faced with an enemy one can neither see, nor hear, nor touch. Such a situation is not documented in any of the manuals.' He paused. 'I reiterate something I have said before, I shall never accept a desk job within the confines of the Admiralty's walls. Let me face an enemy's broadside and die in battle and I will die a happy man.'

'I trust that will not be for a long time,' Dr Whipple quipped.

Oliver leaned forward and reached for a folded letter on the table in front of him. 'On a more serious note,' he said. 'I received word this morning from General Trigge.'

'Is the epidemic coming under control?'

'Unfortunately, it is not. According to his records the number of deaths outside the garrison has risen to over a 100 a day. There is not a single doctor left in the town. They have either escaped or died and left no trace. Sir Thomas has sent an urgent dispatch via Barcelona to Lord Nelson requesting assistance but who knows how long it will be before the message reaches him.'

'That is not good news.'

'No,' he sighed, 'but I have a request to put to you. Sir Thomas Trigge has asked if you can assist the colony's medical officer, Dr Pym, with the sick and dying, both at the garrison and in the town. By obliging him, you will be placing your life in grave danger.'

'Captain Quintrell,' the doctor said sympathetically. 'I am aware you do not fully understand my way of thinking, but I am not a coward or an imposter. I am a good doctor and I have devoted my adult life to the study of medicine and healing the sick.

'If you will allow it, I will gladly go ashore and do what I can to help in the fight against this terrible disease. I shall leave my assistant, Abel Longbottom, here to care for the men on *Perpetual*, but I will need someone to accompany me and provide some assistance. However, I fear, because of the malicious rumours, it will be easy to recruit a volunteer.'

'Doctor, you have not sailed on a fighting ship long enough to realize that all seamen, be they officers of foremast Jacks, are prepared to face death whether it is cloaked in a cloud of miasmic air descending down the side of a mountain, or enveloped in a burst of flaming powder fired from a gun's muzzle at close quarters. What help do you require?'

'A loblolly or dispenser. Someone to carry my bags and assist with the handling of the patients, Things of that nature.'

'Anything else?'

'I would be advantageous that I sleep at the garrison on occasions. That will allow me to attend to the patients at any time, night or day. It will also reduce the risk of carrying any infection back to the ship.'

'Could the garrison manage without your help?'

'I think not. From what I hear, Dr Pym is already unable to cope with the increasing number of deaths being recorded in the town. In answer to your question, I see no alternative. I must go. But I will need the help I mentioned.'

'What of the men you already have?' Oliver asked. 'Can the lad, Tommy Wainwright, do the job?'

'The young man is keen and willing, but he is small in stature and I think he has never suffered the fever. Besides, he will be useful here and will help Longbottom while I am away.'

'What is the situation in the cockpit today?' the captain asked.

'Two new patients. I am keeping them isolated from the other men.'

'Why was I not made aware of this?'

'I have not had the opportunity to prepare my report, and the sickness only presented itself this morning.'

Oliver was not happy with the news. 'What of Longbottom, the surgeon's mate?'

'While I am ashore, Abel will act in my place. I cannot take him and leave the ship with no one to attend the sick berth.'

'So what manner of man do you require?'

'A man who will not baulk at handling the dead and dying. He must have a strong constitution not easily sickened by what he sees or smells. Also, being able to defend himself would be useful. There is danger in the shadows when death lurks around every corner. Finally, I want a man who has suffered from fever in the past and survived. A man who will not die while he is helping me.'

'I will ask for a volunteer from amongst the men,' Oliver said. 'One final question, Doctor. In your opinion how long will this epidemic last?'

'It will pass when the winter arrives and the winds change direction.'

'Two more months?'

'It has happened here before and if this is the same fever as occurred previously, by December it will be over.'

'I pray you are right.'

Oliver had mixed feelings. Although relieved that the doctor was willing to help, he was unsure if it was the correct decision. He also felt guilty. Whatever his opinion of Dr Whipple had been in the past, the surgeon was proving himself to be both conscientious and obliging.

'I am grateful,' Oliver said, 'but for the present, you look tired and need a little rest.'

The doctor smiled a weary smile and replaced his hat. 'Until tomorrow then.'

The captain did not wait until the morning to muster the whole crew.

After lining the men up around the waist, Mr Parry posed the request the surgeon had put to the captain only half-an-hour earlier. However, with not a single response to the first call for a volunteer, the lieutenant scanned the line assessing the faces for a suitable candidate.

'You two. Step forward!' he ordered, pointing to a pair of foremast Jacks.

'I ain't fit,' the first claimed, standing his ground.

'I ain't never had no fever,' the other argued.

Mr Parry looked along the line.

'I'll go.' The deep voice belonged to Ekundayo, the seaman from Santo Domingo who had first sailed with Captain Quintrell on his previous voyage. He took a step forward.

'And why would you want to volunteer?' Mr Parry asked.

'Because young Tommy is my mate. He works in the cockpit and he ain't afraid of no fever nor no breeze of wind. And neither am I. I've seen fever and massacres and worse where I come from.'

'I'll go too.' The voice came from a sailor leaning against the lines coiled to the pin rail.'

'Step up. Show yourself.'

'So,' Mr Parry mused. 'Zachary Irons from Portsmouth. I trust you do not see this as an opportunity to run, because you'll find no escape from the peninsula at this time. Remember Lompa, the mate of yours who ran earlier. He did not fare too well, did he?'

'He was no a mate of mine.'

'So why do you wish to volunteer to go with the doctor?'

'Because I am bored with teasing rope. Because I've had the fever in the Indies. But mainly because I've got a family and I hope and pray, that if any one of them falls sick while I'm away at sea, someone will lend a hand and tend to them.'

Mr Parry turned and looked at the surgeon who was standing beside the captain.

'Let both men report to the cockpit,' Oliver said. 'The doctor will decide which man will accompany him.'

A murmur of disgruntlement came from one of the hands.

'You have something to say about that, Brickley?'

Taking off his hat, the sailor stepped forward. 'Not really sir, only some of the lads would like to know how long we're likely to be stuck here?'

Oliver regarded him for a moment. 'We will be *stuck here*, as you put it, until I receive orders to the contrary. Would you rather be sitting on an outcrop of jagged rock in the freezing Southern Ocean, or being sucked down by the Goodwin Sands in the Channel? I can assure you there are far less agreeable places to be than Gibraltar Bay, and I hope everyman aboard will consider that fact.'

Brickley stepped back.

'If there is nothing else, Mr Parry, kindly dismiss the men.'

Bungs thrust the point of his knife into the mess table. 'It's cursed, I tell you.'

'What is?' Muffin asked.

'Them four chests of Spanish treasure the captain has stowed away in his cabin.'

'Why would it be cursed? More like a gift from heaven, I reckon. It's the only treasure I know of what we didn't have to fight and die for.'

'You don't know nothing, do you?' Bungs said, glaring at Muffin who, as usual, was resting his head against the ship's hull. Then he cast his eyes around the mess and raised his voice. 'Are you all blind as well as dumb?'

The Negro winked at the lad sitting next to him. 'Well, you're going to tell us anyway, aren't you?' Eku said.

'Too right I am. It's clear as crystal to me. That Spanish silver – or whatever's locked in them chests, weren't taken as a prize of war. The reason being, because we aren't at war with Spain. And if a navy ship takes a treasure in peacetime, then it's piracy. Pure and simple. And the pirates – namely the British naval officers what took it – don't want to have the dirty cargo soiling their hands, so they've given it to us to mind.'

'Don't talk daft,' Muffin said.

'You might laugh, but mark my words, cursed it is. And as long as it's aboard this ship it will bring us no good.'

'Stow it Bungs, you're talking out of your ear.'

Eku leaned forward. 'Maybe Bungs is right. Think about it. Them chests came aboard on Sunday morning. By Thursday morning there were five more men in the cockpit suffering with the malignant fever.'

'Aye and two of them died last night. Spitting blood, they were, and faces as yellow as a tar-stained sail.'

'Maybe the sickness was carried on board by Captain Gore?'

'He looked well enough to me,' Bungs argued. 'You mark my words, it's the treasure what brought it and while ever it's aboard this ship, it'll bring us nothing but bad luck.'

'But I bet you wouldn't say no to a share of it.'

'I'd not say no, if it was honest prize money captured fair and square, but I don't want a single bit cut from one of those silver coins. For all I care, the captain can feed it to the fishes. Get rid of it over the side. That's what I say.'

'That's daft talk,' Muffin repeated.

But Bungs was not convinced. 'It's cursed, it is. Just you wait and see.'

CHAPTER 14

The Malignant Fever

To all Ships in the Fleet: 14th October 1804

You are on no account whatsoever to communicate with Gibraltar or receive any letters etc. from any boat or vessel coming from that place on account of the dreadful malady which has broken out there. I am, Sir, &c.,

NELSON AND BRONTE

The letter from General Trigge was addressed to Captain Quintrell with a copy for Dr Whipple. It had arrived by boat early in the morning and had been marked *urgent*.

'Mr Parry, kindly arrange for my boat. I intend to go ashore for a few hours.'

'Aye aye, sir,'

'My regular crew,' Oliver advised.

'I will speak with them immediately. Will the men be leaving you at Rosia Bay and returning to the ship as they did previously?'

'Not in this instance.' Oliver paused. 'I intend to visit Algeciras.'

The lieutenant raised his eyebrows. 'The Spanish port?'

'I believe there is no other. The doctor will be accompanying me. I suggest my boat crew is armed, and I shall require a pair of marines to travel with me also.'

Simon Parry's brow furrowed.

'Don't worry, Simon, I have no intention of staying in the town for any longer than necessary. General Trigge has requested the Doctor visit a close friend of his across the bay.'

'You are tempting providence, are you not?' Simon said.

'By that you mean running the gauntlet of the Spanish gunboats?' Oliver laughed. 'They are a mere façade. I contend their gunfire is little more than a show of bravado. I would remind you that we hold no animosity towards the inhabitants of Algeciras although I cannot say the feeling is mutual. Despite their spiteful games, I believe it merely provides amusement for the indolent crews of the Spanish warships. I compare them to mosquitoes in the moist air. Annoying, but of no serious threat.'

Mr Parry was not convinced. 'They may carry only a single gun, but there are dozens of them on the water. If they launched a combined attack they would be capable of sinking a British ship.'

Oliver made light of his lieutenant's worries. 'Depending on the accuracy of their aim, that is. It would not surprise me if they unintentionally fired on the town, as Captain Gore did in Cadiz. But I jest. I shall take all due care and I have a passport.' He tapped his pocket. 'Signed by the Lieutenant-Governor. Besides, it would not surprise me, once word is passed that I have a doctor with me, to find an escort waiting to greet us. We shall see.'

Mr Parry remained anxious. 'When I suggested you would be tempting providence, it was not gunboats that I was referring to, but the fever.'

'Hmm, the fever indeed. That is the reason for our visit. The British Ambassador to Cadiz, a very good friend of General Trigge, is residing there at the present. Unfortunately his wife has been struck down by a fever, hence the request for Dr Whipple to attend her. Because of the rapid onset of her illness, there is no time to delay.'

'No doubt, an influential aristocratic family,' Simon said.

'No doubt they are,' Oliver replied. 'But from what I hear, this illness does not discriminate between rich and poor, aristocrat and peasant and, unlike the lingering white plague we see every winter in England, this contagion consumes its victims with undue haste.'

Simon Parry chose his words carefully. 'As a friend, Oliver, I must warn you that you are putting both your lives in peril. And, let me remind you of your earlier concerns that the doctor has some closeted weaknesses which have not yet become apparent.'

'As a friend, Simon, I would say to you, there are many times I would not put to sea if I knew what was awaiting me. As for the doctor, it appears my initial assessment of this gentleman was judgemental and prejudiced due to my limited knowledge of accepted medical practices. Captain Gore could not thank him enough for the advice he provided on *Medusa*. General Trigge and Dr Pym both regard him highly and, having watched him attend his patients, I realize he is gentleman of far stronger character and professional acumen than I had given him credit for.'

The lieutenant offered a final warning. 'The word on the North Mole is that all of Andalusia is riddled with infection.'

'I am aware of the rumours, Simon, but if Dr Pym is correct, and the contagion is borne in the air we breathe, it makes no difference whether I inhale it in the Bahia de Algeciras, or Bay of Gibraltar.' He paused for a moment. 'Did any more men report sick at this morning's call?'

'Two more topmen. Their symptoms are the same. Perhaps they are more susceptible because they inhale more infected vapour from the mastheads than the men who remain below deck. I have posted a second marine guard outside the sick berth. No one is allowed to enter without my permission.'

'Thank you, Simon. But what of the rest of the crew?'

'Surprisingly, there are few complaints. The men's main gripe is that they are confined to the ship. Despite what they hear, they want to go ashore. But more than that, they want to sail out of here. I sense an atmosphere of discontent brewing, although the men do not express it to me directly.'

Oliver rubbed the back of his hand across the fine stubble of whiskers on his chin. 'I will return as soon as possible. Kindly attend to the ship in my absence. I know you have the respect of the men.'

The captain's boat had barely crossed the invisible dividing line into the Bahia de Algeciras, when three gunboats emerged from the Spanish harbour.

With the marines sitting on the forward thwart and the captain and doctor in the sternsheets, the small armed vessels swam around them but did not fire. After half-an-hour, the captain's boat was dragged up on a beach close to the town. It immediately attracted the attention of a group of Spanish soldiers.

While the doctor retrieved his bag and walking cane, Captain Quintrell presented his papers to the officer and, on learning one of the men was a doctor, the officer became more attentive. After instructing his men to remain with the boat and not wander into the town, Oliver Quintrell and his ship's surgeon left the beach.

Although he had sailed through the Gut of Gibraltar many times, Oliver had never stepped foot in the Spanish port and was unfamiliar with it. Unlike Gibraltar, the town was cut by two streams which delivered fresh mountain water to its residents – something the colony of Gibraltar was jealous of. Furthermore, being on the west side of the bay, the town received all the afternoon breezes to cool the buildings at night.

Neither the captain nor the doctor spoke more than a few words of Spanish but with the Ambassador's address written on a piece of paper, they followed the directions provided by one of the soldiers. Heading through the town, they wound their way through a maze of narrow streets that led up a hill. The further they went, the tighter the streets became, the tall buildings completely blocking out the midday sun. The shade, however, was welcome, the cooler air pleasant. Climbing a set of steep stone steps, they turned into a cobbled lane leading to an alley with high stone walls on either side.

Hearing footsteps behind them, Oliver quickened his pace but before they reached the end, where the alley opened into a courtyard, two men stepped out from a passageway ahead of them. One was dressed in Spanish garb with a cloak draped across one shoulder and fastened diagonally across his chest. He was very different in appearance to the ruffians and footpads who inhabited the back streets of the boroughs or held up the London coaches. Turning, Oliver saw the glint of a knife flash in the corner of his eye.

It was evident they had been lured into a trap.

'Out of my way!' Oliver cried, drawing his sword.

The Spaniard responded by lifting his arm that had been hidden beneath his cloak. In his hand was a pistol, which he pointed towards the doctor's bag. From the barrage of verbal demands, it was not difficult to interpret what he wanted.

Dr Whipple shook his head. Gripping his cane in one hand, he wrapped his other arm tightly around his bag and held it close to his chest. He had no intention of parting with his valuable surgical instruments and medicines.

'Move!' Oliver shouted. 'This is my only warning!'

As he spoke, the man turned his pistol toward the captain.

Quick as flash, Oliver lunged at him slicing his wrist and dislodging the gun from his hand. With a cry more of shock than pain, the Spaniard dropped to his knees, grasping his wrist to stop the blood spurting from it. After quickly retrieving the pistol, Oliver levelled his sword against the man's throat.

Meanwhile, the second assailant was engaged in a tug-of-war as he attempted to pull the bag from the doctor's hand.

'Call him off!' Oliver demanded of the man kneeling on the ground, but the lout showed no signs of comprehending.

Suddenly, a third man who had been trailing them rushed at the captain but, before he could strike, Oliver spun around and sank his sword into the man's calf. His fists were no match for the sword.

Releasing his bag intentionally, the doctor leapt to his own defence, his walking cane held at arm's length like a rapier. Thrusting forward into the man's chest with the metal tip of his stick, he forced his assailant backwards until he toppled over.

Jumping to his feet, eyes glaring and yelling abuse, the ruffian was ready to launch another attack on the doctor. But a single stinging sweep from the surgeon's cane caught the Spaniard's cheek, the brass ferrule gouging a deep gash across his swarthy face.

At the sound of the would-be thief's piercing cry and the sight of blood gushing from his face, the fellow who had been following them, turned and limped away down the path as fast as he could manage it.

Holding the pistol in one hand and the sword in the other, Oliver stood over his opponent, a satisfied grin on his face. 'Once again you surprise me, Dr Whipple. You have hidden talents.'

But the surgeon was not listening. He was already on his knees, attending to the man he had injured. 'A nasty cut,' he said. 'I am pleased I did not take out the eye. However, I fear the señor will bear the mark of our encounter for the rest of his days.'

After wrapping a bandage diagonally around the man's head, the doctor turned and looked up at the naval captain. 'Stick fighting is a skill I mastered as a boy. It's a fighting art I was thankful to have when I was a student. The back streets of London are undesirable places to wander through, especially at night. I think I should practice more often.'

With the other Spaniard's wrist bandaged and the pair tied together with lengths of cord from the doctor's bag, the captain and Dr Whipple escorted them back to the waterfront and delivered them into the hands of the soldiers on the beach. Following profuse apologies, which they were unable to verbally comprehend, the pair were provided with a military escort and eventually arrived at the residence of the Ambassador, without further incidents.

While the surgeon examined the Ambassador's wife, Oliver was pleased to partake of the refreshments offered to him. From the patio of the house situated high on the hill, the vista across the bay revealed the full expanse of the Rock and the town of Gibraltar nestled at its foot. It was a serene scene that belied the evil currently festering within the territory's defensive walls.

The sight of *Perpetual* basking on the sparkling waters beneath the promontory was reassuring. Apart from the frigate, a few local fishing boats and three hulks were the only vessels on the bay.

Much of the Spanish town reminded Oliver of Madeira. The white lime-washed buildings. The green vines entwining the arches. The brilliant colours of the flowers – magenta, blue, yellow, red. The perfumed scent in the air and the sound of bees. And the view from the top of the hill rekindled memories of the house in Funchal where Susanna lived and of the brief interludes he had spent with her. By now she would be back home, far from the danger she had encountered during her visit to Gibraltar.

Sliding his hand into his pocket, he realized he was still carrying the note she had passed to him when they had met at the garrison. He was sorry he had not managed to visit her before *Conception* sailed. Now he did not know when he would see her again.

His thoughts were interrupted when the doctor returned from his patient.

'How was the lady?' Oliver asked. 'Does she have the fever?'

'She has *a* fever, but she will survive.'

'What did you do?'

'I did nothing. I merely examined her and found her to be covered in a red rash. I believe she has the measles.'

The following day brought rain. Heavy drenching rain, which did not stop from dawn until dusk. From first light, when it began bouncing on the deck, the crew set about collecting drinking water. Old sails, hurriedly hoisted from the sail lockers, were suspended across the deck. They filled quickly, the overflow being funneled into barrels brought up from the hold. The cooper and his mates were kept busy, hoisting, filling, sealing and returning the barrels below. It was a worthwhile task.

For the hands not allocated to help, it was an opportunity to bathe under the downpour, wash their hair or re-wash their salt-hardened clothes. The sounds of splashing, laughing and joking was something that had been absent on the frigate's deck for quite some time. It was a healthy and welcome sound to the officers' ears.

Two days later, Oliver resolved it was time to visit the colonial town and assess for himself the rumours that the situation was fast deteriorating. Accompanied by Mr Tully, he landed at the North Mole. They entered the town through the Waterport Gate a great arch which led directly into Casemates Square.

But compared with the sights, sounds and smells which had greeted him and his men when they had first arrived in Gibraltar, the scene presented before him was very different. This time, the square was silent and virtually empty save for two white robed residents who hurried across, quickly exchanging greetings before parting. An old Spanish women purchased what she needed from one of the few merchants then scurried back into the dismal squalor of the narrow streets.

Between the square and the bay, was a shambles of dilapidated wooden houses. Rising two and three storeys high where several families, comprising dozens of people, all crowded together under one roof. These were the houses Admiral Lord Nelson had condemned during his visit only a few months earlier. He had reported that a pile of lighted matchwood set amongst them would be the best remedy for the dwellings.

In fact if the fire spread throughout the whole town, it would be preferable, he had written.

Oliver agreed with the sentiment. If these were the houses harbouring the contagion, nothing would remove it save from reducing the whole area to a pile of ash.

Seated with their backs against the wall of one of the apartment houses were three men, chins resting on their chests, mouths hanging open as if asleep. But they were not sleeping. They were three of the malignant fever's recent victims, dragged from their houses, waiting in line for collection by the scavenger when he made his next pass through the square.

Oliver indicated to the far corner of the square where Main Street entered. 'This way,' he said to his lieutenant.

It was a little more than an alley with three-storey houses on either side but it led directly to Rosia Bay and Windmill Hill. As they entered the street, the sound of a horn and rumble of wheels could be heard.

'Wait a moment.' Oliver said, nudging Mr Tully aside.

Heading towards the square, was an urchin of little more than five or six years of age. Held in his hand was a tarnished horn, which he blew into occasionally, not to attract business, but to advise the citizens the dead cart was passing. It offered both an invitation for them to bring out their dead and a warning for them to get out of the way.

How different this was to a London funeral, Oliver thought. The glass-panelled hearses trimmed with black bows. An elegant carriage drawn by four black Shire horses. A polished elm coffin. Tall hats, streaming with ribbons, worn by the undertakers. The *cortège* comprising a host of black-clad mourners.

Here in Gibraltar, the funerary party consisted of a wizened old muleteer leading a mangy-haired animal harnessed to a flat cart previously used for conveying barrels of night soil to the neutral zone. Presently it was piled high with stinking human corpses, the wheels creaking under the load.

There were no mourners accompanying it, only flies.

The dead cart's arrival in the square disturbed only the pigeons pecking at the cracks in the paving in search of grain or maggots. An opportunity they never had in the past. When one took flight the others followed, two dozen wings threshing the air in unison. But their flight was soon aborted and the birds fluttered down a few yards away to resume their search.

The few citizens in the square with business to conduct turned their backs when they heard the horn and ignored the procession. The dead cart was a regular visitor, rolling through to the freshly dug ditch on the neutral zone several times a day.

As it rumbled across the market square, one wheel dug into a gap between the paving slabs. Fortunately, the load didn't topple but it swayed perilously from side to side causing one of the bodies to slip from it. Sliding, almost gracefully to the ground, the corpse landed at the feet of the guards walking five yards behind. The pair of untidy young soldiers, short in stature, whose chins had never felt the scrape of a razor, was members of the De Rolls Regiment.

The unlucky pair had been given the garrison's most odious task – to visit every house along the way, knock on every door and ensure all the cadavers had been dragged out to the street for collection. If a house was vacant, it was their duty to inspect all its floors, checking every room and removing any bodies that had been left behind. Once the cart was fully loaded, they escorted it to the north ditch where the bodies were dumped. Then they returned to the town and began the process all over again.

Guarding the dead cart was the garrison's most despised and distasteful duty. Every soldier hated it. They all agreed if a man was ever to walk in the Valley of the Shadow of Death, the streets of Gibraltar led directly to it. And repeating the words of The Lord's Prayer proved no antidote to the epidemic. *Thou shall fear no evil –* was balderdash – the Evil was here for everyone to see.

'Halt!' one of the soldiers shouted, but the scavenger either didn't hear or chose to ignore the order.

'Stop! *Pare!*' the other yelled. 'You lost one!' With very limited Spanish, and an accent, which would have been more acceptable on the streets of Dublin than in a colonial town on the Mediterranean, it was surprising he was understood at all.

The driver turned his head. 'Next time!' the man murmured in reply. 'I pick it up next time.'

'No, now!' the young guard ordered. 'Pick it up, I say!'

Reluctantly, the driver pulled on the reins and brought his mule and cart to a standstill. Shuffling back to see what had happened, he stood over the body, took out a grubby rag, and wiped his brow. A pair of long-legged dogs showed more interested.

'Toss it back on,' the youngest member of the regiment ordered, keeping his distance. The scavenger scratched his groin while he contemplated the nearby wall as a likely place to leave the body until his next pass.

'Throw it up,' the guard repeated, his timid voice hardly audible.

Grabbing the cadaver by the hands, the scavenger dragged it back to the side of the cart but only managed to raise it to the height of the tray. It needed to be lifted another three feet to reach the top of the pile.

'You do it,' the old man said bluntly to the pair. Dropping the body, he stepped back, stuck a fat cigar in his mouth and started chewing on it, paper and all.

Oliver was appalled. The body was that of a female victim, clothed only in a nightshirt. She was a matronly woman, probably of Spanish blood who, in life, would have never revealed even an inch of pale skin beneath her petticoats to anyone other than her husband.

'Lend the driver a hand,' Oliver ordered the troopers, who stood little taller than the muzzles of the muskets they were carrying.

In response, the pair shuffled backwards rather than forwards.

'That is a direct order!' Captain Quintrell called. 'I think General Trigge will not take kindly to learn his men do not obey orders!'

The pair edged forward side by side, clutching their muskets hard to their shoulders, their mouths contorted as if sucking on lemons.

Running out of patience, Oliver turned to his lieutenant. 'Mr Tully, step up here. Take this woman's hands. I shall take her feet. Let us return her to her conveyance.'

With the dogs snapping at their heels, it took less than a minute and the job was accomplished, the woman's body coming to rest across the legs of the other corpses. As it settled, the head of the cadaver beneath her turned to face the naval officer. Despite the blood-stained face hanging upside down, the captain and his lieutenant immediately recognised the red hair, crooked nose and bruised cheek.

Oliver glanced at Mr Tully to see if he had also recognised the face.

Such was the fate of Benjamin Styles, the second pressed man to have run from *Perpetual* soon after it arrived in Gibraltar. Coerced by his mate, Lompa, he had foolishly lied, saying he had spent time in a London jail. That untruth had cost him dearly.

After noting the names of the two guards, nothing more needed to be said. The scavenger took up the mule's reins. The boy blew on his horn. And the two soldiers walked on. Casting their eyes to the ground. They dare not exchange glances with the Royal Navy captain they had failed to take a direct order from. With their muskets wavering on their shoulders, their minds were racked with fear. Fear of reprisals. Fear of contracting the deadly contagion. Fear of death itself.

'I had heard that the discipline at the garrison was lax,' Oliver observed, as he wiped his hands on his handkerchief. 'Such insolent behaviour would never be tolerated on one of His Majesty's ships.'

Continuing along the main street in the direction of Rosia Bay they passed the gothic-styled Roman Catholic Cathedral which still bore marks of the hot shot fired at the city during the Great Siege. It seemed strange, to Oliver, in a British colony to find several Catholic churches, Moorish mosques and Jewish synagogues but to find only one Protestant church. It was also strange to discover that apart from the military and their families, there were very few British residents on the peninsula. The population was made up of people of all colours and creeds.

'Captain! Captain Quintrell!' The cry was urgent.'

Oliver spun around. Zachary Irons, the pressed sailor who had volunteered to accompany Dr Whipple several days earlier, was haring along the street towards him.

'What is it, man?' Oliver called.

Irons had to catch his breath. 'The doctor sent me to find you.'

Oliver feared the doctor had succumbed to the fever. 'Is he ill?'

'No, sir. He sent me to fetch you. But I couldn't find you. I went down to the mole and found your boat. Froyle told me where you were heading. Dr Whipple said I was to bring you to him as quickly as possible.'

'Where is he?' Oliver asked.

'At a house in Gunners Parade.'

'Then we shall hurry,' Oliver said, turning and heading back the way they had come.

'It's not a good place, Captain,' Irons warned. 'So many have died near there. Whole families. It's terrible.'

The sailor's anguish was etched across on his face.

'Are you all right?' the captain asked, as they strode out.

'I'm well enough, Captain, but I feel for the infants. They fall like flies.'

'Do you have children of your own?'

'Yes, sir,' Iron replied. 'A boy of nine, a girl of seven and, if all went well, a child I've never seen. Must be nigh on a year old.'

'And when you were taken by the press-gang, were you heading home?'

Irons nodded. 'Aye, Captain. It's all I'd planned for many a month.'

Oliver glanced at him sympathetically. 'When we return to England, if the war with France is still being fought, your services will still be required and it may be impossible for you to leave the navy.'

Iron shrugged his shoulders. 'I'd thought of that, Captain. I'd even wondered how I could sneak off the ship and avoid the press-gang.'

'Perhaps you should keep those thoughts to yourself,' Oliver suggested. 'War is not pleasant and it is unkind in many ways. It brings certain rewards and satisfactions but because we are in the King's Service, we cannot chart our own course.'

'And if you try to make your own way—' Mr Tully noted.

'—you must pay the consequences,' Oliver added.

'This way,' Irons indicated, turning right up a narrow lane.

The garrison's new library stood at the top of the road. It was a grand double-storey white stone building surrounded by gardens which were ablaze with red geraniums. Oliver wondered if any bodies, other than the beggar's, had been buried there recently. Despite that, it was his intention to peruse the bookcases when he had time. For the present, however, that indulgence would have to wait.

'Tell me, what of the Doctor? Is he able to assist the victims?'

'He does the best he can,' Irons said. 'But it's painfully little. The garrison has plenty of powders and potions, and I have replenished the surgeon's chest twice already. But the medicines he gives seem to do no good. Often when he administers a dose, the patient can't swallow it, coughs it up and spits it back in the doctor's face. Not meaning to, of course.

'But Dr Whipple has got a certain way about him. He sooths his patients and tells the family how best to tend to those who are dying. Oft times, only a wife or mother is left after the rest of the family is gone. As for those who die, he treats them with dignity even when we carry them out onto the street to be carted away. It's a sorrowful scene. So much wailing. It's a wonder the gutters aren't running with tears.'

Suddenly, a voice shouted a belated warning from the balcony above them as a body was tossed down to the street. It landed at their feet with a dull thud, a stream of yellow fluid leaking from its orifices.

Oliver stopped, looked up and shook his head.

'We must hurry, Captain,' Irons said. 'Dr Whipple said it was urgent, and the glass would have almost emptied since I left him.'

They extended their stride, passing the Town Range Barracks on the right where 700 men were usually housed, and the Royal Artillery Barracks on the left where the soldiers remained as a third of the corps had been struck down with the Fever the previous month. Ahead was a shambles of small dwellings – single-storey huts with canvas roofs, dilapidated and dirty with hardly enough space to squeeze between them. They were in far worse condition that the buildings off Casemates Square.

On the right was the Boyd's building. Once gracious, it was now old and rather grubby. Adjoining it were several private houses and a grocer's shop. On the end of the row was a tavern.

'This is where the epidemic began,' Mr Tully said, pointing to the Boyd's building.

Oliver had heard differently.

Zachary Irons led them around the corner to another row of adjoining houses. Their condition was somewhat better. A sign nailed on the wall read:

ACCOMMODATION
Clean rooms let by the day or week
Fresh linen and feather mattresses
Merchants welcome

'The doctor is on the top floor.'

'Thank you,' Oliver said. 'Kindly wait here with Mr Tully. I will call if I need you.'

From the bright sunlight of the street, the narrow staircase inside the building was dark with only a candle burning on each landing. The stairs creaked beneath his feet. The handrail rattled to his touch.

When he reached the second floor, a dark-robed figure stepped aside to let him pass. Oliver paid little heed to the man and continued to climb taking two steps at a time. On the top landing, the dying flame of the candle stub flickered in a lantern. Two doors lay ahead. One was open.

'Captain, thank the Lord.' The surgeon's voice was hushed. 'I am relieved Zachary found you. I was getting anxious. Please come in.'

With his eyes not yet accustomed to the gloom, Oliver glanced to the open window framing the old Moorish Castle on the side of the hill. There was no breeze and the air was dank and heavy. Then he turned and looked to the bed, and his heart sank.

With her long black hair draped across the white pillow, he hardly recognised her face.'

'Oh, dear God. No!'

CHAPTER 15

Susanna

Susanna's eyelids flickered when she heard his voice.

The doctor leaned over her and gently wiped the pink saliva escaping from the corner of her lips.

The freshly laundered sheets were white.

Her face was yellow.

She mouthed his name but no sound came out.

'For pity sake, this cannot be,' he cried.

'Please, Captain. I beg you not to raise your voice. The lady is very ill.'

'Is she—?' he whispered.

'I fear so,' the surgeon said. 'I have done all I can.'

Tears welled in Oliver's eyes. 'But what is she doing here? She was supposed to leave Gibraltar two weeks ago. She should have been safely home by now? This cannot be. It is not fair.'

'Much in life is not fair, Captain, but we must accept it as God's will.'

'But she was due to sail on the Portuguese brig.'

'But she didn't,' Dr Whipple said firmly. 'She chose to stay here and lend a hand with the sick. She wanted to help.'

Then he realized. 'She's been here, all this time. All these weeks. Why didn't she tell me?'

'Perhaps she thought you already had enough problems without her presence adding to them.'

Oliver was distraught. 'What can I do, Doctor? Tell me what to do? Should she be taken to the hospital? Should Dr Pym attend her? Perhaps he can help.'

'I am afraid the hospitals are all full, and Dr Pym would only confirm she bears the signs and symptoms of the contagion. He can do nothing more than I have already done.'

'Then, tell me, what help can I be? I want to stay with her but I cannot. I must return to the ship. Who will nurse her? Who will stay with her? Where is her maid?'

'Her maid, Isabella, died two days ago but I have secured the services of an English lady, the widow of an army captain who served at the garrison for many years. She will give your friend all the attention that is possible.'

'I will pay whatever it costs.'

'I thought that would be the case,' he said sagely. 'You must pardon me for admitting, but I understand your relationship with this lady. She revealed to me how deep her feelings are for you, that is why I saw the urgency to advise you.'

'But why didn't she contact me sooner?'

The Doctor spoke gently. 'Perhaps she feared you would be angry with her for failing to do as you had instructed.'

There was nothing Oliver could say. He pleaded, 'She cannot die.'

'Have some faith, Captain. Not everyone who contracts the fever dies.'

'You must not let her die.'

'I am afraid, that is out of my hands. Until her nurse arrives, Zachary will stay with her, and I will return as soon as I can. Unfortunately, there are many more victims who need my help.' He paused. 'I took the liberty of calling the priest. Were you aware the lady is a Roman Catholic?'

Did he know or not? Oliver couldn't remember. And what did it matter anyway?

'She begged me to call for him.'

'Oliver,' Susanna murmured, 'is that you?'

As he moved to the bed, lifted her hand and sat down beside her, Dr Whipple collected his bag and stood at the door.

'I will leave you together for a little while, and return in an hour. Good-bye Captain. May God be with you both.'

Very early the following morning, soon after the garrison's morning gun, a message was rowed to the frigate from the North Mole. It was for *Perpetual*'s captain.

Having dozed only briefly in his chair overnight, Oliver was fully clothed when Casson handed it to him. It bore the news he did not want to hear. He read only the first line – Susanna was dead.

Closing his eyes, he pictured her face on the pillow, her black hair, her parched face, the blood on the sheet. Then, he remembered her face as she had appeared at their last meeting. Her smooth glowing skin. Her rich lips. Dark eyes. He remembered the sun glistening on her smooth neck. Her comforting voice. Her smile. And the touch of her fingers as she stroked his damaged hand. He would never see her again. Feel her touch. Hold her. Love her.

He thought of the Spanish Admiral, Jose de Bustamente y Guerra and his friend the Major who had stood on the deck of *Médéa* and watched his wife, five daughters and three sons consumed by flames before his very eyes.

How could a man endure such an event and go on living with that memory?

How he hated Gibraltar. He hated the constrains of the service. How he wanted to get away. To leave. Now more than ever before.

He lifted the letter, wiped his eyes and read the rest of the Doctor's words.

As you will be aware, there are no undertakers and no funeral services as there is no-one to attend to the burial of the dead in an acceptable fashion. From what the lady told me, Gibraltar is not her home and, because of the Quarantine Regulations and the nature of her illness, it would be impossible to return her body to Madeira, or even deliver her to your ship for a burial at sea.

Because of this, I have begged permission for her body to be buried in the South Port Ditch Cemetery near Windmill Hill. This is where the soldiers, who have succumbed to the fever, are being laid to rest. Officially the cemetery is not permitting the burial of citizens. Unofficially, for a fee, a space will be found. I felt this would be the best arrangement under the circumstances. I will make every effort to be present when this takes place, though I cannot advise you when this will be.

The letter ended with the doctor's message of condolence. It was signed, Jonathon Whipple.

Oliver was grateful and he was in the doctor's debt.

At least, Susanna would be buried in consecrated ground, even if without the usual ceremony. For a terrible moment he had visualised her body being flung on the top of a pile of corpses on the dead cart and conveyed to the newly dug section of the ditch that stretched for hundreds of yards along the edge of the neutral zone. There, without ceremony, it would have been tipped in, sprinkled with lime and earth, trampled beneath feet and forgotten.

He must arrange to repay the financial debt, but how could he repay the doctor for the attention he had shown.

He would never forget Susanna. She had been the constant glimmer of light that had brightened his darkness during long months at sea.

What was it about her that had been so special?

Why her? he thought. *Why not my wife?*

No, God forgive me for such a despicable thought.

He held his head in his hands.

Like all sea-wives, Victoria had always been faithful, kind, true and forbearing, even though deprived of the man to whom she had committed her life to. And Victoria had been without the joy, satisfaction and company of children of her own.

He had failed. Failed as a husband. Failed as a man. But he promised he would make reparation. He must.

Yet for all his regrets, he could not love the memory of Susanna any less. She alone had given him the intense physical joy, the sensual satisfaction and the deep and lasting love, which only a woman can give a man.

Folding the paper, he touched it to his lips then slid it into the drawer of his writing desk. By closing the drawer, he knew it marked the end of a chapter in his life, and nothing on earth could change it.

CHAPTER 16

Resurrection

Sir Thomas Trigge gazed wistfully through his window overlooking the Gibraltar Strait.

'Captain,' he said, 'I asked you here to advise you personally that I will be departing the rock on the twentieth of the month.'

'Aboard a British naval vessel?' Oliver enquired. He was eager to learn if a ship was due to arrive in the bay. Was it possible it would be coming to relieve *Perpetual?*

'Yes,' the general replied. '*Triumph*, with Captain Barlow. When I leave here, I will gladly convey any letters you have. For the Admiralty, perhaps? I know you, too, are anxious to leave this place. For the present, however, as I have received no instructions to the contrary, your orders are unchanged and you must remain here. My replacement as Lieutenant-Governor of the Colony and Commander of the Garrison will be General Fox. He will take up his appointment in December.'

Oliver was genuinely pleased for General Trigge. He was a worthy man. He had survived the epidemic – possibly because he had spent many years of military service in the West Indies. He had managed a disastrous situation with conviction as best he could while under severe duress. He had arrived in Gibraltar to face an ill-disciplined, mutinous garrison where most of his men were fresh-faced young Irishmen who had never seen action and never witnessed death before. His job had not been an easy one.

For Oliver, however, waiting until December for a new commander, with no prospect of being relieved before that, meant many more weeks sitting in Gibraltar Bay. His men would not be happy when he relayed the news, but he could do nothing but acknowledge the situation.

'Indeed, Sir Thomas,' he replied dutifully.

'From an observer's point of view,' the general said, 'it may appear that I am deserting a sinking ship – if you will pardon the nautical expression – as the epidemic continues to escalate.

'In September the garrison recorded only 31 deaths, excluding those from the Artillery and Engineers, while over 1000 bodies were buried in the mass grave on the northern ditch. But, so far this month, the fortress has suffered 300 deaths including a long-time friend of mine from the First Royal Regiment of Foot. On my desk, I have a list of the names of the men who have died including their ages and where they have been buried. Many of them, I knew personally.

'This contagion is a curse, he continued, gazing at the blue water. It is neither selective by age, rank or regiment. And I am acutely aware that when I vacate my command, I will be leaving the colony in a far more depressed and doleful state than when I arrived. The garrison is more vulnerable now than it has been since the time the British captured Gibraltar from Castile one hundred years ago.

'With the number of soldiers so depleted due to sickness, I have been forced to withdraw troops from the upper galleries near the summit. This means Gibraltar's Mediterranean coast is undefended. I have concentrated my able-bodied men on the gun batteries overlooking the isthmus and the bastions and Line Wall overlooking the bay.'

Oliver sympathized with the dilemma the general was facing.

'The malignant fever is an unfortunate situation which could not be foreseen.'

Oliver pondered over the general's statement. He clearly remembered the questions put to him by the Lord Commissioners.

Have you previously suffered a fever?

Was it possible the Admiralty had foreknowledge of the outbreak of fever, or was the possibility of an epidemic pure speculation? He would never know.

'On a more positive note,' the general continued, 'I am expecting the arrival of a new surgeon shortly and once he arrives, Dr Whipple will be at liberty to return to your ship.

'That is good,' Oliver said.

'Captain, I do not often lavish praise but I must extend my admiration for the tireless efforts and commendable services provided to the fortress by your surgeon. Dr Whipple has been a Godsend both to the garrison and the civilian population. And while putting his own life at risk, he undoubtedly prevented even more deaths than the terrible number that I have mentioned.

'Of course,' he continued, 'from the local population, many deaths will probably have gone unrecorded – infants buried in courtyards, beggars tossed into the sea from the cliffs at Europa Point. The true figures will never be known.

'The navy was indeed fortunate to acquire the services of such a learned man as Dr Whipple and if he wished to re-consider his position, I would gladly recommend him for a post on the Rock.'

'I appreciate your commendation, General,' Oliver said, 'and I will convey your words to him. However, I must confess during our voyage from England, I failed to appreciate the doctor's ability and commitment to saving lives. I now berate myself for not being more mindful. Perhaps the nature of the man's reserved character had some bearing on that.'

'Captain Quintrell, I speak from experience when I say one man out of 200 or 2000 may not stand out, especially if by nature he is humble and unassuming. These are not traits required to advance one's career in either the military or the navy. Title and money, however, play a significant role in my branch of the services. While humility is something we have little time to recognize or appreciate.'

Oliver listened to the address from the old soldier. It was delivered as a father would to his son and reminded Oliver of his grandfather – an honest, hardworking herring fisherman. A man who lacked guile along with any formal education, a man whose fondest wish was that his son and his son's son would achieve more than he had. Oliver hoped he had inherited even a little of the gentle humility his grandfather had possessed.

The general continued. 'During the time he was domiciled at the barracks, I am told, the doctor toiled almost twenty hours out of every twenty-four. His first concern was always the welfare of his patients and not himself. I admit recently my faith eluded me when I visited the hospital and witnessed the rows of men in the throes of death. Threshing. Vomiting. Choking.

'I, too, was sceptical when I first observed your surgeon approaching a patient, not with a plaster or clysters or a vial of medicine, but with a pen and notebook into which he recorded certain details. From those patients lucid enough to answer his questions, he asked their age, country of birth and, of course, how long they had been suffering from the fever. He also enquired of each victim when the illness had begun, what course it had taken and, later, he noted the final outcome.

'To me and my junior officers, it appeared to be a worthless, time-consuming exercise and an imposition on the dying. Surprisingly, however, many of the patients rallied for a while when they found the doctor was taking a sincere interest in them. And when a patient was at death's door, he would sit on the bed beside the victim providing comfort by his sheer presence.' General Trigge sighed long and hard. 'I believe none of us wish to die alone.'

'Did you request the doctor to collect this information?' Oliver asked.

'No, Captain. Deaths occurring at the garrison are recorded, but the information required for government returns is basic and limited. I admit to being a little puzzled myself and questioned the doctor about his extensive record keeping.'

Oliver waited.

'He told me his notes were part of a study he was conducting. He hoped one day to publish his findings in order that the facts, regarding the epidemic, would assist future physicians to better treat the fever if it returns.'

'You think it will return?'

'I fear so.'

With the arrival of a new surgeon to serve at the garrison, Dr Whipple relinquished his duties at the garrison's hospital but, with the help of Zachary Irons, continued to attend the sick in the town. With his nights spent aboard the frigate, Oliver took the opportunity to invite the doctor to dine with him in his cabin. A time for the pair to talk was long overdue.

'I trust you will allow me to speak candidly,' Oliver said.

'Please feel free,' the ship's surgeon said. 'I have nothing to hide.'

'Stories circulate a ship like sharks around a whale carcase. Ugly rumours regarding yourself ran rampant when we sailed from Portsmouth. Unfortunately, those rumours directly targeted your professional reputation and, I admit, made me question your capabilities.

'However, since we arrived in Gibraltar, I have heard nothing but praise for your work from Captain Gore, General Trigge and Doctor Pym. I have seen the extent and care you have extended to patients who mean nothing to you. In Algeciras, I even noted how well you handled yourself in a dire situation. For my own part, I admit that my initial assessment of your performance in the cockpit was unjustified. I put that down to my ignorance of modern medical procedures and I offer you my apology.'

Dr Whipple shook his head. 'That is not necessary.'

'But I want to understand and offer you the opportunity to speak frankly. I assure you whatever you tell me will go no further than these wooden walls.'

'I appreciate the opportunity, Captain. What can I tell you?'

'You boarded *Perpetual* as ship's surgeon,' Oliver said. 'And you explained to me earlier how you had been stepped up to surgeon from surgeon's mate. But you did not explain why you did not complete your training as a surgeon. Might I ask why that was?'

'It was due to the death of my father,' he replied, casting his eyes down. 'Unbeknownst to me and the rest of the family, he had amassed a large gambling debt. So in order to save my mother from being relegated to the poorhouse, the house my family had lived in for four generations was sold. Naturally, my allowances and tuitions fees ceased and I had no other means of meeting my expenses. As a student of Mr Astley Cooper, my annual fees were £500 a year, plus seven guineas for each lecture, and five guineas to attend a dissection.

'A considerable sum.'

'Mr Cooper was an inspiring mentor and because he had been impressed with my progress he had invited me to be a demonstrator for him at his daily lectures. That job entailed preparation and presentation of cadavers for his students. At times, I also helped him with vivisections which he conducted at his private residence.'

Oliver frowned. 'Cutting up bodies in a fashionable area of London!'

'Indeed. Mr Cooper contended that it was preferable to discover how the human body worked by dissecting a cadaver rather than trying to understand how the organs functioned on a screaming subject.'

The doctor's words resonated with the captain. 'The moans of men with arms and legs torn off are never so heart wrenching as the screams of a loved one put to the knife.'

'Men in battle do not feel pain immediately,' the doctor said. 'That it is why it is best for the surgeon to remove an arm or leg as soon as possible. The mind blocks the pain although the pain returns later.'

That was another fact Oliver could relate to. When his hand had been rent in two, he remembered looking at it, considering the blood that was staining his uniform and white silk stockings. He distinctly remembered taking off his neckerchief and binding it around the dripping remnant hanging from his wrist before issuing the next order to fire.

Oliver continued. 'And you helped procure bodies for him.'

Dr Whipple nodded. 'Only once. He had regular suppliers.'

'And I suppose he paid them well.'

'Oh, yes. The bag-'em-up men make a good income. They charge a set price for adults. Ten pounds each. Babies and still-born infants are calculated by the inch, and a special price is paid for a pregnant woman still carrying the foetus within her swollen belly.'

Oliver frowned. 'An unseemly business. I can imagine the state of decay of some of the bodies.'

Dr Whipple was unperturbed. 'No cadaver was ever wasted, no matter what state it was in. With occasional requests for skeletons, badly decomposed bodies were ideal because it took little work to strip the flesh from the bones. But if any fat had to be flensed off, it was traded to the local chandler who was not particular what type of fat went into his candles. He used whatever he could get his hands on and if he received complaints about the smell, he would swear the fat was from a pig.'

Oliver curled his nose. 'But if these resurrectionists were caught, did the surgeon never fear they would reveal his name?'

'*Loyalty amongst thieves* – as the saying goes. They respected Mr Cooper because he looked after them. If they were apprehended, he paid for a lawyer to defend them in court. As a result they were usually released with a fine and were back at work in less than a week.'

'But why would an intelligent man like Mr Cooper do it?' Oliver asked.

'Because like all naval navigators, surgeons need charts. Maps to show the routes taken by veins, arteries and nerves. They need to know where they are heading, what passages are safe to travel and what they are likely to encounter along the way.

'If you witnessed the number of operations I have seen performed on live patients strapped to the table, given nothing to dull the senses, you would agree that practicing on a body which does not feel the knife, is far preferable.'

'But isn't laudanum administered to the patients?' Oliver asked.

'Not always,' the doctor admitted. 'Opiates not only slow the brain but also reduce the patient's desire to breathe. Administer too much opiate and the patient will die from lack of their own breath not from the operation.

'We have a name for our work in the hospital. It is called Pathology. It is the Study of Suffering. As for myself, I found grave-robbing to be a diabolical experience and would never choose to repeat it.'

Dr Whipple continued. 'Greater fear, I have never felt than in a churchyard, after midnight, when the shadows play tricks with your mind. When the swaying branch of a tree is an arm reaching out to grab you. Where every leaf that rustles in the breeze is a footfall behind you. The screech of an owl – a soul in despair. The eyes of a fox – the face of the Devil. Watching.

'In the uncomfortable silence of the night, every scrape of the wooden spade jars in your ears. The crack of the coffin lid when it is rent apart explodes like the sound of a giant oak felled in the forest. The noises reverberate through every nerve in your body. You glance around, not knowing where to look, not knowing what to expect, or when. You imagine voices in the night, faces in the trees, but see nothing. You long for it to be over. You want to be away from that place. You are conscious this is desecration.'

He sipped his wine. 'Then, if the moon suddenly appears through the trees, flickering like a dozen lanterns, you want to run, but you cannot. The grave-diggers whisper. Make jokes. Suck on empty pipes. They have done this many times before. Death is their living. They waste no time. Once a hole is made in the lid, the corpse is hurriedly hauled out, and the shroud or clothing torn off it. Then the body – naked as the day it was born – is stuffed into a large bag.'

'Do the robbers have no respect? Why would they remove the burial shroud which provides the last vestiges of dignity to the deceased?'

Dr Whipple laughed. 'Because the law is an ass. It is a crime to steal a possession such as a loaf of bread, a piece of cheese, a silk handkerchief, even a burial shroud. A man can be sentenced to death or seven year's transportation for such a deed. But a body is a person and not a possession, and there is no law relating to the stealing of bodies.'

Oliver was shocked. 'Then the law should be changed.'

'In due course, that will happen but for the present nothing changes.'

'Do you know of other reputable surgeons involved in such practices?'

'Indeed, some of the most promising surgeons in the land. To those men, the desire to improve their anatomical knowledge justifies their actions. If they wish to become expert anatomists they have no choice.'

'What of the bodies supplied from the prisons?'

'The law only permits the bodies of convicted murderers to be taken from the gallows and conveyed to the dissection rooms for public viewing. But three or four a month is not nearly enough. With lectures and demonstrations occurring daily during the season, several cadavers are needed for every session. And with the promise of a tidy income, the resurrectionists are willing to travel great distances and take risks to supply them. Their work is often aided by greedy parsons, church sextons and the grave diggers who are happy to receive a fee for supplying news of a forthcoming or recent burial.'

'Can nothing be done to stop this heathen practice?'

The doctor shrugged. 'Steel railings erected around a grave seem to have little effect. The best defence is a watch kept over the grave, for two or three weeks, by relatives of the deceased.'

Oliver poured himself another drink. 'But you appear to be an upstanding God-fearing man. Surely you regard life as sacrosanct even after death.'

The doctor took a deep breath. 'There have long been debates about the relationship between body and soul, and men have suffered the most diabolical tortures for speaking the words I now utter. I firmly believe that when death occurs, the spirit departs the body and all that remains is flesh and blood. No different to a side of beef or a ration of pork.'

He continued. 'Until the law is changed and body snatchers can be charged with their crimes in a court of law or surgeons can legally obtain cadavers for vivisection other than from the gallows, the practice of the resurrectionists will continue. It is the only way the surgeon's knowledge of anatomy can advance. AS I said before, it is better for them to practice on a corpse than on a screaming patient.'

'This is your belief?' Oliver asked.

Dr Whipple nodded. 'It was Mr Cooper's belief also.'

Oliver paused for a moment and looked across at the ship's surgeon. 'I have heard of Mr Astley Cooper,' he admitted.

'He is well known in London and well respected at the Borough Hospitals. One day he will be physician to the king.'

'Do you regret you were unable to continue with your training in surgery?' Oliver asked.

'Indeed. When I could no longer afford to continue my apprenticeship with Mr Cooper, I had hoped to maintain my job as a demonstrator at his lectures. However, that was not to be. My position was quickly taken up by another fee-paying student.'

'Is this the reason you applied for a warrant on a navy ship – to give you access to fresh cadavers from sailors felled in battle?'

The doctor appears surprised at the forthrightness of the captain's question.

'No, sir. Without membership of the Royal Society of Surgeons, if I remained in London, I would be nothing more than an apothecary dispensing medicines prescribed by a physician. On a ship, however, my duties are those of apothecary, surgeon and physician, and I can choose to designate whatever potions I see fit.

'Furthermore,' he continued, 'a ship visiting the Indies provides the opportunity to see first-hand exotic diseases, such as leprosy and yaws, which do not often present in the Borough Hospitals. I had also heard that naval surgeons were entitled to receive a proportion of prize money during times of war.'

'And, you had also heard that I had been particularly successful over the past few years in falling upon rich prizes?' Oliver heard the old vein of cynicism creeping into his voice.

'I learned that only when I received my appointment from the Navy Board.'

'If you were to receive a sum of money whilst in His Majesty's service, would you return to the Borough Hospitals and complete your training?'

'Indeed I would. To qualify as a surgeon would be my dearest wish.'

'I commend your intentions,' Oliver said, 'although I doubt there is a man aboard *Perpetual* who would not toss you overboard if he learned of your participation in the evil trade of body-snatching.'

'And why would you not condemn me, Captain?'

'Because I know the surgeon you speak of – Mr Astley Cooper. Several months ago, I visited him at his private address in London for a consultation about my wife's recurring ailment. That visit cost 200 guineas. I consulted with him because he was recommended as the best surgeon in London.'

Dr Whipple was silent for a moment before offering a response. 'Captain Quintrell, I understand why men like you find dissection revolting and offensive. The practice of surgery is not far removed from that. Mr Cooper once advised me that to be a good surgeon one required, "an eagle's eye, a lady's hand, and a lion's heart".' He smiled. 'I have a keen eye and a steady hand, but I could never qualify with the latter. I have the heart of a lady not a lion.'

'Yet you sail into battle on a navy ship and appear afraid of nothing.'

Jonathon Whipple nodded his head slowly. 'While I am intent on hardening my heart, in the meantime, I believe I can provide the services required of a ship's doctor more than adequately.'

'I thank you for you honesty, Dr Whipple. And you must forgive me for not speaking of this before.' Oliver's voice faltered. 'I must thank you for what you did for my friend in the town.'

'I am sorry I was not able to save her,' the doctor replied kindly. 'I only wish I could have done more.'

CHAPTER 17

The Windsor Gallery

'Mr Parry, I will require forty good men to work the guns – twenty sailors and an equal number of marines.'

'Forty *Perpetuals* would be a better choice,' Simon Parry suggested. 'The marines are mere slips of lads lacking in both strength and intelligence, and they have never seen action.'

The captain turned from his first lieutenant to the marine sergeant. 'I cannot blame you for age or lack of learning, however, at times your men do appear to be lacking in discipline. Yet, when I put them to work on the Bay of Biscay, they were eager to perform and quickly learned from my men how to aim and fire a gun on a rolling deck. Now I offer them a chance to return the favour.'

Mr Parry looked sceptical.

'Another opportunity to work together will be good for them.'

'Yes, sir,' Mr Parry replied. 'Which guns shall I have run out?'

'No guns, Mr Parry. I will be going ashore at first light. The garrison needs our assistance. I want volunteers and I am sure there are men who will jump at the opportunity to leave the ship. In case any are reticent and fearful of contracting the fever from the local residents, inform them we will not be going into the town. Tell them they can look forward to breathing fresh sea air directly from the Mediterranean.'

'At Europa Point?'

'No, Mr Parry – at the Windsor Gallery, near the top of the Rock, overlooking Catalan Bay and the Eastern Beach.'

'But I thought the Royal Artillery manned the cannon in the gallery.'

'That was the case until a week ago. For the present, those defences are unmanned because many of the gunners and artificers have died of the fever. The few who remained fit have been brought down to serve on the Line Wall.'

'But the Rock is not under attack, is it?'

'No, not under attack, but yesterday two French ships were observed cruising off Catalan Bay. They headed south but never rounded Europa Point. Whilst the presence of Captain Barlow's advance guard usually deters them in the Strait, *Triumph* has not been sighted for over a week when it was seen heading west to the Atlantic. In its absence, there is nothing to stop the French from sailing into Gibraltar Bay or attacking the promontory from the east.'

'I thought the Great Siege had taught both French and Spanish forces a lesson,' Simon Parry observed.

'Memories fade, as time passes. Presently, the garrison's defences are the weakest they have been in decades. Soldiers are dropping at their guns not from enemy fire but from the fever. And if the French are aware an opportunity to strike exists, they will take it.'

'Beg pardon, Captain. But how could the French know?'

'Sergeant, one only has to step ashore in Gibraltar to know what a cosmopolitan town it is. Several hundred of its citizens are French. Besides that, the guards on the gates have long been taking bribes, as proven with the constant smuggling activities running back and forth into Spain. Plus the traders here are as unscrupulous as anywhere in the world. It would not be hard for word to get out, and with Napoleon's semaphore towers stretching across France, it is very probably the state of affairs on the peninsula is already known across Europe. Add to that the fact General Trigge has recently departed the garrison and until General Fox arrives in December the garrison is without a commander and the colony without a Lieutenant-Governor. If the French intend to launch an attack, now would be an opportune time.'

Captain Quintrell turned to the sergeant. 'The orders I received from the Admiralty indicated I must do all in my power to help protect Gibraltar.'

'Will I be accompanying you?' the lieutenant asked.

'No, Mr Parry, *Perpetual* will be yours while I am ashore. Guard her well. She would make a fine prize for a French privateer. And be ever vigilant of the Spanish gunboats. Let us hope they do not discover we have a consignment of Spanish silver on board. I shall, however, require the bosun, Mr Tully and Mr Nightingale to accompany me.' He turned to the military officer.

'Sergeant Wilkie, you will accompany your men. Choose them carefully. I want no weaklings, boys or anyone who is ailing.' Then he turned his gaze back to his lieutenant. 'The guns in the gallery are

32-pounders. Of the *Perpetuals* – I require sailors from the best crews who can fire and reload in under two minutes. I want no idlers, waisters or topmen. Kindly make a list of those who will be going with me and have the boats in the water before dawn. I want to depart from the beach at first light.'

'Aye aye, Captain.'

When the call went out for volunteers, the cooper and his mates were at the head of the line.

'Count me in,' Bungs crowed. 'Anything to get off the ship for a spell. I like the idea of breathing some sweet air. Better than having the stench of sulphur and vinegar up your nose all day.'

The men pushed forward.

'One at a time,' Mr Parry ordered. 'No, not you, Smithers. Didn't you hear me say the captain doesn't want topmen?'

'Aye, and he's too old anyway.'

Smithers sneered. 'Younger than you.'

'Shut your cakehole!' Bungs replied. 'Hobbles, come here,' he yelled, grabbing his gun captain by the arm and dragging him forward. 'Add Hobbles' name to the list. He's just volunteered.'

Mr Parry questioned the cooper. 'I doubt Hobbles heard a word of what was said.'

'Not to worry, Mr Parry, I'll tell him where we're going later. There's no better gun captain than Hobbles and you know it.'

'But he's not fit. I doubt he can make it up the hill.'

Bungs glanced down at the gun captain's bad leg. 'He'll make it all right. Me and Eku, we'll make sure he does. Aye, and write Ekundayo's name on your list next to mine.'

When the lieutenant glanced at him, the Negro nodded and his name was duly marked down.

'Brickley, I don't want you. You're a topman, aren't you?'

'Yes, sir. But I can worm out a gun as quick as any man.'

Mr Parry shook his head. 'No topmen, I said.'

The sailor mumbled and stepped back.

'What about you, Muffin?' Bungs said, elbowing his mess mate to join the line. 'Why aren't you volunteering? Don't you want a change of scenery?'

'I've got a sore head.'

Bungs laughed. 'Been drinking someone else's ration of rum, have you? A breath of fresh air will do you good. Put him on the list, Mr Parry. I guarantee he'll be all right in the morning.'

'What about me?' Tommy asked.

'I said no waisters or idlers. The captain don't need a loblolly on the Rock.'

'But he'll need a powder monkey,' Tommy argued. 'I did that on my last cruise. And now I'm bigger and stronger, and I can keep a gun supplied double-quick. Strikes me that if you're planning to fire guns, you'll need quills and cartridges. So, you'll need a powder monkey to fetch 'em—'

'Enough!' Mr Parry declared, entering Tommy Wainwright's name as number 10 on his list.

Although dawn had broken, it was still dark in the shadow of the Rock. On the summit, however, the rays of sun rising from the Mediterranean Sea burnished O'Hara's two-hundred foot tower on the top of the promontory.

From the frigate's deck, Simon Parry watched the three boats arriving on the beach at Rosia Bay. After glancing to the ridge, he was relieved to see the strange bulbous arms of the signal tower were still. However, he was concerned the frigate's best gun crews and twenty marines were going ashore and leaving the ship vulnerable. It was a time to be vigilant.

For the men, stepping ashore after weeks confined within the frigate's bulwarks, the feeling of freedom brought with it a burst of euphoria. Although the excursion was to be only for a day, the men's mood changed instantly to that of paid-up seamen returning home after a year at sea.

'Shut your yap,' Mr Tully shouted. 'Stand in line. Double file.'

The uniformed marines made a better show of responding to marching orders and once the sailors had fallen into line behind them, Mr Nightingale joined Captain Quintrell at the head of the troop with the sergeant flanking his marines. Only six of the soldiers were carrying muskets. The rest were pleased to have their hands free.

From the beach, they headed for the main road that ran from the town on the north of the peninsula to Europa Point in the south. But the party merely crossed it and headed part-way up a long set of stone stairs. It was an arduous climb that led to the tower on the top of the promontory. However, half way up, they turned onto a track that ran, with a slow incline, along the lee side of the mountain. It was the scratch across the Rock they had seen from the frigate.

After a while, they were climbing again, the track twisting back and forth in a zigzag to accommodate the incline.

'Looks like we're heading for the top,' Bungs said.

'No talking! Save your breath,' Mr Tully ordered.

The rough-hewn path was little more than a donkey track, just wide enough for the double file to walk shoulder to shoulder. Once on the hill the marines were no longer able to maintain marching step and were pleased to be without their muskets.

For the seamen whose eyes had grown weary looking at miles and miles of endless sea, the view from the side of the Rock was refreshing. Looking west across the bay to Algeciras and the rolling mountain range that rose from behind the Spanish port, while around the bay, a frilled petticoat of breaking surf decorated the treacherous coastline. To the south, from Europa Point, the silver waters of the Strait extended to the north coast of Africa.

The captain stopped occasionally, allowing time for the party to catch their breath and an opportunity for him to refill his own lungs. Walking a quarterdeck did not equip him for such an arduous climb. And he was not alone. For the sailmaker's mates, caulkers, and men who spent most of the voyage working in sedentary occupations, it was a hard climb. The young marines once again fared better.

It was becoming obvious to the captain that the longer *Perpetual* stayed in port, the more unfit his men were becoming. Even the topmen, who could hang from the yards like monkeys and run up the ratlines with the speed of scared rodents, were becoming indolent and lazy. With no need for sail handling, the only exercise their forearms were getting was holystoning the deck. It was of no consolation the frigate's decks had never been cleaner or smoother.

But of real concern to the captain, was the weed tightening it grips on the frigate's hull. Despite the copper plates preventing tiny shipworms eating a honeycomb of holes into the timber, the warm waters of the Mediterranean were promoting a verdant growth of weed sprouting from every joint and nail hole, and it was increasing every day.

After climbing for half-an-hour, the captain raised his arm. 'Halt!'

The sailors stumbled to a stop behind the marines.

'Gun crews, up ahead there is a job for you to attend to.'

The sailors craned their necks to see what awaited them.

'Two weeks ago, a group of Royal Engineers attempted to haul a gun up this track but the soldiers were debilitated with sickness. They reached this point but could go no further.'

The information was passed in whispers down the line. 'It's a bloody 32-pounder!'

'Surely we're not going to fire it here!'

Oliver's hearing was acute. 'No, Mr Entwhistle, our task is to haul it up the hill to the Great Siege tunnel to replace one of the guns that blew.'

'Begging your pardon, Captain, but that's a big 'un. It must weigh near three tons.'

'I am sure you are right, Bungs, but there are enough of you and if you have had your eyes open during the climb you will have noticed iron rings set into the face of the rock at every twenty or thirty yards.' The captain pointed at one alongside where the men were standing. 'They were put in place over 20 years ago and have been used to haul dozens of guns up this hill.'

The blocks and tackle, used by the soldiers on the previous attempt, were lying beside the cannon.

Oliver turned to the bosun. 'Take your mates and rig the lines. I will have the men ready to haul. Take it slowly and carefully. I want no accidents. Thirty yards at a time.'

Running out a gun on a smooth timber deck was something the gun crews were adept at. But running out a gun on a deck that was heeling and pitching took strength and skill and was sometimes near impossible. Yet here on a narrow stony path cut into the side of a precipitous mountain with a steep decline on one side dropping hundreds of feet below, the men were expected to push, pull and heave a monstrous cannon weighing several tons up a hill rising to over 1000 feet. Not only was the gun far bigger than any of *Perpetual*'s guns, but it was seated in an iron carriage. All in all, it was a monster.

But if the hill's incline and the path's limited width were not enough of a challenge, the track was littered with broken rocks, small stones and large boulders that had been dislodged from higher up the slope and rolled down the mountainside. Added to the danger of more falling rocks, the men's footwear was ill suited to the climb. Through the thin leather soles of their slops' shoes, every man could feel the broken rocks beneath his feet.

'We need a team of sodding draft horses to haul this blighter!'

'Thank you, Bungs. I am afraid we do not have a team of horses handy,' the captain advised. 'But you will be surprised what you can achieve once the tackle is rigged. Pull hard and you'll have the gun at the tunnel in no time.'

'Only tunnels I've known was at the bottom of a pit not on the top of a mountain,' Tommy Wainwright said.

'Silence!' Mr Tully shouted. 'Bungs, make sure the barrel is lashed tightly to the cradle. It if teeters, it will overbalance and crush anyone who is in its way. If it rolls down the hill then we will have to start again at the bottom. Our destination is the north end of the rock. You will be relieved to know we are not going as high as the signal tower.'

'Some consolation,' Entwhistle murmured.

Once the lines were rigged, a team of ten men stood to the ropes. Three more were stationed at each side of the carriage to help turn the wheels, while two stood behind for pushing. Meanwhile three sailors were sent to clear the track ahead, rolling the largest boulders aside but taking care not to let them topple over the edge as a single rock could gather others with it and deliver an avalanche of stones on the houses far below. Another pair followed close behind the carriage, armed with crowbars and wooden chocks. Their job was to prevent the cannon from sliding back if the lines snapped.

The marines appeared happy to look on for the present.

When everyone was in place Mr Tully gave the order. 'Heave men! Haul away!'

But the gun did not move. 'Heave, with all your might! Only twenty yards to the next ring!'

With his third call came the crunch of metal wheels as they ground the rocks beneath them.

'She's adrift. Keep hauling! Don't stop.'

With the wheels turning slowly, the team hauled the cannon, first towards the north. Then, when the track zigzagged back on itself, they found themselves heading due south. Despite encouragement from the officers, progress was painfully slow. Half-way to their destination, a band of chattering monkeys bounded down the hill to investigate the intruders in their domain. One of the Barbary Apes, with an infant clinging to its back, leapt onto the gun's barrel apparently to take a ride. The sailors found it amusing.

The marine corporal prodded it several times with his musket and eventually dislodged it, but it promptly climbed back on. He aimed for it again.

'Don't hurt it,' the sergeant warned, 'unless you want the town's folk to string you up.'

The marine shook his head in disgust, but in doing so the monkey was attracted to the wavering plume on his hat. Leaping quickly to his shoulders and dropping back nimbly to the ground, it dragged the hat from his head and ran off. The Irish marine dived after it yelling abuse at the beast. The other macaques screeched wildly in response and scampered after it, followed by four young recruits who thought it a great game.

'That will come out of your pay,' the sergeant called, but his order could not be heard above the excited cries.

'Get back in line this instant!' Captain Quintrell yelled.

The men stopped, turned and slowly regrouped much to the amusement of the *Perpetuals*. The antics of the monkeys and men had been a welcome distraction but it had resulted in the carriage wheels grinding to a halt.

'Back to work, *Perpetuals*,' Mr Tully bellowed. 'Keep your mind on the task. It ain't no different to running out a gun!'

'No different? We're hauling it up the side of a bloody mountain or ain't he noticed?'

'Did you say something, Brickley?'

'No, sir, wasn't me, Mr Tully, sir.'

'Then someone sounded exactly like you. Keep it shut in future.'

After a brief rest, the men took up the lines and hauled again.

Up ahead, Tommy was clearing rocks from the track but suddenly, for no apparent reason, he stopped and sat down allowing the gun to gain on him.

'Get out of the way!' Bungs yelled.

'You there,' Mr Tully ordered. 'Stand up. Get off the track!'

Tommy turned his head and looked questioningly from the lieutenant to the gun that was only a few yard from him and moving closer.

'What's the matter with the idiot? Is he deaf?' Bungs said.

'Get him off the track!' Mr Tully yelled.

'Stop hauling!' the Captain ordered. 'Get that sailor up on his feet!'

The men dropped their lines and cursed as Tommy Wainwright was hauled up by the scruff of the neck and pushed to one side. The gun lost its forward momentum and came to a dead stop. Everyone knew that getting it rolling again was the hardest part.

'You,' Mr Tully shouted to three marines still taunting the Barbary Apes. 'Get down here and clear the track ahead, or lend a hand on the lines. Not far to go. Haul away, men!'

After two hours, the men were near exhausted. By now, the sun had lifted over the ridge running along the top of the Rock, and with it the temperature had risen considerably.

Approximately an hour later, the exhausted crew pushed the big gun into the entrance of the Windsor Gallery – the great cavernous tunnel dug by hand that formed a gallery for big guns. The small cave-like openings in the cliff's face provided natural embrasures for the cannon to be fired through.

A single guard stationed outside the tunnel greeted the captain.

After a brief conversation, Captain Quintrell learned that the signal tower on the Rock had been active during the morning but, as it was not visible from the tunnel's entrance, it was impossible to know if it had stopped. However, their position, high on the north-east corner of the Rock, provided a broad vista over the mile-wide isthmus joining the British colony to the mainland of Spain. It also provided a panoramic view over the Mediterranean Sea.

Unfortunately for the captain, from this position he was not able to see *Perpetual*. He considered the frigate's vulnerability. *If the French are aware of the epidemic and the state of the garrison, do they also know about the treasure he had been entrusted with?* The occupants of the old hulks also posed a potential threat, the traders-cum-smugglers had already demonstrated they would stop at nothing. Then there were the occasional bad apples in his own crew to consider. He remembered a handful of greedy men who had chanced their lives in the freezing Southern Ocean for a lump of ambergris. What would such men do for chests full of silver? Added to that were the Spanish gunboats of Algeciras. They were as annoying as mosquitoes as they flittered across the bay but still constituted a threat. The sooner this job was over and he could return to his ship the better.

'Steady men,' Mr Tully warned, as he watched the cannon being manoeuvred through the entrance leading into the Rock. Chiselled out by hand in 1782 by the military artificers of the Corps of

Engineers, the mouth of the tunnel was broad enough to accommodate a London coach and four. The rock floor was angled on a slight declivity and led into a long tunnel bathed in blackness.

Lashed with ropes to hold it back, the massive cannon now wanted to run on its own and was more unmanageable than when it was being hauled up the hill.

'Don't let it get away!' Captain Quintrell called.

After the searing sunlight, the tunnel within the Rock was dimly lit. Only a few well-spaced lanterns hung from the walls, each glim as insignificant as the glow of a single firefly in a meadow. But at each gun embrasure rays of sunlight streamed from the hole in the rock face. Curtains of rope dangling across the apertures didn't block the view. Their purpose was to conceal the holes from the outside.

Wide eyed, to accommodate the darkness, the sailors eased their load past the first three embrasures. The 32-pound gun's metal wheels ground slowly down the decline heading to the next vacant hole in the wall where a gun could be positioned.

A group of artificers, working further down the tunnel, were surprised by the approaching noise and voices, and came back to investigate. A corporal, carrying a lantern, appeared out of the darkness and presented himself to Captain Quintrell. He advised the naval officer where he would find a vacant embrasure. It was fifty yards further down the gallery.

When the cannon was finally rolled into place, Oliver slid aside the rope curtain and looked down. It was a near perpendicular drop. The Eastern Beach was to the north and Catalan Bay slightly to the south over 1000 feet below.

While Oliver assessed the capability of the gallery's guns, Mr Nightingale announced loudly, 'Three sail of ships to the north.'

The captain darted to the nearest opening to look through. No doubt the ships were the reason the tower had been signalling.

Everyone stopped and waited.

With a glass supplied by the corporal, Oliver studied the ships. 'Frenchies. Heading this way.'

With Mr Tully keeping watch, Oliver spoke with the military officer in charge. 'How many men do you have?'

'Only half a dozen, sir, but we're not gunners. We're artillery artificers. We're here to care for the ordnance, and keep watch.'

Not very well, Oliver thought. 'Does the garrison post guards at Catalan Bay?'

'No, sir. The Line Wall ends before it reaches the beach. Besides, there's nothing worth guarding down there, just a couple of fisherman's huts. As for the men on the wall, I heard that most had been moved to Windmill Hill, because of the sickness.'

'Did the garrison never consider the possibility of a landing party arriving on the Mediterranean Coast?'

'I don't know, sir.'

'Sergeant, have this gun ready for firing as quickly as possible.'

'You intend to test the gun, sir?' *Perpetual*'s sergeant of marines asked.

'I intend to fire the gun, Sergeant. In fact I intend to fire five guns with the help of your men.'

'You there,' he called to the artillerymen in the tunnel who appeared to have nothing to do. 'I need cartridges and shot. Show the powder monkey where the arsenal is and lend a hand. Be quick about it!'

'They're hauling their sails, Captain,' Mr Tully warned. 'Looks like they intend to drop anchor off Catalan Bay.'

He turned to his two lieutenants. 'Each of you, take a position and select a gun crew. Sergeant, your men can work another two guns. I shall remain with this one. Gentleman, you wanted to see some action. Prepare your guns and be ready to run them out on my command.'

Priming the guns was not a problem, but loading a 32-pound cannon ball into a barrel then angling it to a decline without losing the ball, was no easy task. Furthermore, adjusting metal carriages was very different to the wooden carriages and quoins the sailors were used to.

The first shot pushed up into the captain's gun rolled out as soon as the cannon's muzzle was depressed. It dropped with a dull thud on the rock floor, rolled forward and fell for 1000 feet collecting an avalanche of scree on the jagged rocks below.

'Fools! Do you want to announce we are here? Look to the wedges,' the captain shouted, pointing to a bag containing circlets of rope.

With grommets and wads the size of Dutch cheeses inserted into the barrel, the heavy ball was held firmly in place. Now there was nothing to do but wait to discover what the intentions of the French ships were.

CHAPTER 18

Catalan Bay

Only a hundred yards off the fisherman's beach at Catalan Bay, the three French ships hove to.

'They are opening their gun ports,' Mr Nightingale called.

'Hold your fire!' Oliver's voice echoed along the length of the gallery.

From his vantage point, he could see boats being lowered into the water from the three frigates. Uniformed troops were lined up along the decks.

'Wait,' Captain Quintrell ordered. 'They are transporting soldiers. Two hundred men or more!'

He turned to the corporal in charge of the artificers. 'Send one of your men with an urgent message to the garrison. Tell the commander that a French force is about to make land on the east coast.'

'But the lookout at O'Hara's Folly will have seen them,' he argued.

'There is no line of sight from the top of the Rock to the beach below. Did you hear my order, corporal? Do it now. Send a message down the hill this instant!'

Once each boat was filled with troops, it was pushed off from the frigate's side and immediately began pulling for the shore only a hundred yards away. Already there were six boats on the water, each carrying near four dozen men. With no defences on the beach at Catalan Bay, there was nothing to stop them landing there or slightly further north on the Eastern Beach. From here they could cross the isthmus beneath the old Moorish castle and enter Gibraltar's township via the Land Port Gate.

With no sign of any defensive fire from the garrison's forces on the northern line-wall, Oliver had one thought. He must stop them before they reached the beach. He glanced from the aperture in the cliff. The angle of fire was incredibly steep. Could the guns be angled sufficiently? He could but try.

'We will stop the boats, and sink the ships,' he ordered. 'Run out your guns, men!'

When the order echoed through the tunnel, any weariness the men had felt after the long climb up the hill was forgotten. Running each gun forward, pushing its barrel through the curtain of rope, heaving its muzzle through the natural porthole in the cliff face then elevating the carriage to allow the barrel to point almost vertically down to the sea below, appeared almost impossible. But the crews worked well and the guns were made ready.

To an observer on the water, the muzzle of each cannon was no larger than the eye of a seagull nesting on a ledge.

'Prepare to fire!' the captain yelled.

With bunches of teased oakum stuffed in their ears, and neckerchiefs or scarves wrapped around their heads, all the men had to do was wait for the command.

'Fire!'

The thunderous noise was ear-shattering and, despite the earplugs, even Hobbles heard it. With a flash of orange flame and a thick cloud of grey smoke, five 32-pound projectiles were shot out from the cliff face.

The cannon reared on their ungainly metal carriages like angry stallions. And while the gun crews feverishly wormed, sponged and reloaded the barrels with another ball, the officers and gun captains peered through the curtains to see where their shots had landed,

The shot from the marines' gun at the most northerly end of the tunnel had landed closest to its target. The poor aim of the second gun had sent their shot drifting too far to the left. The *Perpetual*s, unused to firing at such elevations, had delivered their shots hundreds of feet over the French frigates' masts. They quickly made adjustments and prepared to fire again.

The marine captain was waiting. He had his gun ready. Firing from the top of a battlement was what his men were best trained to do.

Hobbles assessed the distance, considered the wind and likely drift, checked the barrel's depression and adjusted the angle even further.

'Run out your guns,' Oliver shouted.

The iron wheels ground towards the openings. The muzzles poked through the rope curtains.

'Ready.'

The gun captains waited, excitement simmering.

'Fire!'

Five 32-pound balls hissed through the air and again splashed into the sea sending columns of water shooting as high as the ships' masts. The shots fell close, but not close enough.

'I want the next one in the waist!' Oliver demanded.

It was obvious to him that there was panic on the decks of the ships below. The frigates' captains knew they were under attack but apart from the puffs of smoke emitted from the face of the cliff, they could not see the guns that had fired at them. Nor could they elevate their own guns to bear on a target 1000 feet above them.

Oliver was elated. 'They cannot touch us here, men,' he said. 'Never did I walk a safer gundeck. I want a hole the size of this embrasure in the side of one of those ships. A double ration of rum for every man when we get back.'

There was obvious confusion on the stretch of water between the fighting ships and the beach. Of the six boats making for the shore, three continued pulling for the sand while the other three tried to pull around and return to the frigates.

Putting his head to the curtain, Oliver listened. The faint sound of musket shots was drifting up from below, yet there had not been sufficient time for a message to be delivered to the Lieutenant-Governor. Hopefully it was the garrison's troops that had responded to the sound of gunfire and arrived to defend the beaches.

'Fire!' Oliver yelled.

Thunder roared through the gallery with the destructive noise that rendered artillery men deaf before they reached the age of twenty. Tongues of orange flame spat out from the Rock's sheer face but when the captain's gun recoiled, the rope curtain failed to prevent the cloud of smoke and shower of sparks being sucked back into the tunnel with it.

The men coughed and spluttered. Their eyes watered.

'Is this the fresh air we were promised?' Bungs asked.

'Tend to your gun!' the captain reminded him.

Heads quickly poked through the mantle to check where the shots had landed. Each man gulped a mouthful of fresh air in the process. Several yards too far from Mr Nightingale's shot. Too short from Mr Tully's gun. Then the delayed firing from one of the marines' guns sent the blast reverberating along the tunnel.

'Direct hit!' Mr Tully shouted. 'One of the mains has gone.'

The men cheered.

The response from the French frigates was a display of defensive broadsides delivering darts of smoke and licks of flame spitting out from the hulls over the water. The shots hit the scree slopes sending lethal splinters rocketing across the beach. Some hit the boat crews and others splashed into the water. But the enemy was hundreds of feet above where the shots fell.

Other balls ricocheted off the cliff face and rolled down the scree gathering up an avalanche of rubble as they fell.

A direct hit from the largest French frigate dashed one of the fisherman's huts to kindling. Small overturned boats on the beach also fell victim to the broadsides, but the muffled thuds from the gundecks barely carried to the sailors and marines in the Windsor Gallery high above.

'Fire at will,' Oliver ordered.

A shot splashed down between the frigate and one of its boats. Another landed amidships, splitting the longboat cleanly into two halves, shooting its bow clear of the water along with bodies and lethal splinters.

The crews in the gallery cheered while Oliver checked the scene from the embrasure. Within minutes there was nothing left of the boat, save for a few floating bodies and oars.

'Well done, men,' he called.

Under a rain of lethal iron splashing dabs of white on the smooth azure tones of the Mediterranean, two boats pulled desperately for the shore while the others turned and struggled back towards the ships' sides. Even from a distance it was easy to see how desperate the soldiers were to climb aboard.

'Re-load!' the captain called. 'As fast as you can. Fire!'

The horrendous noised reverberated inside the tunnel walls.

'You got him!' Mr Tully yelled. 'Landed in the starboard chains. She'll lose her mast in a minute. Mr Tully was not wrong. The main on the large frigate teetered then, when the remaining lines could take the strain no longer, they snapped. The mast leaned slowly then fell tossing men, spars, lines and canvas into the sea.

A gaping hole in the other frigate's side was sucking in seawater and rapidly drowning the ship. As the water took hold, the ship heeled gracefully spilling men from the yards. It went down in a froth of bubbling water. Soldiers, who had managed to climb aboard, had no alternative but to leap back into water where they were quickly dragged down by their wet uniforms and backpacks.

A few soldiers made it to one of the surviving boats without being hit by the lethal projectiles raining down on them. Once in the relative safely of the boat they had three options. They could pull for the fisherman's beach to be taken prisoner in a plague-infested colony, pull for the frigates, which were under bombardment from the sky, or head north and attempt to row back to France.

As the firing continued, three shots landed almost simultaneously on the smallest frigate. Dropping with deadly force from a great height, the huge balls drove through the wooden decks as easily as a sharpened quill through a piece of paper. When they reached the hull, the ribs were rent apart spewing up a fountain of sea and quickly drowning the hold.

"Huzza! Huzza!'

'Give them one more,' Oliver demanded. 'Fire!'

A well-aimed shot grazed the rudder of the only frigate still afloat. She was attempting to make a run to the north. It was evident to Captain Quintrell the French captain was not prepared to haul his colours, nor was he prepared to stand and fight any longer. He had no defence against an airborne attack. Running was his only option.

Clustered around the embrasure, Oliver's men cheered. The euphoria was equal to any victory won at sea. The captain was delighted also. The British Navy had sunk two French ships and sent another running home to tell its tale to the Emperor. Apart from a few streaks of smoke smeared across the sailor's faces, his guncrews had not sustained a single injury, not even a broken finger nail.

'Well done, men. You have sent Napoleon a clear message – the Rock does not welcome French visitors. Now let us clear this gundeck and return to *Perpetual*. I am sure Mr Parry will be wondering what has become of us.'

'We don't have to haul the gun down the hill, do we?' Muffin asked, dolefully.

'No, it will remain here.'

Muffin sighed. 'Thank the Lord for that.'

Sitting at the back of the tunnel in the darkness, Tommy Wainwright took his hands from his ears. 'Is it over?'

'Yes it's over,' Eku said. 'Time to head back to the ship. Are you all right?'

Tommy nodded. 'My head is thumping.'

'Mine too,' said Bungs. 'I never heard so much noise.'

'Time to go,' Eku said, offering his hand to help Tommy to his feet.

'I don't feel good,' Tommy whispered.

'You'll be fine,' the Negro said. But when they emerged into the daylight, the whites of Tommy's eyes told another story. They were the colour of old stained linen.

Although the hours had slipped by as easily as sand through a glass, it had been a long day and the men were hungry and weary. But they were pleased with their efforts. Hauling the heavy gun to the top of the rock had been a hard climb. Coming down without it was going to be much easier.

The sergeant of the Marine Corps was pleased too. Captain Quintrell had praised his men for their achievements. Following the captain from the tunnel, he formed his men into an orderly double file and once everyone was out of the gallery, they began the march down the mountainside.

Despite the smoke they had inhaled, the *Perpetual*s were in good voice chattering, joking and singing. It took harsh words from Mr Tully to silence their elated spirits. Hobbles said nothing but wore a broad grin on his face. His gun crew brought up the rear of the party.

'So what's up with you?' Bungs asked Tommy, who was lagging behind. 'Cat still got your tongue?'

Tommy didn't answer.

'It makes no sense to me,' the cooper drawled. 'Yesterday you begged Mr Parry to let you come along and serve as a powder monkey. Yet while we were in the tunnel, I never once saw you with so much as a quill in your hand. What were you doing?'

Tommy gazed around searching for the distant voice he could hear in his head. Suddenly his eyes glazed, rolled back and closed. His knees collapsed from under him and he keeled over. Within seconds, he was rolling down the hillside.

'Fool?' Mr Tully yelled. 'Can't he walk straight?'

The party came to a halt. The men moved to the edge to watch the loblolly's tumble. Having been standing alongside him, Eku immediately shot down the hill after him skidding on his hands, feet and the seat of his pants until he reached him. Fortunately, not far below them, the path doubled back stopping his fall.

Splayed across the track, Tommy's face and arms were cut and blood was streaming from his nose. He opened his eyes.

'Are you all right?' Eku asked softly.

Tommy looked at him blankly.

Mr Tully snaked around the bend in the track. Captain Quintrell was close behind.

'I need two men to carry him back to the ship,' the captain called.

'I will take him,' Eku said.

'Can you manage him alone?'

'I've carried much heavier burdens than this,' Eku said, picking up the youth and cradling him in his arms.'

Oliver accepted the offer. The West Indian was probably the strongest man in his crew.

'When we arrive at the ship, take him directly to the sick berth. Tell the surgeon to ignore the cuts and bruises. Tell him the boy is ill.'

Eku looked into the captain's eyes.

Oliver met his gaze and nodded.

Nothing more needed to be said.

'Is it the fever?' Bungs asked, after helping Eku deliver the boy to the cockpit.

'I fear so,' Dr Whipple replied, bathing the blood from Tommy's face. 'Delirium is a symptom of this disease, and I should warn you that death is often a close companion.'

'I want to stay with him and care for him,' Bungs begged.

The surgeon hesitated. 'What of your regular duties?'

'Duties be damned! They can wait. Besides we ain't at sea. I'll tend to the lad for as long as it takes.'

'And Mr Muffin?'

Bungs was shocked. 'What of Muffin?'

'Isn't he one of your messmates also?'

'Yes, but—?'

'He's in the cot over there. Mr Tully brought him in just before you arrived. The lieutenant said it took the sailor all his strength to climb aboard. He said it was a wonder he didn't topple into the bay and drown.'

'I didn't know he was sick,' Bungs said, apologetically. 'Then I'll mind them both and my mate will help me. Won't you, Eku?'

The West Indian agreed.

'And what of the danger to your own health?'

Bungs laughed. 'An old tar like me? I've had a dose of everything there is to have. Nothing ain't gunna kill me, 'cept a direct hit at close quarters. And the same goes for Ekundayo here. Ain't that right?'

'That's true,' the West Indian said.

Dr Whipple looked from the two men to the three other swinging cots in the sick berth. 'Because there are others I must attend to and, because I am without the services of my loblolly, I accept your offer of help. If you can administer care to young Tom and Mr Muffin, I will be most grateful but I will have to tell the captain what you are doing.'

Over the next three days, the crew was kept busy replacing the caulking on the gun deck. The quantity of old rope they had teased was put to good use. As they worked, they inhaled deeply preferring the smell of boiling pitch in their nostrils to the smell of death drifting across the bay from the town.

For two dozen men who could swim, netting was slung around the ship's sides which allowed them to scrape a layer of weed spouting from between the copper plates below the water level.

Although unable to provide any guarantee to his men that their situation on the bay would change in a day, a week, or even a month, Captain Quintrell wanted to be ready to leave as soon as his orders came through and feel confident he could make a safe and swift passage back to England.

During that time, Tommy drifted in and out of delirium and, while his nose bleed caused by the fall did not recur, blood began oozing from Muffin's nose and the corners of his eyes. The foul black vomit came the following day. Bungs dutifully bathed his patient, dressed him a clean shirt and gave him every possible care.

On the morning of the fourth day, Tommy Wainwright opened his eyes to the sound of whispered voices. The patient in the next cot was being taken out. His name had been recorded in the surgeon's log as a victim of the contagious fever.

Tommy was unaware it was his messmate, the Muffinman, and he never had the opportunity to say goodbye.

It was a time of mixed feelings when Tommy was declared fit enough to leave the sick berth and return to eat with his friends. He received a round of huzzas when he walked through the mess.

'Welcome back, you young scallywag,' Bungs said, ruffling Tommy's mop of hair as he slid along the sea chests to his usual seat directly opposite the cooper.

Tommy smiled back from his perch next to Eku. Although he'd been told about Muffin's death, it was confronting to see the empty place where the sailor usually sat with his head resting against the ship's side as if he was asleep.

'So what have you two been doing while I've been sick?' Tommy asked.

Bungs and Eku looked at each other across the table.

'Just minding us own business,' Bungs said, winking at the Negro. 'Ain't that right?'

'Too right,' Eku answered. 'Just minding us own business.'

CHAPTER 19

Admiralty Orders
December 1804

'Touching his breast pocket, as he stepped aboard, Captain Quintrell reassured himself the orders he had received from the Admiralty via the Acting Commander of the Garrison were safe. All that remained was to go below and open them. A half-smile curled on the corner of his lips – one of satisfaction rather than joy at the prospect of receiving news he was to be returning home.

Once within the confines of his cabin, he broke the wax seal and removed the sheets of paper from the envelope and read. Then, he frowned. These were not the orders he had expected. After reading his instructions twice over, he laid the dispatch on his desk, mulled over its content for a time then passed word for his first lieutenant to join him.

'Come in, Simon, please sit.'

Simon Parry was also eager for news. 'You have your orders, Captain?'

The tone of Oliver's reply fell somewhere between an announcement and a guarded apology. 'You will be pleased to learn that our duty here has come to an end. We are at liberty to proceed to sea.'

'The Lord be praised,' Simon said. 'The men will be delighted when they learn of it.'

Oliver nodded tentatively, wondering if the crew's initial euphoria at hearing the full extent of the news would be short lived.

'It's officially over,' Oliver announced. 'The epidemic has come to an end. The garrison has recorded no deaths in the past few days and not a single soldier has fallen sick in the last week. The same applies in the town'. He leaned back and stretched. 'It's like a curse has been lifted and the change is remarkable. You can see the relief on the soldiers' faces. You can sense it on the parade ground. It's like the atmosphere on the gundeck after the smoke has cleared and every man gets on with his business as if nothing had ever happened.'

'That is indeed good to hear.'

'The garrison also received word from Lord Nelson that his own surgeon from *Victory* is to be transferred to Gibraltar, and an eminent physician from London is heading this way.'

'A little late perhaps, would you not agree?'

'Sadly, yes.'

'On the nineteenth of this month General Fox will arrive and take up his post as Lieutenant-Governor of the colony and Commander of the Garrison. Plus more troops will be arriving to replace those who died of the fever.'

'Is it known how many died?'

'Between October and November, the garrison lost over 1000 men and the town lost half its population – almost 5000 souls. One in every two people fell victim to the contagion.'

Simon shook his head. 'Let us pray it never returns.'

Oliver echoed his sentiment.

'The *Perpetuals* should be grateful they were confined to the ship,' Simon said. 'That alone must have saved some lives.'

Oliver pondered over his lieutenant's statement. 'It's hard to know. In total Dr Whipple recorded only five deaths on the ship due to fever, but I think that was nothing to do with where the men went, or what they did, or the quarantine regulations, or the services he provided in the sick berth. Personally, I believe it was pure luck.'

Simon Parry was curious.

'Consider Captain Gore's men. They never once stepped ashore in Gibraltar or in Cadiz, but news, just arrived from England, states that when *Medusa* arrived in Plymouth, he had fifty sailors confined to the sick berth. I wonder how many sailors were buried on the Bay of Biscay.' Oliver paused. 'It appears no amount of fresh sea air was able to prevent the pestilence from spreading.

'However, that is now a thing of the past and we must concentrate on the future. With ships at liberty to enter Gibraltar Bay, trade will resume, the garrison will re-group under a new commander and before long the colony will be flourishing again.

'As to my commission,' he said, tapping his finger on the dispatch. 'I have my orders. Do you have all the men aboard?'

'Yes, sir. All accounted for at this morning's muster.'

'Including the doctor?'

'Yes.'

'And what of the shipwrights I was promised from the naval dockyard? I will not sail without a carpenter.'

'They are due to arrive first thing in the morning.'

'Good. I have no desire to linger in this place any longer than is necessary. Are you satisfied all has been made ready to sail?'

'Aye, Captain. Am I permitted to notify the men?'

'You are—'

'Excellent.' A satisfied smile spread across Simon's face. 'Spirits have been low, but this news will be like a double ration to the men.'

But Oliver was not through. Standing up, he gazed into the empty fireplace. 'December in England can be cold,' he mused.

'But a warm hearth is always a welcome sight,' Simon added. Then he paused, inclining his head. 'Is there a problem, Oliver?'

'Do we have ample water?'

'We could fill some barrels on the Portuguese coast and, if we are fortunate to meet rain on the Bay of Biscay, there will be sufficient for us to reach Portsmouth without the need for rationing.'

Oliver turned and faced his lieutenant. 'We are not going home, Simon. The Admiralty has other plans.'

The lieutenant raised his eyebrows.

'We head into the Atlantic. Our first port of call will be the Portuguese Azores.'

'Not Madeira?'

A shudder ran down Oliver's spine, although his face showed no indication of the thoughts flashing through his mind. 'No, Simon, not Madeira. In the Azores we shall take on food and water for a six-month voyage.'

The lieutenant waited.

'Our destination is the Southern Ocean – the newly established settlement of Hobarton in Van Diemen's Land, the small island to the south of New South Wales.'

'That will not please the men. They have been praying for the day we return to England. A voyage such as this will take four months to reach our destination and the same amount of time, if not more, to return.'

'I do not write the orders, Simon, I merely follow them.'

'If I might be so bold as to state the obvious, we have on board a substantial amount of Spanish treasure.'

'I am fully aware of that.'

'Are you also aware the men are not happy about it? They claim it is cursed.'

'Sailors are a suspicious lot,' Oliver observed.

'But to convey it half-way across the world and back would seem foolish in the extreme.'

'Yet it is that very commodity which determines our destination. My orders state,' he said, glancing at the letter on the desk, 'that I must:

...deliver a consignment of specie – coins of various denominations – to the Lieutenant-Governor in Hobarton to be placed in the settlement's Treasury to be used for the purpose of administration of the new colony on Van Diemen's Land.'

'But you admitted yourself the treasure that was detained at Cape Saint Mary and is being held in Britain, rightly belongs to the Crown of Spain. The value must be considerable'

'Over one million dollars in silver bullion, almost two million in silver dollars, a million in gold plus pigs of copper, bars of tin, sealskins and oil.'

Simon leaned back in his chair. 'Incredible.'

'In the meantime, regarding the four chests removed from *Medusa* and delivered aboard *Perpetual,* the Admiralty has already allocated an equivalent amount of money which has been put aside ready to be returned to Spain assuming an agreement is reached. Therefore, what we have on board should be regarded merely as a cargo of coins for the colony from the British Treasury.'

'Interesting.'

'As you know, Simon, sending a large amount of currency by sea is a hazardous operation. In their wisdom, the Admiralty therefore resolved it is safer to transport a consignment of coins from Gibraltar than from the Thames or Spithead.'

The lieutenant was still puzzled. 'But in a new British convict colony, what immediate value is a consignment of Spanish reales and silver dollars?'

Oliver explained. 'The colony of Van Diemen's Land is a fledgling settlement of only a few thousand men and at the moment there is no legal currency. Apart from promissory notes, all goods and services are paid for in gold or any specie which is available –

Dutch guilders, silver ducats, doubloons, Spanish reales and silver dollars cut into pieces of eight.

'Building a settlement from bare earth takes men, therefore convicts from the prison hulks are being shipped in their hundreds to supply the labour force. Convicts, despite their crimes, must be housed, fed and clothed. Roads, bridges, dockyards and warehouses must be built, along with a courthouse, jail and lieutenant governor's residence. This requires a considerable amount of money, not to mention the day-to-day upkeep of troops required to keep peace in a colony consisting almost entirely of felons. The money we deliver will be used to help build a settlement Britain can be proud of.

'As to our voyage, I will speak with Mr Mundy about our course. From the Azores, we will make for the coast of Brazil, water in Rio de Janeiro then head south to harness the Roaring Forties to carry us directly to Van Diemen's Land.'

Simon smiled. 'It is ironical, in effect we will be returning the coins along the path the treasure fleet sailed on its voyage to Cadiz, and in so doing flaunting it under the noses of the Spanish Dons. Surely that will make us a prime target?'

'Let us trust that the Spanish are not aware of our cargo, and that Napoleon's forces will be fully occupied in Europe. Hopefully word of what we are carrying will not precede us.'

'Is that possible?'

Oliver Quintrell shrugged. 'Let me put this to you. How did the Admiralty in London know of this consignment at least a month before the four Spanish treasure ships set sail from the River Plate, before one ounce of silver was loaded onto a ship, even before Admiral Bustamente was appointed Commander of the Fleet? How did the Admiralty know it would arrive off the coast of Cadiz in early October?' Oliver delivered his own answer. 'Spies, Simon, spies. We have ours and they have theirs. Secrets cannot be guaranteed.'

Oliver smiled. 'The only thing I can assure you of is that we will be leaving behind this place where the very air we breathe is our worst enemy. I am sure there is not a sailor aboard who will argue that fact. What I cannot promise or foresee for the future is action or prize money – only fate will determine that.'

CHAPTER 20

Epilogue
10 December 1804

As *Perpetual* weighed anchor and made ready to sail from the Bay of Gibraltar, a solitary seaman standing on the beach at Rosia Bay raised his arm in a gesture of acknowledgement to the frigate.

In his pocket was a copy of a letter addressed to Admiral Lord Nelson, Commander of the Mediterranean Fleet, from Captain Oliver Quintrell.

In it, the captain requested:

...that the bearer of this letter, Zachary Irons, a topman, who has served faithfully on His Britannic Majesty's Frigate Perpetual, be permitted to sign on the next ship returning to Britain, and that on arrival in an English port, the aforementioned sailor be paid the wages due to him and that he be discharged from any further requirements of the Service...

A few days earlier, Captain Quintrell had asked the sailor, 'What would you do if you were returned to England?'

'I would collect my pay then return home to my wife and children and make sure they were wanting for nothing.'

'And after that?' the captain had enquired.

'I would seek another ship and return to sea.'

'A ship of His Majesty's Navy?'

'No, sir. Wishing no disrespect, Captain, but a Company ship – an East or West Indiaman.'

'Then when you step ashore next time, I suggest you keep well clear of the press. They are likely to be out in force.'

Standing on the deck of His Majesty's frigate *Perpetual*, along with two carpenters and their boxes of tools, a young shipwright waved farewell to the boat that had just delivered him and his mates to the frigate. It was heading back to the naval dockyard where the tradesmen had been engaged for the past few months.

'God love us!' Bungs cried, shaking his head in disbelief. 'If it ain't the lad from Buckler's Hard. You're a sight for sore eyes.'

Will Ethridge smiled and extended his hand to the cooper who he had served with aboard *Elusive* two years earlier. 'Good day to you, Bungs,' he replied. 'It's good to be back.

*   *   *

AUTHOR'S NOTE

Gibraltar and the epidemic

The epidemic which devastated the populations of Gibraltar and Andalusia in 1804 was Yellow Fever. But, at the time, neither the disease nor the cause of its spread was known. The *Malignant Fever* was blamed on many things – overcrowding, lack of hygiene, the Levanter wind blowing off the Mediterranean and the miasmic air of Gibraltar Bay.

It was not known in 1804 that the Yellow Fever virus was transmitted by mosquitoes and that the Barbary Ape (macaque monkey) was the vector.

Sylvatic Yellow Fever allows the infection to spread from man to mosquito to monkey to mosquito to man. But that fact was not discovered until many years later. In 1895, Theobald Smith discovered that animals acted as vectors, and in 1927 Max Theiler proved the fever was viral. In 1932 he developed a vaccine to combat Yellow Fever and in 1951 received the Nobel Prize in Medicine for his achievements.

In 1804, half of the population of Gibraltar died of the disease and tens of thousands died in Spain. Similar epidemics followed in 1810 and 1813.

The Battle of Cape Saint Mary

The infamous Battle of Cape Saint Mary was reported in British Naval dispatches. It was also described in the Memoir of Captain Graham Moore of His Majesty's frigate *Indefatigable*. While Patrick O'Brian and C.S. Forester both used this battle in their fiction stories, they infiltrated their own characters into the event. In *Admiralty Orders*, the author has maintained the integrity of the action, the ships and the captains involved exactly as documented.

However, in this story some treasure is delivered to Captain Quintrell on board *Perpetual*. This is a figment of the author's imagination.

As was predicted, Britain's capture and detention of the Spanish treasure ships precipitated war with Spain. The declaration was made by King Carlos on 12 December 1804.

Sunken Treasure

In 2007 the wreck of *Nuestra Señora de las Mercedes* was discovered where it sank off the coast of Portugal. In November 2012, after a five-year legal battle between a US salvage company and the Spanish Government, the treasure recovered from the seabed was finally returned to Spain. It was reported to be worth $500,000,000 (£316,000,000) at 2007 value.

The Siege Tunnels

Excavated initially with crowbars and sledgehammers, work on the tunnels began in 1782 to create an impregnable defence system within the Rock. The Windsor Gallery was the first to be completed and have guns installed. More tunnels were dug in the nineteenth and twentieth centuries. Today the labyrinth of tunnels stretches for 33 miles (52km) within the great promontory.

In November 2012 the author visited the siege tunnels in the Rock of Gibraltar and recommends it as a unique experience.

Water Tanks and HMS *Victory*

Following the demands of Earl St Vincent and Admiral Lord Nelson for water tanks to be built at Gibraltar, the work began in 1799 and was completed in 1804. Six enormous tanks were cut out of solid rock. Five of the tanks measured 60 x 4.5 x 6.5 meters. The largest tank was 60 x 4.5 x 7.2 meters wide. They were dug below ground level, but were above the level of the bay allowing for the water to be fed to lighters or directly to the ships by gravity or hoses.

In 1805, following the Battle of Trafalgar, HMS *Victory* was towed into Rosia Bay for repairs and to take on water from these tanks.

Surgeons and Resurrectionists

Sir Astley Cooper (1768-1841), the world's richest and most famous surgeon later served as surgeon to the Prince Regent and Queen Victoria. His exploits with vivisection and experimental operations on both human and animal patients is told in a remarkable book, *Digging up the Dead* by Druin Burch.

Burch writes: "He set up an international network of body-snatchers, won the Royal Society's highest prize and boasted in Parliament that there was no one whose body he could not steal. He experimented on his neighbours' corpses and the living bodies of their stolen pets."

Digging up the Dead is a riveting account of gothic horror combined with fertile idealism in the Age of Enlightenment. It makes remarkable reading.

In 1800, The Royal College of Surgeons was established which elevated surgeons to the same level as physicians.

Characters in the novel

Apart from the addition of Dr Whipple, Captain Quintrell's crew consists mainly of the officers and men who sailed with him in the two previous books in this series.

In *Admiralty Orders (Book4 in the Oliver Quintrell Series)*, cameo appearances are made by various real-life historical characters such as Sir Charles Cotton and Lord Cochrane, also Captains Barlow, Gore, Hammond and Sutton, who were the serving frigate captains at the Battle of Cape Saint Mary. Lieutenant-Governor Sir Thomas Trigge and Dr Pym were both serving in Gibraltar in 1804.

Some of the references used in researching this book:

ACCOUNT OF THE EPIDEMIC FEVER which occurred at Gibraltar in the Years 1804, 1810, and 1813, taken from official documents, military and medical, and from the communications of Joseph D.A. Gilpin, M.D. Deputy Inspector of Hospitals. (accessed on-line).
DIGGING UP THE DEAD: Uncovering the Life and Times of an Extraordinary Surgeon by Druin Burch, (2008).
FRIGATE COMMANDER by Tom Wareham, (2012).
MEMOIRS OF A FIGHTING CAPTAIN, Admiral Lord Cochrane, (2005).
MEMOIR OF SIR GRAHAM MOORE, Reprints from University of Michigan Library, (1844).

NELSON'S REFUGE – *Gibraltar in the Age of Napoleon* by Jason R Musteen, (2011).
REPORT ON GIBRALTAR AS A FORTRESS AND A COLONY: *Respectfully addressed to the Right Honourable The Lord Viscount Palmerston, G.C.B. by Sir Robert Gardiner.* (1856).
ROUGH MEDICINE *Surgeons at Sea in the Age of Sail*, Joan Druett, (2000).
BLOG POST: *The People of Gibraltar* by Neville Chipulina
Plus Naval Chronicles, personal letters and other sources.

I trust you have enjoyed reading the three books in the Oliver Quintrell Series. Why not join the captain and his crew in another adventure on the high seas?

The Unfortunate Isles is Book 4 in the series.

Made in the USA
Columbia, SC
20 May 2020